# Murder on the Rocks

ALSO BY T E KINSEY

## Lady Hardcastle Mysteries:

A Quiet Life in the Country

In the Market for Murder

Death Around the Bend

Christmas at The Grange

A Picture of Murder

The Burning Issue of the Day

Death Beside the Seaside

The Fatal Flying Affair

Rotten to the Core

An Act of Foul Play

A Fire at the Exhibition

An Assassination on the Agenda

The Beast of Littleton Woods

## Dizzy Heights Mysteries:

The Deadly Mystery of the Missing Diamonds

A Baffling Murder at the Midsummer Ball

# MURDER ON THE ROCKS

A Lady Hardcastle Mystery

T E KINSEY

THOMAS & MERCER

Published by Thomas & Mercer, Seattle

www.apub.com



EU Product Safety Contact:
Amazon Media EU S.à r.l.
38, avenue John F. Kennedy, L-1855 Luxembourg
amazonpublishing-gpsr@amazon.com

ISBN-13: 9781662521584
eISBN: 9781662521577

Cover design by Tom Sanderson
Cover illustration by Jelly London

Printed in the United States of America

# Murder on the Rocks

# Chapter One

Lady Hardcastle was looking out of the train window as we clickety-clacked through the Somerset countryside. 'Don't you just adore a train journey?'

'We've had some fun ones, that's for certain,' I said. 'And some terrifying ones. Do you remember the night train from Bucharest?'

'Oh yes. Or that tiny line in Dubrovnik when the local gang leader thought we must be British spies.'

'We were British spies.'

'I suppose so. But we weren't spying on *him*.'

'No, that's true.' I contemplated the view across the fields for a few moments. It really was rather beautiful in the winter sunshine. 'But yes, apart from those two – and at least a dozen other hairy trips – I do, indeed, adore a train journey.'

There was a knock at the compartment door, and a white-jacketed steward slid it open and poked his head inside.

'Please excuse the interruption, ladies, but I see you've reserved a table in the restaurant car. Lunch will be served in fifteen minutes.'

Lady Hardcastle turned towards him with a smile. 'Thank you . . . ?'

'Pearson, madam.'

'Thank you, Pearson. We shall be there presently.' She pointed towards the front of the train. 'That way?'

He shook his head and pointed in the other direction. 'That way, madam. You can't miss it – just follow the sound of spilling soup.'

And with that, he was gone.

'Say what you like about the convenience of the motor car, young Flossie, but until you can serve me a three-course luncheon as we drive along the King's highway, the Great Western Railway has much to offer.'

I gave a small shrug. 'I can't argue with you there. You'd be wearing most of your meal by the time we arrived at our destination.'

'Just so.' She stood and hefted her Gladstone bag from the luggage rack. 'Shove your book in here for now, dear. We'll sort everything out when we change trains at Plymouth.'

'Shove?' I said.

'Yes, dear. Shove it in.'

I placed my book carefully in the bag, nestling it among magazines, a newspaper, a hairbrush, a box of powder, a leather case containing a manicure set, and goodness knows what other unnecessary tat she was hauling about with her.

She snapped the bag shut. 'Come then, tiny one. Let us adjourn to the restaurant car to see what they have to offer.'

We made our way along the corridor and through the doors joining the carriages. I wondered, as I so often did, whether it would be possible to uncouple the carriages while the train was in motion. How useful that would have been on some of our journeys, leaving our pursuers impotently shaking their fists in the doorway of their rapidly slowing car as we sped off into the distance.

'No,' said Lady Hardcastle.

'No what?'

'No, you can't uncouple the carriages while the train is in motion.'

I frowned. 'How did you—?'

'You wonder about it every time we move along a train.'

She wasn't wrong.

We soon found the restaurant car and I smiled to myself with satisfaction at its clinking glasses and jingling cutlery on starched white linen.

Pearson the steward ushered us to a table set for four. 'We're quite busy for lunch today so we have no more twos, but I thought you'd be more comfortable at a larger table anyway, so I took the liberty.'

We thanked him and sat down.

As we perused the menu, a gentleman entered the car and beckoned the steward. A murmured conversation followed, which ended with Pearson shrugging apologetically and gesturing down the carriage at the already-full tables.

'It's a good thing you booked a table,' I said. 'There doesn't seem to be room for the more spontaneous diners on board.'

Lady Hardcastle turned in her seat to look at the dismayed man near the door. He was smartly dressed and had a decorated cardboard box under his arm.

She turned back towards me. 'He seems like a nice enough fellow. Would you object to some company?'

'Not at all,' I said. 'It's a long journey and you've heard all my sparkling anecdotes dozens of times before.'

'I was present for most of the adventures recounted in them.'

'You were. So we need someone else to talk to, I think.'

She beckoned the steward, who moved along the swaying carriage with a grace I was sure neither Lady Hardcastle nor I could manage. The forlorn would-be diner hovered near the door with his package, seemingly unsure what to do.

'Yes, madam?' said Pearson. 'Some water, perhaps?'

'Thank you, no. Actually, yes, that would be splendid. But that's not why I called you over. Is that gentleman looking for a table?' She tilted her head backwards to indicate Forlorn Man.

'He is. But I've had to turn him away – we're fully booked, as you can see.'

'Ah, but we have plenty of room at our table. If he wouldn't be uncomfortable dining with strangers, we'd be more than happy to have him join us.'

'That's very kind of you, madam. If you're sure you don't mind . . .'

'Not at all. It's not that we're weary of our own company, you understand, but a fresh view of the world would make our journey much more enjoyable. Bring him over if he'll come.'

Pearson glided off and returned moments later with the now grateful and relieved passenger. 'Ladies, this is . . .'

'Dymond,' said the man, putting down his box on the floor next to the chair Pearson was holding out for him. 'Paul Dymond at your service. Like the precious stone, but with a Y.' He paused. 'But there are no Ys in Paul, obviously.'

Pearson smiled. 'This is Mr Dymond with a Y. I shall be back in a few moments to take your orders.' He left to attend to other diners.

Lady Hardcastle gestured for our guest to sit. 'Welcome, Mr Dymond. I am Emily, Lady Hardcastle . . .' She paused.

'And I'm Florence Armstrong,' I said. 'Miss.'

'How do you do,' said Dymond. 'It really is most kind of you to allow me to share your table. Thank you.'

'Think nothing of it,' said Lady Hardcastle. 'We were just saying to Pearson—'

'To . . . ?'

'Pearson,' repeated Lady Hardcastle. 'The steward.'

Dymond nodded. 'Aha. Sorry, do go on.'

'We were just saying how welcome company would be. An engaging conversation can make a long journey seem so much shorter, don't you think?'

'I suppose so, yes. Though give me a good book and a comfortable place to sit and I can be quite content with my own company.'

'I know exactly what you mean,' I said. 'With a warm fire at this time of year.'

'Oh, most definitely,' said Dymond with a nod. 'London has been exceptionally cold.'

'You've come all the way from London?' said Lady Hardcastle. 'Good heavens. You must have been travelling for ever. We only joined at Bristol and I already feel as though we've been on the train since the dawn of time.'

'It's not so bad. I have a book and a comfortable place to sit, so the time is passing quite pleasantly. It was only unexpected hunger that forced me from my compartment. That and the loud snoring of the gentleman I've been sharing it with.'

He caught sight of me trying to get a better look at the box at his feet. Not my finest hour – I always imagined myself more subtle than that.

'It's a bear,' he said. 'I collect them.'

I smiled. 'A bear?'

'The Americans call them teddy bears, but this one is German.'

He picked up the box and opened it. Inside was not, as I expected, a brown toy bear, but a black one.

'It's a *Titanic* Bear,' said Dymond. 'Steiff – do you know Steiff? They make bears. Steiff made the *Titanic* Bears to commemorate the victims of the disaster. He's a sad bear, but he has pride of place in my collection. I didn't like the idea of leaving him unguarded with only my snoring compartment companion to see off potential thieves, so I brought him with me.'

'He's magnificent,' I said. 'I had no idea there were collectors of bears.'

'There are collectors of everything,' he said with a smile of his own. 'Not many collect bears, mind you, but there are a few of us. They appeal to me for some reason.'

'And are you on your way home to Devon?' asked Lady Hardcastle.

'No, I'm visiting a friend at Exeter. He has managed to acquire a couple of bears from America and he's said I can have one. I'm taking the *Titanic* Bear to show him. Do you live in Bristol or are you travelling home to Devon yourselves?'

'We live near Bristol,' I said.

'And we're off on something of an adventure,' said Lady Hardcastle. 'An acquaintance of ours – another American, as it happens . . . I wonder if he has any teddy bears. I shall ask him. But bears or not, he has invited us to spend the weekend with him at his . . . I'd ordinarily say "country house", but it's not quite a house and it's not really in the country.'

Dymond laughed. 'That's intriguing. So what is it?'

'Well, it used to be a fort, but he's renovated it and turned it into a . . . a retreat, I suppose one might say. And it's not in the country because it's on a little island a mile or so off the coast. He plans to open it as a resort where the well-heeled can get away from it all for a few days in unashamed luxury.'

'I say. That does sound exciting. I take it he's a wealthy chap.'

'Rich as Croesus. His father's company made a fortune in munitions during the Civil War. During the Reconstruction they diversified into . . . well, into everything as far as I can make out. Railways – or "railroads", I should say – oil, mining, factories. By the time he inherited the company in the eighties, you name it, they had a hand in it. For nearly twenty years he ran the many businesses with great success, but around the turn of the century he had some manner of Damascene moment and decided that the rapacious acquisition of wealth didn't sit well with his conscience. He divested himself of his many holdings and retired to England, where he potters about indulging his love of antiquities.'

'But he's still rich, you say?'

'Oh, he got out of the Robber Baron game, but he kept the money. I believe it's all held in various trusts – you know what rich people are like with their tax avoidance wangles – but it's all available to him whenever he wants it. He certainly has enough to spare to invest in this new venture. A crisis of conscience didn't extend to his becoming some sort of medieval ascetic.'

Dymond laughed again. 'And who is this partial paragon? Might I have heard of him?'

'JB McIntyre,' I said.

Dymond goggled. 'I've definitely heard of *him*. Good gracious. Well, that sounds like a splendid adventure indeed.'

At that moment, Pearson arrived at the table, as if from nowhere. How *do* waiters do that?

'Are you ready to order?'

'I'll have the terrine, please, and then the Dover sole,' said Lady Hardcastle.

I had barely glanced at the menu when we sat down and hadn't looked at it since. 'Er . . . I'll have the same.'

Mr Dymond clearly hadn't looked either, and followed my lead. 'And for me, please.'

'An excellent choice,' said Pearson. 'We have a rather nice Chablis to go with that, although I can also recommend a German wine from Mosel if you're in the mood for something a little different.'

Lady Hardcastle noticed our uncertainty and tried to hide a smile. 'Actually I was thinking of champagne. Unless either of you would prefer the Chablis. I find the bubbles go well with a cream sauce.'

Mr Dymond seemed even more uncertain now but not, I felt, because he couldn't make up his mind. I wondered if he was worried about the price. 'Well . . . I . . . er . . .'

'My treat,' said Lady Hardcastle. 'Let's have the champagne.'

Pearson retreated with a smile and a bow.

'That really is most generous,' said Mr Dymond, 'but I can't—'

'Nonsense,' said Lady Hardcastle. 'I was going to order champagne anyway, and Miss Armstrong and I can't possibly drink a whole bottle on our own at lunchtime.'

This was a charmingly reassuring lie. We'd downed two bottles of champagne between us at many a lunchtime, though that was usually by way of maintaining our cover while on missions for the Crown. That's what we told ourselves, anyway. But it made us look less like drunkards to gloss over that unflattering truth, and it gave Dymond the opportunity to accept Lady Hardcastle's generosity without feeling uncomfortable.

'Well, thank you very much,' he said. 'I don't often get the chance to drink champagne, so it's much appreciated.'

Conversation turned away from bears and rich Americans as the train trundled on, and lunchtime passed in a pleasing blend of good company, good food, and at least one additional bottle of champagne.

Dymond seemed to enjoy himself, too. Eventually, though, the ever-attentive Pearson came to the table to tell him that we would soon be arriving at Exeter. He said his goodbyes and returned to his compartment to gather his belongings in time to get off the train.

We carried on to Plymouth.

◆ ◆ ◆

The journey continued, seemingly for ever. We changed trains at Plymouth and a small branch line took us almost to the coast, where we were met at the tiny station by a man with a cart. Lady Hardcastle introduced us and he said, 'Ar,' before loading our luggage on to the cart and gesturing for us to climb up on to the bench beside it. The only other words he uttered as we clip-clop-creaked along the Devonshire lanes were to the horse – whose name, we learned, was Jemima.

Ere long, as the poets say, we arrived outside a small fisherman's hut at the bottom of a cliff. Our taciturn driver unloaded our bags, adding them to the pile of luggage that squatted near the hut, and then made use of the large cobbled area to turn Jemima and the cart.

He gave us another heartfelt 'Ar' in response to our offer of thanks, accompanied by a polite nod when Lady Hardcastle pressed a few coins into his hand. Having checked that all was still well with Jemima and her harness, he heaved himself back to the driver's seat and resumed his conversation with the horse as they trundled back up the lane.

We finally turned our attention to the stone jetty that stretched out from the turning circle, and the battered old fishing boat moored alongside.

We were not alone.

Our fellow guests were standing on the jetty, but were keeping well clear of the fishing boat. They had watched our arrival in silence but, once the cart had gone, a short, plump man with a beaming smile half hidden by an impressively luxuriant moustache came over to us.

'What ho, ladies,' he said. 'You must be Lady Hardcastle and Miss Armstrong.'

'I suppose we must,' said Lady Hardcastle with a smile.

'Ha,' he barked. 'Well, you don't *have* to be. You can be whomever you wish. Of course you can. I, however, am afforded no such luxury.

For my sins I am forced forever to be Granville Bridgewater. Come. Meet the others.'

We how-do-you-do'd and followed him a few yards along the jetty to where the rest of the party were milling about in the limp sunshine.

A particularly large wave hurled itself gleefully at the side of the jetty, causing two of the ladies standing there to shriek as the water splashed their legs.

Bridgewater chuckled. 'I told them we should be standing up there by the hut where the carts turn round but they insisted on being nearer the sea.'

As we arrived, the group turned towards us.

'My friends, I have the honour of introducing Emily, Lady Hardcastle, and Miss Florence Armstrong. We've all read of their exploits in the newspapers, and now here they are in the—' He stopped and reddened.

'It's all right, Gran,' said a short, dark-haired woman. 'You can say "flesh". Just don't say "trousers". Or "bloomers". Definitely avoid that.' It wasn't a particularly bright day and yet the lady was wearing an extremely stylish pair of very dark glasses. She was also holding an elegant walking cane in her right hand.

'Well . . . I . . . er . . . yes. Quite. I suppose I'd better start with Mrs Clarice Everett since she's the one making all the noise. She's the musician of our little group. Violin, you know. Make whatever rude gestures you like – she can't see you. Blind as a bat, poor thing.'

'Kiss my—' The crash of another boisterous wave blotted out the preferred location of the kiss, but we were all able to guess what she meant.

Bridgewater seemed entirely unfazed. 'With Mrs Everett is her long-suffering husband, manager and accompanist, Edgar.'

The tall man, whose arm Clarice was holding, inclined his head but said nothing.

'Next to them is my equally long-suffering wife, Dorothy.'

'Call me Dotty, dears,' said the woman. 'Everybody does.'

'Then we have our good friend Robert Sidwell-Plant and his wife, Patience.'

The Sidwell-Plants were standing slightly apart. They were both tall, slender, and exquisitely well dressed. Like Everett, they inclined their heads in greeting but said nothing.

'Last but not least is the youngster among us, George Wilson. Don't let his youthful good looks fool you. Got a wise head on those young shoulders. Chap knows his onions, what?'

'How do you do?' said Wilson. 'Bridgewater makes me sound like a greengrocer, but I'm nothing so grand, I'm afraid. Still, I suppose I ought to be flattered – always nice to be thought of as a chap who knows his onions.'

Lady Hardcastle smiled. 'Always. As long as he doesn't think you a rap*scallion*.'

Wilson gave an appreciative smile.

Bridgewater, though, was confused. 'A what? A rap—' He chuckled as the penny dropped. 'Oh, I see it now. Very droll, Lady Hardcastle. Very droll.'

She inclined her head in acknowledgement of the compliment. 'It's a delight to meet you all,' she said. 'But I'm afraid it will take me some time to remember any of your names. You'll have to forgive me if I completely forget who you all are. I'll try my best but . . . well . . .'

'Don't worry, darling,' said Dotty. 'I can't remember who we all are and I've known us for years. Just call everyone "Honey-Bun" and you can't go far wrong.'

'Thank you, Honey-Bun,' said Lady Hardcastle.

This earned her a chuckle from the assembled throng and I began to think we might have quite a pleasant weekend with this lot.

Clarice Everett suddenly turned her head towards the sea. 'The boat's coming.'

'I say,' said Dotty. 'How on earth did you—'

'I can hear it, you idiot,' said Clarice with a sigh.

'Oh, yes, of course. So sorry.'

Now that it had been pointed out, I, too, could hear the boat, and I turned with everyone else to look for it. JB's island, with the old fort perched menacingly upon it, was obvious enough, but it took a while to spot the boat.

Finally, I saw it, and showed it to Lady Hardcastle, who acknowledged me with a nod. It occurred to me that with her famously keen eyesight she'd probably already seen it, but she was kind enough to give me the credit.

The others saw it, too, and even though it was still some way off, they stopped talking and watched it – there's something about an approaching boat that draws all attention entirely to itself.

It was a magnificent craft. It looked to be more than seventy feet long and the white-painted hull gleamed even in the wan light of the February sun, while the varnished mahogany gunwales and deck positively sparkled. The sound that Clarice had heard came not from the puff of a steam engine but from the steady chug of a diesel motor. Sparkling, slender, elegant and very, very modern. This was clearly the maritime plaything of our host, JB McIntyre.

It took another ten minutes for the launch to pull alongside the jetty, during which time I had the opportunity to size up our weekend companions. I decided, based solely on our first meeting and the muttered snatches of conversation I was able to hear while we waited for the boat, that Dotty and Granville Bridgewater were likely to be the social heart of the group.

The Sidwell-Plants – Robert and Patience – were more aloof and might be heavy going unless they opened up with a couple of gin and tonics inside them.

Clarice . . . I couldn't make her out. Spiky, certainly, but her bloomers remark had made me laugh, so perhaps she was more fun than I thought. Of them all, she was the one I'd heard of. Her recent concert tour had garnered enthusiastic reviews from even the newspapers' most staid and jaded music critics, and I'd been disappointed that we'd not been able to hear her when she'd played in Bristol.

As for her husband, Edgar, I had no idea. He'd said nothing at all since we arrived and had merely looked at everyone with a faint air of disapproval.

Spikiness and sullen broodiness notwithstanding, I hoped they might play for us, but resolved not to be too disappointed if they did not. They were there, like the rest of us, for a relaxing break at JB McIntyre's new weekend retreat and it seemed churlish to expect that they might also have to sing for their supper.

George Wilson was closer to my age and seemed like a jolly enough fellow. He had a salesman's charm and patter that might make him easy to get along with, as long as his boyish enthusiasm didn't become wearing if we were exposed to it for too long. He was more than averagely good-looking, too, and from the way she kept stealing glances at him, he had certainly caught Patience Sidwell-Plant's eye.

The motor launch was piloted by just one man and I began to feel a familiar indignation on behalf of a lone servant sent to do the work of at least two or three. Not only would he have to greet his master's guests and see them safely aboard the launch, he'd have to carry all our luggage down the jetty and stow it securely before piloting us out to the island.

A door slammed behind us and I turned to see a bearded man in sea boots and oilskins shambling round to the far side of the hut. He returned moments later, pushing a handcart on to which he proceeded to load the group's luggage.

By the time the launch drew alongside, he had wheeled the cart down the jetty and was in time to catch the line the boat's pilot threw ashore and to tie it expertly to one of the iron rings set in the stones. Between them they made the launch fast and put out the gangplank.

The boat's . . . captain? Was he a captain? A pilot? Handler? Driver? Whatever his job title, he came down the gangplank and gave us all a warm smile.

'Good afternoon, ladies and gentlemen. Thank you for being patient. My name's Crawford and this swarthy reprobate is Tommy Vickerman. He brings our post and supplies out to the island, but I'm the one who takes the guests.' He pointed to the fishing boat. 'Don't never get on that old bucket with Tommy 'cept in an emergency. And then only if you don't have no other choice.'

The bearded man gave a nod and a chuckle. 'He i'n't wrong. I only gets on it cos I can't afford nothin' better.'

'If you'd like to come this way,' said Crawford, 'you can make yourselves comfortable while we get your dunnage squared away, and we can be off. Mind your step now.'

Crawford retreated back up the gangplank to receive us on deck, while Vickerman stood with his foot on the base to help us on our way.

Lady Hardcastle and I lingered at the rear, watching the group as they lined up.

I wasn't wholly surprised to see confident young George Wilson stride to the front and board first. He refused help from Crawford as he hopped on to the deck and made his way towards the open platform at the stern with a cheerful grin on his face.

Patience Sidwell-Plant left her husband behind and followed Wilson just as confidently, though she did take Crawford's proffered hand and acknowledged his assistance with a curt nod.

Granville Bridgewater allowed Dotty to precede him and kept an attentively caring eye on her as she wobbled up the broad plank, before making his own way aboard with just as little agility.

Edgar Everett led Clarice to the foot of the plank and quietly said, 'Slight step,' as he drew her forwards. 'Raised battens about a foot apart.'

Edgar moved slowly, but Clarice, who was feeling her way with the cane, was significantly more confident. Nevertheless, Sidwell-Plant took it upon himself to walk closely behind her and seemed poised to catch her if she stumbled.

'I can feel you behind me, whoever that is,' said Clarice. 'Please don't crowd me.'

'It's me. Robert. I just wanted to—'

'Well, don't.'

The three of them boarded safely and went with the others to the stern.

Lady Hardcastle was next, with me taking up my usual protective position at the rear. I'd boarded many boats in my time and should have felt quite at home, but still the bounciness of the gangplank and the gentle sway of the boat took me as much by surprise as they always did.

By the time we arrived at the stern, the others had all gone into what I heard Bridgewater call the 'saloon'. We joined them and made small talk while Crawford and Vickerman loaded the luggage.

From the shore, Guardians Rock looked very much like any of the dozens of small islands dotted around Britain's coastline. As far as mainlanders were able to tell, it was just another craggy lump of rock too far from land to be casually useful, but close enough that it might one day be pressed into service if the need arose.

At some point, it seemed, a need had arisen, and a king – it was usually a king, or at the very least a bellicose prime minister – had seen fit to build a fort upon it, as they had upon many of the other tiny islands. I had no proper idea who the coast of Devon might need to be protected from, but it was usually the French. If not them, then the Spanish. Neither nation had ever made a serious effort to attack Britain by sea, but it was impossible to tell whether that proved the effectiveness or the pointlessness of the island forts.

Essential or futile, Guardians Rock and its fort grew more and more impressive as we approached. Much of the island was bounded by sheer cliffs of at least fifty feet high, with just one accessible point on the landward side where a quay had been built in a small inlet.

The bulk of the island was flat above the cliffs but the ground rose steeply towards a high plateau at the centre, upon which the sizeable fort had been built.

Stone walls seemed to grow from the rock itself, inset with windows and arrow loops. The central area of the roof was gabled, with Tudor chimneys not entirely unlike those of The Grange back home in Littleton Cotterell. By this point I was prepared to go out on a limb and guess that the fort had been built at the instigation of Henry VIII.

Crenelated platforms extended from either end of the gables, presumably providing a stable base for the fort's guns in its working days, but which were now, I hoped, equipped with comfortable garden furniture for alfresco entertainment when the weather allowed.

Lady Hardcastle and I went out on to the after-deck of the launch as we approached the quay, the better to get a first, proper glimpse of our destination, and – almost as importantly – to get us away from Granville Bridgewater's relentless joviality. I had been worried about young George Wilson, but so far it was Bridgewater who was proving to be the tiresome one.

Crawford lined up the launch for its approach to the quayside, built into a tiny cove protected on three sides by yet more towering cliffs. From our vantage point we were the first aboard to see our weekend host, JB McIntyre of Philadelphia. Dressed in English country tweeds and standing beside a barrel, he caught sight of us and gave the friendliest of waves. We waved back with equal friendliness, but then both sides realized our collective error as we tried to work out what to do with our arms and faces during the long minutes between this initial greeting and our eventual arrival.

When the launch finally docked, though, our premature hail was rewarded with the most effusively enthusiastic greeting.

Lady Hardcastle and I were the first down the gangplank once JB and Crawford had secured it, and JB launched himself at us like one of Sir Hector Farley-Stroud's ebullient spaniels.

'Emily,' he said as he tried to hug her. 'So wonderful to see you. Thank you for coming.'

Lady Hardcastle was certainly not averse to a friendly pat on the arm, and was very much inclined to hug her good friends, but this surprisingly familiar greeting took even her by surprise. She handled it well, though, and returned his brief embrace with only the faintest trace of bemusement.

'It's entirely my pleasure, JB dear,' she said once he had released her. 'We couldn't possibly pass up the chance to see your magnificent new drum.'

'My drum?'

'Your drum. Your home.'

'I've not heard that one. It's not really my home, though. For now it's just my weekend retreat.'

'Soon to be a magnificent luxury resort. We're very keen to see it.'

'Thank you.' He made to hug me next but turned the movement into a two-handed handshake at the last moment. Perhaps something in my expression put him off. It wasn't intentional, but I was a little relieved nonetheless.

'And welcome to you, my dear Miss Armstrong. Or do we know each other well enough now for me to call you Florence?'

'Whatever makes you most comfortable,' I replied. 'As my mother always said, "You can call me anything you like as long as you call me early for my dinner."'

He laughed. 'I like that. Let me just greet the others and we can all make our way up to the fort together.'

'Well, this is quite a bit different from the places we usually weekend,' said Lady Hardcastle when he had gone.

'Where *you* usually weekend,' I said. 'For I am but a poor, humble servant girl. I spend my days in thankless toil below stairs for a cruel and capricious mistress.'

'Oh, do shut up, there's a poppet.'

'Righto. But "we" haven't weekended anywhere for ages – we've been too busy.'

'Ah, but when we did, we weekended at some of the finest homes in Britain. Some of the finest in Europe, indeed.'

'We did, it's true. And more than one of them was a castle. But this one, as our American pal Ellie Wilson might say, is "something else".'

'Something entirely else. It looks a tad forbidding from the outside – one wonders what his architect has done with the inside.'

I nodded towards where JB was shaking George Wilson warmly by the hand and exhorting him and the others to follow. 'I don't think we'll have to wait long to find out. If McIntyre doesn't show us all soon I think he'll burst with excitement.'

We joined the group and followed our host up the stone steps cut into the side of the cliff. They were broad, with a sturdy wooden balustrade, and at first seemed very easy to climb. By the time we reached one of the landings about halfway up, though,

Dotty Bridgewater's face was a fetching shade of scarlet and she asked to stop.

Edgar Everett gave an impatient *pfft* and carried on leading Clarice towards the top, with Robert Sidwell-Plant still hovering at her back with his arms slightly wide, like a goalkeeper ready to save a penalty. Patience rolled her eyes and followed them.

But Lady Hardcastle and I stopped at the landing with Dotty, as did her husband, whose face had acquired a similar carmine hue.

'I think stopping for a moment is a marvellous idea,' said Lady Hardcastle. 'No point in exhausting ourselves before the weekend has even begun.'

'Quite right, too,' panted Bridgewater. 'Just get my breath back, then we can press on. Don't want to miss the tour.'

'That's a good point, actually,' said Lady Hardcastle. 'I definitely want to find out more about this fort of JB's.'

Just these few moments' pause had improved Dotty's colour no end. 'Then let's not hang about, darlings. Onwards and upwards, as they say.'

We set off once more.

JB and the others had waited for us at the top of the steps, and once we arrived they, too, set off again.

The island itself provided the raised platform on which the fort stood, and the ground rose from the grass and gorse like a miniature mountain. The top had been flattened off – either by nature or gunpowder – and a castle had been built above it.

The path was freshly gravelled and led up a gentle slope towards the fort. Now we were almost upon it, the fort – though tiny compared with a proper grown-up castle like Dover or Windsor – was surprisingly imposing.

From a distance it had looked a little more like a Tudor manor house than a fort, with its white-faced walls and tiled roofs. But now we were closer it was a good deal more formidable. The walls might be fitted with windows but they were sheer castle walls, and I was willing to wager they'd be thick enough to withstand a decent pounding from a ship's guns.

I wondered about this incongruity – a fearsome fort looking like a family home – but then it occurred to me that the side we could see was the side facing the land. Perhaps the local lord had objected to having an ugly fort just off his coastline and had insisted on one or two homely touches to the exterior to make it less of an eyesore.

We couldn't see the side which faced the Channel and its potential invaders, but I was willing to bet it was a good deal more forbidding in appearance. It was fine keeping the lord and his tenants comfortable, but you wouldn't want invaders to feel welcome.

'They certainly knew how to build a fort in the olden days,' I said. 'I'd not fancy taking it by force.'

'You'd be lucky to get close enough to try,' said Lady Hardcastle with a nod. 'A handful of well-manned guns up on those platforms would make matchwood of an approaching ship. You'd not be able to return fire – your guns would all be angled to shoot at other ships, not castles in the sky.'

Eventually, we reached a modestly sized but impressively sturdy, iron-bound front door.

'Welcome to my fortress,' said JB proudly as he opened the door for us. 'Come on in.'

I hadn't quite known what to expect, but the luxurious yet somehow also cosy hall on the other side of the formidable door still came as something of a surprise. The walls were hung with modern tapestries while the flagstone floor was covered with some sort of rush matting. It was a fort . . . but not a fort.

There were appreciative oohs and ahhs from the rest of the group.

JB pointed. 'We're going to put a reception desk over there in the corner. That door there leads to a small bunch of unused rooms and we're going to convert the whole thing to an office and an apartment for the hotel manager.'

This elicited another round of appreciative mutterings.

Apparently pleased with our reactions, JB led us round the rest of his weekend retreat like visitors to a historic castle on a guided tour.

On the ground floor we caught a glimpse of the well-equipped, modern kitchen from where JB's cook-housekeeper, Mrs Crawford, gave us a cheery wave. Beyond the kitchen, we were told, were the butler's pantry and the Crawfords' own comfortable flat – JB was at pains to emphasize the 'comfortable' part.

The rest of the ground floor was given over to a cosy sitting room and a substantial library, both of which had windows looking out to the English Channel. I guessed that the next landfall would probably be Guernsey. Or perhaps Jersey. I resolved to consult the atlas I noticed on the bookshelves to confirm my guess as soon as I had a moment. As with the hall, the walls were hung with modern tapestries, but now the flagstone floors were covered by luxuriant rugs.

A narrow, curved staircase led to the first floor, where JB took us to a beautiful 'long gallery'. I was getting a tiny bit disorientated by this point and I wasn't entirely certain how it sat in relation to the rest of the fort, but in my imagination it was directly above the library. It was certainly a similar shape and now served a similar function: it was JB's museum and housed his nautical collection.

'I figured the guests would appreciate it,' he said.

Maps and charts, mostly of the waters off the north-eastern coast of America and Canada, lined the walls. Cabinets and display cases held knick-knacks and doo-dahs from an assortment of ships, ancient and modern, as well as ships' logs, letters, photographs and medals. There was a captain's jacket with what looked like a bullet hole in the chest on a tailor's dummy. My attention was caught by a display of scrimshaw and I wondered at the skill and patience of sailors who could carve such beautiful and intricate work while being tossed about by the stormy waters of the North Atlantic.

Everything was precisely arranged and fastidiously labelled.

'I can't stand mess and disorder,' said JB with a chuckle when Sidwell-Plant mentioned the neatness. 'You know that. I have to straighten everything up, "sort it all out" as you fellas say.'

There was a cabinet devoted to firearms and it contained a number of pistols and revolvers of assorted vintages, as well as boxes of ammunition of various types, presumably for the weapons on display.

Next to it was another cabinet containing a selection of knives of all shapes and sizes; some were tools, while others were very obviously weapons. Bridgewater was intrigued but, like everyone else, his attention quickly turned elsewhere.

Because the thing that immediately captured everyone's imagination was what looked like an ivory spear. It was about five feet long and was carved with a spiral pattern.

'I say, JB,' said Bridgewater, 'where the devil did you get that? Could do a chap a lot of damage with a spear like that.'

JB smiled. 'It's not a spear – it's a narwhal tusk. Actually, it's a tooth, but we call it a tusk.'

'And what's a narwhal when it's at home?' asked Patience Sidwell-Plant.

'It's an Arctic whale,' said JB. 'And the males grow one of these extra-long teeth. Points straight out of the front of their face. Kinda like a swordfish, if you can imagine it.'

'Whatever for?'

'Same reason males do anything – to impress the ladies.'

There were smirks and chuckles from the group.

'Seems dashed impractical to me,' said Patience. 'How do you kiss a chap with a five-foot tusk sticking out of his face?'

More chuckles.

'Extremely carefully, one imagines,' said Bridgewater.

JB frowned. 'I'm not entirely sure narwhals kiss. But this tusk's just a small one. They can get up to ten feet long. Those are the males the lady narwhals really go for.'

'I still say it would make a good spear,' said Sidwell-Plant. 'You're sure the people who live up there in the Frozen North don't use them?'

JB was still baffled. I remembered from our previous meetings that he still wasn't quite used to the English habit of making a joke of absolutely everything. He was a funny man with a well-developed sense of humour, but in JB's world there was a time for levity – and this, it seemed, was not that time. I wondered if his other friends had noticed that, too, and were teasing him.

Bridgewater and Sidwell-Plant began to mime a fight between two men armed with five-foot ivory spears. George Wilson joined in, taking a fencer's stance and miming, using the tusk as a sword. The three of them were giggling like schoolboys over their mock battle, but JB had already moved on.

A fair amount of the floor was given over to bedrooms, and I thought I counted six, served by three comfortable, surprisingly modern-looking bathrooms. We passed them quickly on our way to the other side of the building.

Next we were shown a luxuriously carpeted drawing room furnished with an improbable number of comfortable armchairs and a gleaming Blüthner piano. Despite its impressive size – the room was large enough to accommodate a billiards table at the far end – it was nevertheless warm and inviting.

My gaze lingered for a while on the piano, and I once more allowed myself to hope that it might be put to use to accompany

Clarice later on. At the very least, Lady Hardcastle could bash out a couple of tunes.

Next door was the dining room with its long, oak table.

Something about the arrangement of the rooms was troubling my servant mind, but it was Sidwell-Plant who voiced the pertinent question.

'Good place to have the dining room,' he said. 'I could look at that view of the Devonshire coast all day. But why put it upstairs? Shouldn't it be nearer the kitchen? I don't envy your man Crawford having to haul your supper up those stairs.'

JB gave a little chuckle. 'Ah, but that's because you've not seen my pride and joy. Look over here.'

He walked over to a pair of small doors on the wall next to one of the windows and opened them. Inside was a reasonably sized, completely empty cupboard. He pressed a button on the door frame and the interior of the cupboard began to move downwards, soon revealing a steel cable attached to the top of what we could now see was a box mounted inside a wood-lined shaft. The whole thing moved silently but reasonably swiftly, and the box was soon out of sight.

'It's a dumb waiter,' said JB. 'We have them a lot in the States and I just couldn't resist having one fitted here. They did a good job with it, don't you think?'

'It's marvellous,' said Sidwell-Plant. 'But how does it work?'

'It's all electrical. We got ourselves a diesel-powered generator in a shed out back. Powers the whole place.'

'Every modern convenience,' said Bridgewater. 'You should have seen the contracts we had to draw up to get all this stuff built. And the planning applications? Good lord – you wouldn't believe it. My office has never been so busy.'

'Still some work to do there,' said JB. 'We still need to get your General Post Office to approve running a telephone line out here, then we'll be all set up.'

'It seems you're already rather well set up as it is, JB dear,' said Lady Hardcastle. 'As Sidwell-Plant says, this is all simply marvellous.'

JB beamed. 'Why thank you, Emily. Now, friends, let's get you settled downstairs in the sitting room and I'll have Mrs Crawford bring us tea and cake while Crawford finishes taking your bags to your rooms. Then you can all rest awhile after your journeys and we can meet at six-thirty for drinks in the library.'

# Chapter Two

I unpacked for Lady Hardcastle before settling into my own room. She didn't need me to, but it gave us a chance to talk privately about the fort and our weekend companions while I fussed about. And, honestly, I quite enjoyed doing things for her.

With that little task done, I secured her agreement that I could have first dibs on the bathroom opposite our rooms – we had decided, unilaterally, that it was 'our' bathroom – and settled in for a soak. It was good to wash off the travelling dust and I felt much invigorated by the time I dried myself and padded across the corridor to my room.

I had so far given no thought to the fact that, despite the chilly February weather, the fort was warm and cosy. When I had drawn my bath and the steaming water had poured in from the tap, I hadn't been surprised. But now as I dressed for dinner in a bedroom with no fire in the grate, I began to ask myself where all this heat was coming from. A glance round my room revealed a cast-iron radiator and I was once again struck by the modernity of JB's weekend place. A centuries-old English fortress updated with twentieth-century technology. Or nineteenth at the very least. I knew the Romans had central heating, but . . . let's just say it wasn't what you'd expect in a sixteenth-century island fort. JB's future guests were going to be well looked after.

I briefly wondered where the furnace and boiler might be, but my musings were interrupted by a knock at the door.

'Just a moment,' I called as I struggled to finish buttoning my evening dress.

'Are you indecent?' It was Lady Hardcastle.

'Positively vulgar most of the time, but I'm fully dressed if that's what you mean. Just come in, for goodness' sake.'

The door opened and a familiar, grinning face peered round it. 'My, don't you clean up well?'

'I'm a vision. Just get in and close the door before someone sees me.'

She did as she was asked.

'You seem to be having trouble there, dear,' she said.

'I can't do these blasted buttons. I don't know why people design dresses like this.'

She stepped over to help. 'What you need, young Flossie, is a lady's maid. I have one. She's simply marvellous. They're all the rage in certain circles.'

I harrumphed. 'So I'm told. But if I'm so essential, how did you manage without me?'

'I didn't,' she said, turning round to reveal the unbuttoned back of her dress. 'Be a poppet and do me up, would you?'

'I'm surprised JB doesn't have some sort of automaton to take care of this sort of thing,' I said as I fastened her dress.

'Wouldn't that be wonderful? A mechanical maid who could cook and clean, fasten dresses and fix hair and who never, ever, gave its employer any cheek.'

'You'd miss my sparkling repartee,' I said as she turned back to face me. 'That's your favourite necklace – you don't often wear that. When did you sneak it into the trunk?'

'It was a last-minute thought. I remembered JB chortling one day about how Dotty Bridgewater and Patience Sidwell-Plant have some sort of competition between themselves as to who can wear the most extravagant jewellery. I didn't want to be left out.'

It was a beautifully ornate piece set with more diamonds than I'd ever seen in one place and had been a gift from her late husband, Sir Roderick. She seldom wore it, despite my repeated insistence that she should, and I was pleased, if a little surprised, to see her finally enjoying it. The matching earrings set off the ensemble perfectly.

'They don't stand a chance,' I said. 'They'll be hard-pressed to match that.'

'Not tonight, at any rate. But I gather it's their habit to escalate the competition as the weekend progresses, saving the most impressive pieces for a spectacular final rubber on the last night. I'm playing my best hand far too early to be in with a chance of winning their little competition.'

'You'll cause a few splutters, nonetheless, even if you're reduced to wearing the same tired old thing every night.'

She sighed a happy sigh. 'I used to wear it every night when Roddy and I were young.'

'I know. I was the one who used to have to put it away in its case when you got home from another of your parties.'

'While I made notes of all the state secrets I'd overheard during the evening.'

'I didn't know you were doing that, though. I thought you were just too lazy to put your things away when you were done with them.'

'Oh, I was. I remain so. But at least then I had an excuse.'

'Slattern.'

'Nag.'

I patted her down and straightened the necklace. 'Shall we go and join our companions for a preprandial bracer?'

'I thought you'd never ask.'

We made our way downstairs together and found the library by following the sound of conversation and laughter.

JB greeted us as we entered. 'Welcome, ladies. I must say you two look a picture. Can I get you something to drink? The *spécialité de la maison* is the Old Fashioned.'

'I'm not sure I've ever had one of those,' said Lady Hardcastle.

'What about that hotel in Manhattan?' I said. 'Didn't we have them there? Whiskey – with an E, obviously – with syrup and bitters.'

'Now there's a gal who knows her liquor,' said JB with a smile. 'But I'm sure I can rustle up something else if that's not to your taste. I don't have any ice, though. Can't seem to get anyone to deliver it.'

'An Old Fashioned will be splendid,' said Lady Hardcastle. 'And the absence of ice is fine. Please don't worry.'

'Ah, but I do worry. Can't have a drink without ice.'

'I noticed that, when we were in America,' I said. 'Why is it that your compatriots think that?'

JB chuckled again. 'Seems we're just the victims of a marketing genius. Story I heard is a fella bought an ice lake up in the north somewhere and was determined to make his fortune selling his ice all around the country. Trouble was, people only used ice to keep their food from spoiling and everyone had just about enough ice for their needs. So he hit upon this wild notion. He employed men to go to bars and ask for a drink with ice. Bartender says, "Sorry, sir, we don't have no ice." And the men are to say, "Oh, but it's the latest fashion. Everyone in . . ." And then he's supposed to say the name of a nearby town, somewhere the bartender will see as competition. "Everyone in Squirrelburg is taking their drinks with ice these days." A couple of days later, the ice salesman shows up and says, "Can I interest you in buying some ice?" And pretty soon, we can't get drinks without ice and the ice man retires to count his fortune.'

Lady Hardcastle laughed. 'And is that true?'

'Heck if I know, but it's a good story either way, don't you think? Now I hear tell of another fella in Fort Wayne, Indiana, who's invented a refrigeration machine. Can you imagine it? Pretty soon we'll be able to make our own ice whenever we want. It's a brave new world that has such people in it, as your bard fella said.'

'Human ingenuity knows no bounds, it seems,' said Lady Hardcastle.

Dorothy Bridgewater approached us. 'Is JB prattling on about his gadgets and thingumajigs again?'

'"Doohickies" is the word, my dear Mrs Bridgewater. I'm prattling on about doohickies. And I haven't gotten to the best one yet. Do you have a phonograph, Lady Hardcastle?'

'Oddly, no. One would imagine I was exactly the sort of person who would, but I never seem to have managed to get round to buying one.'

'But you've heard them, sure enough? A tiny, tinny sound coming out of a great fluted horn of a thing? What if I told you there was another fella in San Francisco who's invented a device for amplifying electronic signals? Imagine if you could turn the sound of a phonograph record into an electronic signal – like a telephone, but much higher quality. You could use a machine based on Mr de Forest's Audion device to play it out through a loudspeaker. It would be like having the musicians in your room.'

Dotty tutted. 'You already have musicians in your room, JB dear, and you're neglecting them. Now fetch Lady Hardcastle and Miss Armstrong a drink, then go and talk to the Everetts. They look a little lost standing there in the corner.'

'I'm on my way,' said JB.

Dotty touched my arm. 'He's a lovely man, but he does go on so. You just have to know how to handle him.'

I smiled. 'He's very enthusiastic about modern inventions. I've always rather liked him.'

'Well, quite. But he still needs to see to his other guests and you two still don't have drinks. Come over and join us while you wait.'

◆ ◆ ◆

JB was an excellent dinner host. Whether it was a skill he'd learned, or a gift he'd been born with, I shall never know, but he made everyone feel comfortable and welcome as we took our places at the long dining table.

Crawford arrived once we were seated and took a terrine on an elegant platter from the dumb waiter which he placed in the middle of the table. He fussed about with a rack of finely sliced toast and small bowls of chutney before withdrawing. As we began to help ourselves, JB tapped his fork on his wine glass.

'Welcome to dinner, my dear friends,' he said. 'Thank you for coming to see my new . . . drum.' He winked at Lady Hardcastle. 'You're my first proper guests and I wanted to share my excitement about the project with you all. I surely do appreciate you making so much effort to be here. Within a year this will be England's premier retreat, providing luxury accommodation for discerning guests away from the hurly-burly of twentieth-century life.'

Raised glasses and a chorus of 'Pleasure to be here' and 'Thank you for inviting us.'

He inclined his head in acknowledgement. 'See, now I know most of you know each other, but I don't think you've all met Lady Hardcastle and Miss Armstrong 'cept on the boat. And I also know how skittish you Brits are about asking each other anything more than your names and how you're finding the weather.'

'Not bad for the time of year,' said Bridgewater through a mouthful of food.

Dotty tutted.

'I'd never ask anyone their name,' said Patience Sidwell-Plant. 'One has to be introduced.'

JB smiled indulgently. 'Actually you're right – you can't even ask that, can you? And you'd rather die than ask anything more personal. Can't ask an Englishman what he does for a living, for instance – that would never do. You're dying to know, but you just can't bear to ask. So let this Yank take all the embarrassment on your behalf and make some introductions for you.'

He gestured towards Lady Hardcastle.

'To my left here, we have Emily, Lady Hardcastle. Scientist, musician, photographer, artist – if she'd been born five hundred years ago she'd have been one of the leading lights of the Renaissance.'

'If I'd been born five hundred years ago, JB dear, I'd have been hanged as a witch. The good folk of fifteenth-century Europe weren't wildly enthusiastic about the idea of women actually *doing* things.'

'The good folk of twentieth-century Europe aren't a great deal more excited,' said Clarice.

'Well, in that case, I'm glad *we* got you and not them,' said JB. 'Wouldn't want to see you hanged.'

'Or burned at the stake,' said Bridgewater. 'Can't bear a burnt steak.'

I braced myself for a Hardcastle lecture, but it was Clarice who spoke up once more. 'We only burned heretics in England, Gran – witches were hanged.'

'That's as may be,' said Bridgewater, 'but I couldn't resist the steak pun. Can't let facts get in the way of a good joke, what?'

'If you make just one good joke over the course of the weekend, Gran darling, I'll eat my violin.'

Bridgewater laughed. 'Give me a few moments, my dear – there's probably something in there about old catgut in your catty old guts. I'll get there eventually.'

'I'll not hold my breath. But I love you for trying.'

Bridgewater laughed again. Clearly this was how the two of them talked to each other. Either that or Bridgewater was impervious to criticism. To be honest, it was too early to tell.

JB waited indulgently for them to finish before adding, 'And now, Emily is famous throughout the land as a solver of mysteries. An amateur gumshoe.'

'A wellington?' said Dotty.

'Don't be daft, Dots,' said Bridgewater. 'She's a sleuth. A detective.'

'I know *that* – I've read about her in the newspapers – but JB said she was a gumboot.'

Lady Hardcastle picked up a slice of toast. 'I do own a pair of wellingtons, if that's any help. It can get quite muddy in Gloucestershire.'

JB pressed on. 'Next to you, Lady Hardcastle, is Edgar Everett, a celebrated piano accompanist in his own right, but now perhaps better known as the husband and manager of one of England's finest violinists.'

Edgar smiled. 'And proud to be so.'

'For the rest of you,' continued JB, 'next to Everett is Miss Florence Armstrong, who works with Lady Hardcastle.'

'So you're a gumboot, too, what?' said Bridgewater.

'I've been called worse,' I said. Part of me wanted to tell them I worked *for* Lady Hardcastle, not with her, and that I was actually her lady's maid, but these days I wondered how true that was. I also knew from tedious experience that that particular revelation usually just caused embarrassment anyway, so for now I was happy to be a gumboot.

'Next to Miss Armstrong,' said JB, 'is George Wilson. He's a dealer in antiquities, among his other talents.'

'My very modest talents,' said Wilson. 'I dabble in this and that.'

'Don't put yourself down, my boy. Wilson here found many of the knick-knacks and *objets* in my collection, some of them very rare. And he's just managed to track down a little something I've been after for quite a while. Should be a terrific addition to the display in the long gallery – something to intrigue the visitors.'

Wilson smiled.

'Granville Bridgewater at the other end of the table is my English attorney – "solicitor", I should say. Can't quite get used to that. Back home a solicitor is the guy who comes to your door trying to sell you something you don't need.'

'Can't say that's entirely different from my own line of work,' said Bridgewater. 'Not sure anyone actually *needs* my services.'

'I'd be lost without you,' said JB. 'Bridgewater handles all my English legal matters.'

'I can do the Welsh ones, too, if you like.'

'I'll keep that in mind. But not Scotland, right?'

'No, not Scotland.'

'Like crossing a state border. Same as I have to have a New York lawyer and a Pennsylvania lawyer.'

'Exactly so.'

'Sure. So then we come to the other side of the table and Clarice Everett. I sold her short a little while ago when I said she was one of England's finest violinists – I would say she's the finest solo violinist in Europe.'

Clarice smiled. 'You're very kind to say so, JB.' Deftly holding a slice of toast in one hand, she discreetly slid her finger across her plate until she located her slice of terrine and then used the knife in her other hand to spread a little on her bread.

'I call 'em as I see 'em, darling Clarice. Next to Mrs Everett is my accountant and business manager, Robert Sidwell-Plant.'

'And I can do that anywhere in the world,' said Sidwell-Plant. 'One doesn't need special qualifications to count things and examine ledgers.'

'Still takes a special mind, though, Bobby. Don't do yourself down. Mrs Dorothy Bridgewater is next. She has the misfortune to be married to Gran—'

'Oh, don't say it like that, JB,' said Dotty. 'I'm very lucky to be married to him.'

'No,' said Bridgewater. 'Sounds fair enough to me. I think you're an absolute saint for putting up with me.'

'Well,' said JB, 'saint or not, Dorothy is also something of a horticultural expert. She's helping me design the gardens here on Guardians Rock.'

'We'll make a little Eden off the Devonshire coast,' said Dotty, proudly.

JB beamed. 'I hope so. And last but not least, we have Patience Sidwell-Plant. Now, Patience has been working with my architect, Henry Lovelace, and is the one responsible for all the decor here in the fort, so she's the one you have to congratulate for the fantastic way the place looks.'

'Marvellous job, m'dear,' said Bridgewater. 'And where *is* Lovelace? I thought he was coming this weekend.'

'Couldn't make it, I'm afraid. Had to go up to Northamptonshire to fix some problems on another project. But that's it – that's all of us.'

'What about you, JB?' said Bridgewater. 'Who the devil are you?'

'I'm just some Yankee with more money than sense. And I judge from the delicious aroma coming from the dumb waiter that I'm saved from further embarrassment by the arrival of our main course.'

Crawford appeared again and cleared the now-empty terrine platter and our plates to a sideboard before unloading the dumb waiter once more. The delicious aroma that JB had mentioned had been growing steadily stronger throughout the fort since before we sat down to eat and was coming from the bouillabaisse Crawford placed on the table in its rustic French *marmite*. Once more he fussed about, this time with bowls and spoons, before loading the dumb waiter with the dirty crockery and then disappearing.

The fish stew looked and smelled wonderful and I knew that, whatever else happened over the course of the weekend, we wouldn't go hungry.

After dinner we retired to the library once more, where JB plied us with cognac and port. Dotty and Patience were chatting, and from the snatches of conversation I could hear, they were discussing their respective plans for the next phase of the fort's redevelopment. Sidwell-Plant was trying to impress Clarice with his knowledge of the classical repertoire, while Bridgewater told a long-winded joke to an obviously bored Everett.

Crawford was on hand to dispense cheese and crackers, and JB brought Mrs Crawford in so that we could all congratulate her on the magnificent meal. She stayed and talked to Dotty and Patience while JB brought Wilson over to join Lady Hardcastle and me.

'So, how do you like my new place?' asked JB. 'I'm trying to gauge reactions. The Bridgewaters and the Sidwell-Plants have all been involved in the conversion in one way or another, but you three and the Everetts are seeing it for the first time.'

'Well, I for one,' I said, 'think it's wonderful. I'd be reluctant to go home to the mainland if I'd booked a stay here.'

'Oh, thank you. We worked hard on it. Lovelace and his builders did a terrific job, then the ladies over there came in to turn the Tudor fortress into a palace.'

'I agree with Flo,' said Lady Hardcastle. 'It's a devil to get to, but it's well worth the trip.'

'Oh, you don't know the half of it,' said JB. 'All our provisions have to come over from the mainland a couple times a week. That old pirate Tommy Vickerman brings the mail and supplies on his ratty old fishing boat and he'll be making the trip more often when the place is up and running. I'm staying here for a spell while we organize a few things, so I'm relying on him to keep me fed.'

'When's he next due?' asked Wilson.

'Not till Tuesday for provisions – we've got enough to last us until after you've all gone home. But that won't be the next time he comes.'

'No?'

'No, my boy. I've got a little surprise for you. Seeing as how it's St Valentine's Day tomorrow I thought I might introduce you to someone. I met a photographer in London and I want her to take some pictures of the place. But I also thought she's perfect for you, so I invited her to join us. I was hoping she'd be here today, but she couldn't make it so she's coming over with Vickerman tomorrow morning. I said I'd send Crawford for her in the yacht, but she insisted on seeing the fishing boat.'

'Oh, JB, really,' said Wilson. 'You're trying to marry me off now?'

'Couldn't help myself. She's a peach. You'll love her.'

'The poor girl. Does she know why she's coming?'

'She's coming to reconnoitre the place for her photos, just like I said. The possibility of a St Valentine's Day romance is just my little surprise bonus.'

'You really are too much, JB.'

My attention, by this point, was beginning to wander a little. I couldn't help but notice the comings and goings of the other guests, who had been excusing themselves and disappearing before slipping back into the room several minutes later. I knew why, of course, and began looking for an opportunity to make my own discreet visit to the WC once I realized that Clarice and Everett had gone and not returned. Their performance in the drawing room was imminent, I felt, and I wanted to be comfortable while we listened to the glorious music I was anticipating.

Lady Hardcastle was holding forth on the subject of . . . actually, I couldn't work out what she was talking about. Something to do with Moby Dick or Nantucket, it seemed. Or possibly both. A half-remembered limerick about a man from Nantucket made me smile and I took my leave.

I wasn't the first to arrive at the drawing room. Everett was already seated at the piano when I entered and was playing something I half recognized.

Lady Hardcastle seemed to read my mind as I sat down next to her. 'Schubert.'

'Thank you,' I said. 'How did you—?'

'From your expression. The crease between your eyebrows gives you away when you're trying to remember something. It's subtly different from your confused face, and nothing at all like your irritated face.'

'I had no idea I was so transparent.'

'I can read you like a piano score, Flossie dear. In this case, Schubert's Impromptu Number 4.'

'In which key?'

'A-flat, if memory serves.'

'Show-off.'

'You did ask.'

It took a while for the rest of the weekend guests to assemble, and Everett kept playing, almost lost in a world of his own. At length, the piece ended to a pit-pat of applause from the room and JB, having judged us all finally to be present, stood up.

'Now that everyone's here,' he said, 'I think we can let Clarice begin. I didn't want any of you to miss this.'

An anticipatory murmur ran round the room as the audience of eight settled to listen. At a nod from Clarice, Everett began the introduction, then she swept up her bow and began to play.

The sound was transcendent. It had always puzzled me how such a straightforward instrument could sound so different in the hands of an amateur and a virtuoso. Taut horsehair pulled across a string, making it vibrate – how was it possible to do that badly? How could it be possible for one person to make a scratching screech and another to produce a sound so perfect it made audiences weep?

I was completely enraptured and I felt rather than saw Lady Hardcastle turn towards me as though about to speak, and I could guess what she was going to say. I touched her leg and shook my head to stop her interrupting. I really didn't care what the piece was, I just wanted to listen.

Clarice played on. The room melted away and all that was left was music. Even the composer, whoever he was, could never have imagined that this piece he'd spent so long perfecting could ever have this effect in the hands of a maestro.

Clarice, too, was totally immersed. Unable to see her audience, it seemed that for her there was just the violin in her skilled hands. There was no 'performance', no element of showing off, she was making that beautiful sound purely for its own sake, for the pleasure of the music.

There was silence when the piece ended, and I noticed I wasn't the only one who had to wipe away a tear before we could applaud.

Even starchy Sidwell-Plant, whose upper lip I imagined to be so stiff he would rather die than show any sort of emotion, had to take a moment to collect himself before he could utter an awed 'Brava'.

Clarice smiled and it struck me that it was the first time I'd seen her do that. This was clearly her calling; this was why she got out of bed in the morning. Everything else she might have to do as she went about her day was nothing compared with the unalloyed joy of playing the violin.

Even Everett looked pleased. Or less displeased, at least.

He launched into the second piece and we were off to the magical land of music once more.

The evening came to a natural end soon after Clarice's performance was over, and we all said our goodnights before heading off to our rooms. Travelling is always exhausting and everyone was keen to get some sleep.

My plan was thwarted, as my plans so often were, by Lady Hardcastle, who insisted on me joining her for a nightcap. She had taken some of JB's very fine cognac from the library along with two glasses, and she poured us both a decent glug before sitting on her bed and gesturing towards the armchair by the window.

'Sit yourself down, Floss. What a place, eh?'

'What a place, and what a night,' I said as I swirled the brandy in its balloon. 'If anyone had told ten-year-old Flossie Armstrong she would one day be spending the weekend in a converted fort listening to one of the finest musicians in the land—'

'In the world, I should say.'

'Without a doubt. But even if they only suggested it would be the finest in the land, ten-year-old Flossie would have laughed in their face.'

'Punched them in their stupid face for their impertinence, I shouldn't wonder.'

I gave a rueful nod. 'Quite probably. And yet here I am. Thirty-five-year-old Flossie is doing just that while sipping extraordinarily good, stolen cognac—'

'I'll take it back, don't worry. I couldn't possibly keep it. This' – she indicated the distinctive bottle with its fleur-de-lis stopper – 'is Louis XIII and probably cost JB more than the average Englishman earns in several months. Several years for some, I shouldn't wonder.'

'Unusual that he leaves it lying about. Most men lock the good stuff away and keep it only for themselves.'

'JB McIntyre is that rarest of creatures: a generous rich man.'

I nodded. 'I've always thought him rather nice for a squillionaire.'

'I have, too. His pals seem all right, as well.'

'A decent bunch,' I agreed. 'Edgar Everett could stand to cheer up a bit, and Sidwell-Plant could be less . . . fussy around Clarice—'

'I keep thinking it's a good thing she can't see him trying to "protect" her or he'd probably get a fat lip.'

'Exactly. But he means well and I've spent weekends with far less pleasant people.'

'Those dreadful people in Sussex that time, do you remember?'

'I do. Or that weekend we spent in Norfolk with that Hungarian couple who were posing as an art dealer and his wife.'

She tutted. 'Ghastly. And art thieves are usually such good company.'

I laughed. 'Charmers to a man. But this lot really do seem to be charming. And I doubt any of them will be stealing anything.'

'They all seem far too well-to-do to be involved in anything so unseemly. Fancy a top-up?'

I looked at my empty glass. 'I'd better not. I think I'll turn in. I have to be at my sparkling best for whatever we all decide to do tomorrow.'

She sighed. 'Very well. I'll see you in the morning.'

I returned to my own room and was asleep within seconds of clambering into my bed.

# Chapter Three

I woke to the sound of seagulls and lay for a few moments trying to fathom out exactly where I was. Fort. Weekend. Music. Warmth. Ah, yes, warmth.

The heating was still working well and I mused for a few moments on whether some similar system might be possible at home. There's something comforting – almost primevally so – about gathering close to the fire on a winter's evening, but it's even more comforting to be able to get up and walk about the house without fear of chilblains.

Lady Hardcastle had mentioned no plans for getting up, but the antique ship's chronometer on the windowsill told me it was already half past seven so I decided to get up and see what the day brought.

Washing and dressing in the warm room was a joy and it felt more like preparing for the day on a summer's morning than a dreary Friday in February. Even my hands were warm as, ablutions done, I knocked on Lady Hardcastle's door.

'Who is it?' came a sing-song voice from within.

I opened the door and peered in. 'If it's not me, then our secret knock has been compromised and we need to change all our codes at once.'

'Flossington! Come in, tiny one.'

I entered, closing the door behind me. 'Flossington?'

'It's something I'm trying out. Do you like it?'

'Not even a little bit.'

'Shame. You're dressed.'

'I thought it might scandalize JB's pals if I were to swank about the fort in the altogether.'

'You make a sound point. But isn't it a little early?'

'It's almost eight and I can smell breakfast. I thought it was time we were up and about.'

'But it's supposed to be a relaxing weekend away. We're supposed to come and go as we please.'

'Technically, it's only Friday so it's not the weekend yet. And your whole life is spent coming and going as you please, anyway. You have fifteen minutes.'

I left her mumbling and returned to the corridor. I half thought about going for a walk – but without a watch, and without knowing where I might see another clock, I wouldn't be able to judge the passage of the quarter of an hour I'd given her. And for the pettiest of reasons, I didn't want to allow her more time than that.

Instead I waited in my own room, looking out of the window at the grey skies and the white-capped sea.

Just as the clock on the windowsill showed that her fifteen minutes were up, there was a knock on the door.

'Who is it?' I chimed.

'It's me, you tiny oaf. Breakfast awaits.'

We went down the passageway to the dining room together.

◆ ◆ ◆

JB sat at the dining table with the Everetts. Rather charmingly, he stood as we entered. Rather predictably, Edgar Everett did not.

'Good morning, Lady Hardcastle,' said Clarice. 'Good morning, Miss Armstrong.'

Lady Hardcastle grinned. 'I say, well done. What gave us away? Footsteps from two sets of ladies' shoes?'

Clarice smiled. 'That and your perfume. It's rather—'

'Overpowering? Sorry about that. I got a little carried away.'

Clarice laughed. 'I was going to say distinctive. But it's not just that: two ladies came in, but only one perfume. I noticed last night that Miss Armstrong doesn't wear perfume so it wasn't much of a leap to reason it was you two.'

'I've never found a perfume I could bear to have wafting up my conk all day,' I said.

'Ah, but after a while, one's snoot becomes accustomed to it and just ignores it,' said Lady Hardcastle. 'One can't smell one's own perfume.'

JB gestured to the sideboard. 'I hope the selection is to your satisfaction, ladies, but do holler if there's anything we've forgotten. If we have it in the storehouse, Mrs Crawford can cook it up for you quick as a wink.'

'Thank you, JB dear.'

'I want you to be comfortable, but I'm testing the place out, don't forget. I want to make sure we get everything right so when we open in the fall, our guests want for nothing.'

We approached the sideboard and began loading our plates. I wasn't sure there was anything more Mrs Crawford could possibly add. Apart from kippers. Luckily, I wasn't in the mood for kippers so I wasn't going to complain.

JB addressed Clarice. 'So it's true what they say about losing one of the senses. The remaining four are intensified.'

Clarice snorted. 'Oh, JB, I expected more of you. Of course they don't. How could they? You have a keen scientific mind – by what biological mechanism do you imagine that would happen?'

'Well . . . I . . . ah . . . that is to say . . .'

'We just pay more attention to them, that's all. You rely very heavily on what your eyes tell you so you don't need to give much thought to what you hear and smell. I can't see anything, so I get my information about who and what's around me by the way people and things sound, by the way they smell. It's not a magic trick, nor is it some miracle of nature. It's just concentration, memory and imagination.'

We took our overloaded plates and sat down opposite the Everetts.

'What other details can you glean from sound and smell?' asked Lady Hardcastle as she buttered a slice of toast.

Clarice thought for a moment. 'Less than you'd hope, but more than you'd think. Fabrics make different sounds, for instance, so I can usually tell whether a lady is wearing satin or linen. Someone who has very recently come in from outdoors will have a crisp, outdoor smell about them, but only for a minute or two. It's more pronounced in cold weather, but it's still noticeable in the summer.'

'Fascinating. Sorry if I'm boring you. You must have to talk about this a lot.'

Clarice smiled ruefully. 'Not as much as you might think. People are dismayingly incurious for the most part. Mostly I have to endure sympathy and the assumption that my blindness makes me feeble-minded. When people realize my musical accomplishments, I become "an inspiration".'

'Are you not an inspiration, though?' said JB. 'Despite your . . . your handicap, you're one of the greatest musicians of the age. How can that not be inspirational?'

Clarice spun her head and looked directly at him. 'How does my blindness affect my ability to make music?'

'Well . . . you can't read the score, for one.'

'I use the Braille music notation system. What else?'

'Well . . . I . . . ah—'

He was saved from further floundering by the arrival of George Wilson.

'Good morning, one and all. I was afraid I might be late.'

'No such thing as late here, young 'un,' said JB. 'Come and go as you please. *Mi casa es su casa,* as they say down in Mexico.'

'Do they, indeed?'

'They surely do. My house is your house. I want all my guests to feel comfortable. If you want breakfast at four in the afternoon, we'll accommodate you.'

'I say. Very generous, JB, very generous. But there's hardly any need for that. I just didn't want to miss spending time with everyone.'

'Well, help yourself from the sideboard there and come and join us.'

While George was doing that, Bridgewater and Sidwell-Plant came in together.

'Morning, all,' said Bridgewater. 'Glad we're not late, after all. The memsahib will be here presently. I left her fussing with her jewellery box.'

'I have no idea what Patience is doing,' said Sidwell-Plant. 'I'm sure she'll be with us soon enough. She does love a good breakfast.'

We joined the chorus of good mornings.

I was about to ask Clarice more about Braille music – as someone who could read music but preferred to play by ear, I was keen to hear the opinion of a professional. My question was put to one side, though, when Dorothy Bridgewater burst into the room in a state of some agitation.

'My ruby necklace. It's gone.'

'Course it isn't,' said Bridgewater. 'You've just mislaid it. Or that dull-witted lady's maid of yours forgot to pack it. It's not like you don't have other jewellery with you.'

Dotty huffed. 'I packed it myself. And checked it twice. I wanted to wear it to the St Valentine's Day dinner tonight. Rubies are very romantic. But now it's gone. The case is empty.'

'That's most frustrating,' said Lady Hardcastle. 'But it might simply have fallen out of the case. We'll help you look for it after breakfast.'

Dotty was already skilfully constructing an impressive pile of food on one of JB's elegantly decorated breakfast plates. 'Oh, I'm not sure I can eat much breakfast. But thank you, dear. That would be most comforting.'

She sat down and Lady Hardcastle patted her arm. 'We specialize in finding lost jewellery.'

'Do you, dear? I thought you specialized in catching murderers.'

'Well, we do that, too, but we found a missing pearl necklace a couple of Christmases ago.'

'How exciting. I don't think that one made the newspapers.'

'No, it was a private affair.'

'We recovered a stolen emerald, as well,' I said.

Lady Hardcastle grinned. 'Oh, we did, didn't we? That was when we first moved to Littleton Cotterell in '08. So, you see, Dotty dear, we're quite the dab hands at finding missing gems. You'll be ready to beat Patience in your little competition in no time.' She winked.

'It'll be quite easy to beat me,' said Patience Sidwell-Plant from the doorway. 'Someone's stolen my diamond brooch.' She glared at Dotty.

◆ ◆ ◆

Breakfast proceeded somewhat frostily.

Dotty and Patience glared at each other.

Bridgewater seemed uncharacteristically flustered by the news and, presumably to cover his obvious discomfort, attempted to lighten the mood with his customary banter. Sidwell-Plant, meanwhile, endured his weak witticisms with less than his usual patience. In truth, neither man seemed quite as relaxed about the disappearances as they were pretending.

JB and I talked stiltedly about the differences between British and American English.

Lady Hardcastle and Clarice talked animatedly about music as though oblivious to the atmosphere around them.

George Wilson seemed uncomfortable, and slightly bewildered, and kept to himself.

Edgar Everett said nothing and just glowered at his food.

It was a relief when Dotty finally declared herself sated after her third plateful of breakfast and suggested to Lady Hardcastle and me that we might set off to hunt for her missing rubies.

'And what about my diamonds?' asked Patience.

'We shall look for them all,' said Lady Hardcastle. 'Come with us. We'll make an adventure of it.'

Patience harrumphed, but appeared to acquiesce.

Lady Hardcastle looked to JB. 'You don't mind us poking about the fort, do you, JB?'

'Not at all. I want these things found as much as anyone.'

'Does anyone else have any objections to our entering your rooms?'

There were none.

'You're wasting your time,' said Everett. 'It'll be the servants. Those two are definitely up to something.'

'What do you mean?' asked Lady Hardcastle.

Everett simply shrugged and returned to his food.

Lady Hardcastle turned once more to JB. 'Is anywhere out of bounds?'

'Nowhere. Go as you please. If a door's unlocked, you can go in. If it's locked, just ask Crawford for the key.'

'Thank you. Come on then, ladies. Let's retrieve your gems.'

We trooped out into the passageway, and I had to reorientate myself. I wanted to head for the stairs, but I'd forgotten that the dining room was on the first floor. Most of the bedrooms were on this floor, too, beginning with the Everetts', which was right next door.

'I'm not at all sure I'm comfortable poking about in other people's bedrooms,' said Dotty as Lady Hardcastle put her hand on the iron door handle.

'I'm perfectly happy,' said Patience. 'That brooch cost a small fortune. Actually, quite a large one – I could probably buy my own place in the country for what that pretty little trinket cost. And I'm getting it back no matter who I have to upset.'

Lady Hardcastle turned away from the door. 'Well, that puts a different complexion on things,' she said. 'I'd assumed the pieces were expensive, but not house-in-the-country expensive.'

'The rubies would probably buy two houses in the country,' said Dotty, the competition still inexplicably on her mind.

'Why on earth didn't you say?' asked Lady Hardcastle.

Dotty shrugged. 'It seemed a little vulgar to talk about money like that.'

'Well, I'm not above talking about money,' said Patience. 'So let's get this door open and get on with it. I've never been sure about Edgar. Nasty chap. I wouldn't put it past him to steal our jewellery out of spite.'

'Spite?' I said.

'Dotty and I play our little game of trying to trump each other's jewels, and he seems to think it diverts attention from his wife's music. Or, more likely, it's that it diverts attention from him. He never seems especially happy that she's the star of the show. But I can imagine him pinching the bijouterie just to teach us a lesson.'

'The money would come in handy, too,' I said.

'Well, quite.'

Lady Hardcastle gave a nod. 'The other possibility is that it's all some sort of practical joke. I'm temporarily at a loss to fathom what the payoff might be, but rather an unfunny joke than an actual tealeaf in our midst. Admittedly, Everett doesn't seem like a man given to making practical jokes – or jokes of any kind for the matter of that – but if you think him capable of acting out of genuine malice, then it still fits.'

'As long as we're not actually accusing anyone of theft, then I suppose it's all right,' said Dotty.

Lady Hardcastle smiled and opened the door. 'At this point, we're accusing no one of anything, dear, but we can't find these valuable pieces without looking. And we can't claim to have looked unless we look *everywhere*.'

We followed her in.

The room was almost unnaturally tidy. I imagined Lady Hardcastle's brain whirring, trying to fathom how anyone could possibly live in such a neat room, but it made perfect sense to me. The floor was clear, with all the furniture pushed back against the walls, so that it was possible to walk from the door to the bed, and from there to the washbasin without any obstructions. There was nothing to trip over, and that's the way Clarice would need an unfamiliar room to be.

'It shouldn't take us long if we work together,' said Lady Hardcastle. 'Check drawers, suitcases, trunks and bags. Under the bed, too. Look in shoes in the wardrobe. Anywhere that could hold a ruby necklace and a diamond brooch.'

We did as we were asked but found nothing. Lady Hardcastle briefly had to take over when Dotty refused to rootle through Edgar Everett's sock drawer, but the search was otherwise incident-free.

We moved on.

'Oh, but this is our room,' said Dotty. 'I've already looked here.'

'Nevertheless,' said Lady Hardcastle, 'we should check it just as we will all the others. We can't claim to have conducted a thorough search if we leave rooms out.'

'Then would you mind if I didn't accompany you? It would be altogether too mortifying to have to be there while you rummage through my unmentionables.'

I tried not to chuckle.

Patience made no such attempt. 'I, for one, am intrigued to see the marvels of twentieth-century engineering that serve as your foundation garments, Dotty dear.'

'You see?' said Dotty. 'Mortifying. We're not all blessed with your willowy figure, Speedy darling. Some of us need a little help, and I'd rather not be there when you find out quite how much.'

'Speedy?' asked Lady Hardcastle as we began our search.

Patience sighed. 'My little sister was unable to say Patience and called me Pacy. The name stuck and family and friends called me Pace or Pacy from then on. Gran Bridgewater, as you might have discerned, fancies himself as something of a wit and he changed Pacy to Speedy one evening as a reaction to my *im*patience at the bridge table.'

'Do you mind?'

'Would there be any point? It's affectionate at least. Had he a better vocabulary he might have settled on "restless" or "fretful" or some other word for impatient, so it could have been worse. At least Speedy makes me sound like a woman of action and accomplishment.'

A thorough search of the Bridgewaters' room revealed no missing jewellery but did, as promised, provide an insight into the architectural scaffolding techniques of haute couture.

George Wilson's room was gem-free, as were both mine and Lady Hardcastle's.

We moved to the empty room reserved for today's late arrival but there was nothing there save for clean towels.

The cupboards were searched, as was every nook and cranny in every bathroom.

We were careful in the long gallery not to damage any of JB's exhibits but we still didn't find what we were looking for.

'Upstairs?' said Lady Hardcastle when we had completed our search of the first floor.

'There are a few rooms up there,' said Patience. 'Though I think JB's suite is the only one that's occupied. There's nothing but an empty corridor on the dining room side of the fort.'

We searched the bedrooms and the various storerooms on the second floor. Still nothing.

By this point, Patience was clearly bored, and we left her in her room.

We started to make our way downstairs but Lady Hardcastle paused and pointed. 'What about those doors. Do they lead outside?'

'Yes,' said Dotty. 'Out on to the terrace. It was the main gun platform when this was a fort, but JB has it decked out as a sun terrace now.'

'Is there anything out there?'

'A shed for the furniture, that's all.'

'We'd better have a look.'

And so we dutifully trooped out into the rising wind, checked the shed and trooped back. We found spiders – what were they doing out there? How did they get here from the mainland? What did they find to eat? – and some rather nice outdoor furniture, but nothing else of note.

We returned indoors and made our way down to the ground floor.

'What I don't understand,' said Dotty, 'is who had the time to take my necklace. It was with me in our bedroom. Then everyone was down in the library for drinks. Then we had dinner. Then we all went to the drawing room to hear Clarice. No one had a chance to ransack both our room and Patience's.'

I shook my head. 'That's not entirely true. There was about half an hour between the end of dinner and the start of Clarice's performance when everyone was coming and going. No one was in sight for the whole time. And if the thief had planned everything properly, it would be easy for them to do the deed and sneak back unnoticed.'

She sighed. 'So it could be anyone.'

Lady Hardcastle patted her arm. 'We'll find it. Them. You know, it really could all just be a practical joke.'

'I've never been fond of practical jokes, you know. They always rely on making the victim look foolish. And I feel quite foolish enough most of the time without someone deliberately making fun of me.'

'We just have to take it with good grace. They're probably waiting for us to exhaust ourselves with this fruitless search before plucking them from a coat pocket with a flourish and then laughing themselves hoarse at how silly we've all been. We'll smile ruefully and pretend we don't mind.'

'Hmm. I certainly wouldn't put it past Gran to do something like that. Sometimes I wish I didn't love him quite so much – he can be *so* exhausting.'

I laughed. 'There doesn't seem to be any malice in him.'

'None whatsoever, dear, but sometimes one feels that life would be a good deal less hard work if every interaction didn't have to begin or end with a joke.'

'Is he that good an actor?' asked Lady Hardcastle. 'He certainly seemed most perturbed by the disappearance of your rubies.'

'Oh, he could have been on the stage, dear. Honestly, sometimes I think he'd rather have done that than be a boring old solicitor.'

We made our way to the library to begin our search of the ground floor.

'Do you know the Crawfords?' asked Lady Hardcastle.

'Not well. You've been to JB's place in London, haven't you? He has a valet and a housekeeper there, as well as a couple of maids-of-all-work. I've met them all at one time or another but he doesn't bring them with him. He hired the Crawfords locally, specifically for the fort – when the place is up and running they'll be the senior staff. I've spent very little time here – just long enough to measure the garden and make some sketches – so I've only really nodded hello.'

'Ah. I'm just trying to gauge how they'll react when we search their rooms. I don't want it to look as though we're accusing them of anything. We're not accusing *anyone* of anything – we're just trying to find some misplaced items.'

'I have no idea, dear. I'm sorry.'

'Let me take the lead when we get to their flat,' I said. 'I'll make sure they don't feel like suspects.'

This seemed to satisfy the other two and we continued our room-by-room search, finding – as I was coming to expect – absolutely nothing.

◆ ◆ ◆

We entered the servants' quarters through the kitchen, where Mrs Crawford was already busy preparing lunch.

She didn't seem at all fazed by the unexpected arrival of three houseguests at the top of the short flight of steps leading into her domain. 'Hello, m'dears. What can I do for you? Lunch i'n't till twelve, but I've got some fruitcake if you're feelin' peckish.'

I smiled. 'We're quite all right, Mrs Crawford—'

'Call me Peggy, my luvver. I can't be doin' with all that Mrs Crawford nonsense.'

'I shall. But we don't need anything to eat. Or at least I don't think we do.' I looked to my companions.

'Actually, I wouldn't mind a slice of that cake if you're offering,' said Dotty.

'Be my pleasure. I'll cut you a piece dreckly – I just need to set this pastry to restin'.'

She took her mixing bowl and disappeared into the pantry.

'Dreckly?' whispered Dotty.

'Directly,' I whispered back. 'She'll do it as soon as she can.'

Peggy returned. 'Now, then, who else wants a slice of cake?'

Lady Hardcastle and I both declined, but Dotty took the proffered piece and munched eagerly.

'We're actually on a mission,' I said. 'Mrs Bridgewater and Mrs Sidwell-Plant have both managed to mislay a couple of small items and we're helping to search for them. They're just tiny things so they could easily have been caught up in towels or linens when you or Mr Crawford—'

'Now, you should definitely call that gurt noodle Jago. Mr Crawford makes him sound like a solicitor or sommat.'

'—when you or . . . Jago were tidying up. We won't get in the way, but we'd be grateful if we could look round your flat to make sure nothing got kicked under a dresser or anything like that.'

'You do what you need to do, m'dear. Valuable, these lost things, are they?'

'Not especially,' I said. 'But you know how frustrating it is when things go missing.'

'Oh, I do. You look round. Jago i'n't here, but he won't mind, neither.'

I smiled. 'Thank you, Mrs— Thank you, Peggy. Oh, have any of the other guests been down to see you?'

'No, m'dear. You're the first.'

We left her to continue her lunch preparations and went through to the next room, the butler's pantry.

It was full of the usual butlerish paraphernalia – polishes, cloths, corkscrews, a decanting cage – as well as a selection of small tools. There was no sign of the jewels.

A short passageway led to the Crawfords' sitting room, then another to their spacious and comfortable bedroom with its private bathroom beyond.

By the time we returned to the kitchen Crawford was back from whatever errand he'd been on.

'Hello, ladies,' he said with a warm smile. 'Peg tells me you'm lookin' for sommat. Anythin' I can do to help?'

'No, thank you, Jago,' I said. 'We only really came down here so we could reassure Mrs Sidwell-Plant we'd looked everywhere. You have a lovely home here.'

''T'i'n't bad, is it?' he said, proudly. 'Better than the old pub we lived in backalong, eh, Peg?'

Peggy nodded, sagely. 'Oh-ar. Definitely. Fallin' down, that were.'

'You ran a pub?' asked Lady Hardcastle. 'How wonderful.'

'You wouldn't say that if you'd seen it,' he chuckled. 'And the customers? Rogues and scoundrels the lot of 'em. I'd much rather be workin' for Mr McIntyre and livin' here.'

Peggy nodded again. 'Much rather.'

'Well, we shan't detain you any longer,' said Lady Hardcastle. 'Thank you for indulging us.' She paused and then pointed to a door in the corner of the kitchen. 'What's through there?'

'Just a storeroom and the wine cellar,' said Peggy. 'Sundry bits and bobs, mostly, but we keeps it locked because of the booze. No real need while it's just Mr McIntyre's friends visitin', but we wants to get into the habit afore the payin' guests start arrivin'. You know? But there won't be nothin' of the ladies' in there.'

'Of course. And that one leads outside, one presumes.' She pointed to a substantial, iron-bound door.

'That's right. We uses it for deliveries, mostly – saves us draggin' things in through the hall.'

Lady Hardcastle smiled and nodded. 'Aha. Well, good day to you both. And thank you again.'

◆ ◆ ◆

We made our way out into the great hall just as JB came in from outside, accompanying a strikingly beautiful woman of about my age and size. She was expensively dressed but her smile was most definitely the first thing anyone would notice. She seemed thrilled to be at the fort.

'Oh, JB, this is wonderful. Just look at the way the light comes in from those upper windows. And the decor – oh, my. Your friend did this, you say?' Her accent was hard to place. Southern England, certainly. Probably upper-middle-class London, but it was hard to tell.

'Patience Sidwell-Plant, yes,' said JB. 'You'll meet her soon. Dotty Bridgewater here is designing the gardens.'

There was a brief round of how-do-you-do's as JB introduced us to the newcomer – whose name, we learned, was Lily Thacker.

Lily dazzled us once more with her smile. 'I'm so sorry I couldn't come over with you all yesterday but I had an appointment in Exeter I simply couldn't get out of.'

'No matter,' said JB. 'At least you're in time for lunch today.'

'Indeed. And now I'm finally here I'm very much looking forward to getting to know you all. Oh, and you absolutely must let me photograph you – you're all so . . . interesting.'

I tried my hardest not to laugh. If I'd been given a choice on what it was about us all that made us promising photographic subjects, I'd have opted for 'beautiful'. I'd have settled for 'alluring'. 'Ravishing' would have been nice. 'Gorgeous', perhaps. 'Bewitching'? Even 'winsome' would have been better than 'interesting'. It made me feel like a sideshow attraction. 'Roll up, roll up. Come and see Florence Armstrong – she's . . . interesting.'

'And we must talk about photography at some point, too,' said Lady Hardcastle, who, to be fair, was not only beautiful but also very interesting.

'We must,' said Lily with another smile.

The Everetts had come down the stairs and were crossing the hall on their way to the door.

'Hi, Clarice,' said JB. 'Hi, Everett. Off for a walk?'

'Just a stroll round the island before luncheon,' said Everett.

'Good idea. But come on over here and meet our final guest before you go. Clarice and Edgar Everett, may I present Miss Lily Thacker, a photographer from London.'

I'd got the London part right, at least.

'Lily, this is Clarice Everett, the famous violinist, and Edgar, her equally famous husband.'

Clarice held out her hand towards JB.

'Oh, my goodness,' said Lily. 'How wonderful to meet you. Will you both be playing? May I photograph you?'

Having located her by the sound of her voice, Clarice turned a little so that she was facing Lily. Her nostrils flared slightly as Lily shook her hand. 'I have no objections. It's not as though I'll be embarrassed by how awful I look.'

'Oh,' said Lily with a nervous little laugh. 'I suppose not. Thank you.'

Everett looked at Lily with a slightly puzzled frown but then tipped his hat, and he and Clarice continued to the door.

'Well, ladies, I should leave you to your search while I show Lily to her room. And then there's a young gentleman I'd like you to meet, Lily. I think you two will really get along.'

'Search?' she said with a puzzled frown.

'A couple of items have been mislaid,' said Lady Hardcastle. 'Nothing to worry about.'

JB led Lily towards the stairs.

Lady Hardcastle waited until they'd gone. 'Aside from the locked storeroom in the kitchen, I think we've searched everywhere in here. Is there anything outside?'

'There's a privy out on the lower gun platform,' said Dotty. 'And another storeroom next to the kitchen door. Oh, and a toolshed down in the garden, but I doubt anyone would have had time to get there and back without being missed, even if they did manage to find their way in the dark.'

'Then we'd better have a quick look in the lav and the larder before we call it a day and get ready for lunch. I think you're right – no one could have gone out to the garden.'

Dotty looked crestfallen.

'Don't worry,' I said. 'We'll fathom it out. We always do.'

She gave me a wan smile and we made our way to the door.

# Chapter Four

I changed for lunch.

Let me say that again, but slower this time:

I . . . changed . . . for . . . lunch.

It wasn't exactly unprecedented. I had played the role of many an upper-class lady on espionage missions in the past where changing clothes every time the clock struck was, for reasons still unknown, de rigueur. But in my personal life, this was a major development.

I had long derided the need to pack multiple outfits for Lady Hardcastle for a country house weekend when all she really needed was an indoor dress, some outdoor clothes and an evening dress. Throw in appropriate shoes, a nightdress and undergarments, and you were packed. There was no need, I always insisted, for a morning dress, a lunchtime dress, an afternoon dress and an evening dress for each day of the stay (all complete with complementary shoes or boots), together with the outdoor clothes and boots (preferably more than one outfit in case there were outdoor activities on different days), nightwear and underwear.

And yet this is where I now found myself. The dress I had worn that morning, which would have seen me through to Monday as long as I was careful not to spill anything on it, was now to be cast back into the trunk, not to be worn again on this trip except in the direst sartorial emergency.

I sighed as I pinned on my favourite picklock brooch and checked myself in the glass. Obviously, I looked splendid. But I had looked splendid before. I couldn't be sure what else I might have done with the time it had taken me to complete this needless transformation, but I was willing to bet the price of the dress that it would have been more fun and more useful than replacing one perfectly serviceable outfit with another.

I went to Lady Hardcastle's room to see if she needed any help.

I gave the agreed knock.

'Who is it?' came the sing-song reply.

I sighed. 'It's the plumber, ma'am. I've been advised that there's a decrepit old boiler in this room. I'm here to see if she needs to be condemned.'

'Not today, thank you.'

'Just open the bloody door.'

'Open it your-bloody-self – it's not locked.'

I went in to find her still not fully dressed, holding up an afternoon frock in front of herself and checking its effect in the full-length glass. 'What do you think?'

'I think if you're going to be flouncing about in your unmentionables you ought to lock the door.'

'Honestly, dear, if anyone is desperate enough to want to see this' – she gestured up and down herself – 'they're welcome. And I wasn't flouncing, I was contemplating.'

'Fair dos.' I pointed to the bed. 'Then you ought to contemplate the green one. It looks like the weather is closing in and the blue will look better tomorrow when the light is greyer.'

'Thank you. You have an eye for these things.'

She struggled into the green dress. I probably should have helped, but it was more entertaining not to.

'Do you have thoughts on this morning's shenanigans?' she asked once she and the dress had been properly introduced.

I began some remedial work on her hair. 'Jewellery's easy to hide. It's easy to miss, too, but I'm reasonably sure we didn't. I find it hard to accept the idea of things "vanishing into thin air" but that's what they seem to have done. The less paranormal explanation is that the thief has the pieces about their person. Either that or we were too hasty in accepting Peggy Crawford's assertion that the lost property was unlikely to be in her locked storeroom.'

'Hasty, perhaps, but politic, I felt. It looked as though we suspected them of something when we rootled through their private quarters. Asking her to unlock the door would have been a direct accusation of theft. It might turn out to be justified, but I'd rather keep them both on our side for the time being. I'm sure we'll get another opportunity to look in there.'

'By which time they might have moved the stolen gear.'

'That's a chance we'll have to take. Servants, as you so often remind me, are a valuable resource, and not just because they make nice pies and keep the place clean.'

'Talking of nice pies, do you fancy a spot of lunch?'

'I thought you'd never ask.'

We set off for the dining room.

JB was already there, as was Lily Thacker, whom he had seated next to George Wilson. They seemed to be getting along very well, much as JB had hoped.

He indicated the seats opposite them and we made ourselves comfortable.

The Everetts were next, and he sat them with Lily and Wilson.

The Sidwell-Plants came in with the Bridgewaters and JB sat them with clumsy obviousness so that, although the Bridgewaters were together, the Sidwell-Plants were deliberately separated.

With Lily, Wilson, Everett, Clarice and Sidwell-Plant on one side, and Lady Hardcastle, me, Patience, Dotty and Bridgewater on the other, the Sidwell-Plants were as far from each other as possible without actually moving the earlier arrivals.

Crawford began loading platters on to the table from the recently arrived dumb waiter and we began helping ourselves to the delicious baked mackerel.

'Did you find it?' asked Patience.

'Sadly not,' I said.

'Then what on earth has happened to it?'

Lily's ears pricked up. 'Is this the thing you were all looking for earlier? What is it?'

I didn't quite know what to say. We were all acting as though we were friends but Lily was the newcomer and, as far as I could make out, no one but JB knew her. Would he want her to think there was a thief at the fort? Would we want to allay any fears by telling her we thought it was all just a joke? If we did that we would tell the prankster we knew what they were up to. Would that help or hinder? Would—

'Someone has stolen my diamond brooch and Dotty's ruby necklace,' said Patience.

Apparently we didn't mind telling Lily at all.

'Well,' said Dotty, slowly. 'We don't know that for sure. We've certainly both misplaced expensive items.'

Patience shook her head. 'I might accept that if just one of us had "misplaced" something. Especially if it were you. But it's far too much of a coincidence that we've both "misplaced" exactly the same sort of something on exactly the same evening.' She looked around the table, pointing at the other guests with her table knife. 'Those pieces are worth an absolute fortune. If one of you has taken them – even if it was just done as a prank – we'll find out who. And when we do . . .'

She left the specifics of the threat to our imaginations, but I definitely wouldn't have wanted to be in the thief's shoes.

◆ ◆ ◆

Lunch settled into the usual empty chit-chat and admiration of JB's weekend home. When we were finished, Lady Hardcastle went off to the long gallery with JB and Wilson to talk about Nantucket whalers. Or Spanish treasure ships. Or Nelson's posting to Antigua. Or possibly all three. Whatever it was, they were all very excited about it. I was not.

JB invited Lily to join them but she declined. I couldn't find it in myself to blame her.

Dotty had gone off for a postprandial nap, while her husband and his pal Sidwell-Plant had retired to the drawing room to play billiards.

The Everetts had silently evaporated. I knew not where they had gone.

This left me, Patience and Lily still at the dining table with no real plans.

'I wouldn't mind taking a good look round JB's library,' I said after an awkward pause. 'Would either of you care to join me?'

'Oh, rather,' said Lily with unanticipated girlish enthusiasm. 'I'd live in a library if I could.'

'Good lord,' drawled Patience. 'I'd live in a palace if I could.'

'I've visited quite a few palaces,' I said. 'They're not nearly as luxurious as you imagine. And they're *very* cold in the winter. Draughty, you see?'

Patience regarded me curiously. 'Well, aren't you a surprising one? You can tell us more on the way to the library.'

'Oh, yes, rather,' enthused Lily. 'Where were these palaces? Oh, do say they were somewhere wonderful. Have you danced with crown princes?'

'As a matter of fact, I have,' I said.

'You have not,' said Patience with a *pfft*.

'One grand duke, two generals, an admiral, and more colonels than I can count. Oh, and a Romanian princess.'

'A Romanian princess?' said Lily. 'How on earth—?'

'She's teasing you, Lily dear. As if anyone's danced with that lot.'

I gave them both a smile and a shrug.

By now we were passing the door to the sitting room.

Voices were coming from within. Raised voices.

As one, we paused to listen.

'. . . useless cripple. You'd be nothing without me. Nothing. If your legions of admirers had even half an idea of how pathetic you are they'd turn away from you in disgust.'

Patience, Lily and I looked at each other agog. It was Everett, and he was clearly talking to Clarice.

I made to step into the room. This had to be stopped.

Patience held me back and shook her head.

'He might be dangerous if he's in a temper,' she whispered.

'Not half as dangerous as I am,' I said, and shook my arm free.

I moved once more towards the door. I hadn't yet noticed that the tirade had ceased and was nearly bowled over as Everett burst out of the sitting room and stalked off down the hallway towards the stairs.

The ladies and I looked at each other again and went in to see what we could do for Clarice.

She looked very shaken. 'Who's there?'

'Flo, Lily and Patience,' I said. 'We—'

'You heard. Of course you did. I'm so sorry.'

'Good lord,' said Patience. 'You've nothing to apologize for. What on earth—?'

'I'm sorry you had to hear it, that's what I meant. No one should have to hear him when he's like that.'

'Least of all you,' I said. 'Does this sort of thing happen often?'

'He's a very jealous and bitter man,' said Clarice. 'When we met he was the star. His piano playing was the talk of London. And his compositions were making people sit up and take notice, too. And now? Now he's the accompanist to the brave, blind violinist. Very much second fiddle. But without a fiddle. He resents every moment of my success and he takes it out on me.'

'Does he hit you?' I asked. I was more than prepared to hit him back if she said yes.

'Oddly, no. I think he'd love to, sometimes. I can hear it in his voice. But he's afraid of what people might say if they found out he'd struck a blind woman. I should be thankful for small mercies, I suppose.'

'Why don't you just leave him?' said Lily.

Clarice sighed. 'I honestly don't know. Inertia, I suppose. It's easier to put up with his spiteful tantrums than to contemplate a life on my own. I pride myself on being self-reliant, but now the thought of having to start that new life fills me with dread. I'd have to find somewhere to live. And what about my work? He handles all the bookings – how would I do that? I mean, I could probably find a way to do it all, but for the price of a small amount of humiliation once in a while, I already have someone to take care of it.'

Patience took Clarice's hand. 'I've said it before and I'll say it again now: you can come and live with me. There's acres of room at the house where you could live and practise, and I know plenty of people who could book concert appearances for you. We'd have a wonderful time.'

Clarice laughed. 'You've always been so kind. But what would Bobby say?'

'Bobby can go and jump in a lake. Actually, I rather wish he would anyway. I mean it, Clarice. If you ever decide to leave that ghastly bully, you just give me a ring. I'll have a car round to your place in a trice, and to the Devil with them both.'

'Thank you. I doubt I shall, but thank you, anyway. There is one very practical thing you can do for me if you wouldn't mind, though.'

'Name it, darling.'

'I'm still not very familiar with the layout of this damn fort. Would you mind awfully showing me the way back to my room.'

'Of course. Are you sure, though? Won't Edgar be there?'

'No, he always goes off to sulk on his own when he's in a temper like that. He'll be hiding out somewhere.'

'I'd be happy to,' said Lily. 'Will you come with us, ladies?'

'I think I'll keep an eye on things down here,' I said. 'I'll make sure he doesn't disturb you.'

'Oh, do be careful,' said Lily. 'He doesn't strike Clarice, but he might not think twice about walloping you.'

'Oh, I do hope he tries,' I said.

Lily gave me a puzzled look.

'I'll stay here with Florence,' said Patience. 'I have a suspicion she might be the one to put your money on if things cut up rough.'

Lily gave her a puzzled look, too, but led Clarice out into the corridor. I could hear her chattering as they climbed the stairs.

Patience made herself comfortable in one of the sitting room's many fashionable armchairs while I looked out of the window at the darkening skies.

'I'd kill for a cup of tea,' said Patience. 'Do you fancy one?'

I turned. 'I've rarely been known to refuse. Any idea where the bell is?'

'Somewhere well thought out but bafflingly hard to use, knowing JB. He's the most impractical practical man I've ever known. "Well, young Patience, see, I put it there because that meant the shortest possible run for the electric cable. Most efficient place for it." "But no one can see it, and half of us can't reach it." "Well, gee, I never thought of that."'

I laughed at her uncannily accurate impression.

'I say,' said a voice from the doorway. 'You two seem to be having fun. What am I missing?'

Lady Hardcastle entered.

'We're trying to find the bell – we want tea.'

'Oh, yes, tea,' she said. 'What a splendid idea. But why the bell hunt? It must be here somewhere. JB would never neglect something as essential as a bell.'

'Which is exactly what we were discussing,' I said. 'So your challenge is to find it. If you think you're up to it.'

'A shilling says I find it before either of you.'

'You're on.'

Patience laughed. 'Are you two always like this?'

'*She* certainly is,' we said together.

Patience laughed again. 'Well, I'll keep out of your way and let you get on with it.'

I turned to examine the area around the window and, quite by chance, happened to catch a glimpse of something brass, partially concealed behind the heavy, tied-back curtains.

I moved a little to properly block it from view, doing my best to make it seem as though I was merely trying to get myself into a better position to scan the room.

Lady Hardcastle began a systematic search of the walls either side of the door.

With my left hand shading my eyes like a sailor looking out to sea, I stood on tiptoes and looked about the room.

'You'll never beat me like that,' said Lady Hardcastle as she moved on to one of the short side walls.

'We shall see,' I said, and continued my mariner-ish search.

I let her get halfway along the side wall nearer to me before I said, 'Oh, look. Here it is. Found it.'

Lady Hardcastle harrumphed. 'You rotten cheat. You knew it was there all along.'

'Indeed no – I didn't spot it until after I'd accepted the wager. I just thought it would be funnier to let you sniff up and down the walls like a—'

'If you say "pig hunting for truffles" I shall write you out of my will.'

'Oh, I wasn't going to say anything of the sort, but now I can think of nothing else. Oink-oink.'

I rang the bell and moved towards an armchair. She spotted my move and raced towards it, sitting down before I could reach it.

'Child,' I said.

'Cheat.'

I sat in another chair.

Patience laughed anew. 'I love you both. You're a breath of fresh air after what we just witnessed. Thank you.'

'Goodness,' said Lady Hardcastle. 'What did you witness?'

I briefly described the incident between Clarice and Everett.

'I hope you thumped him one,' she said when I was done.

I shrugged. 'I certainly thought about it, but he was off down the corridor before I'd fully assessed what had just happened.'

Patience had remained silent during my recap of events and looked away when I turned to her for confirmation of one of the details.

I was going to ask her what was wrong, but at that moment Crawford arrived, puffing slightly.

He looked around the room. 'Was it you who rang? I can't make head nor tail of that blasted bell board. I went upstairs to the drawing room at first but there i'n't no one there. Then I realized I'd got the drawing room and the sitting room mixed up.'

'It was us,' said Lady Hardcastle with a smile. 'Do you think we might have a pot of tea, please?'

'O' course, m'lady. It is "m'lady", i'n't it? I remembered Mr McIntyre sayin' one of the guests was Lady Sommat, but I'm blowed if I can remember which of you it were.'

She laughed. 'It's me, but I really don't mind if you forget. As Miss Armstrong here said earlier: "I don't mind what you call me as long as it's early for dinner."'

He gave a throaty chuckle. 'I shall always try my best. But it's tea you want for now. I think the missus has made some biscuits, too, if you fancies a nibble.'

Patience frowned. 'We've only just had lunch.'

'Actually,' I said, 'I never say no to a biscuit. Thank you.'

'I shall be back in two shakes,' he said as he stepped smartly out of the room.

◆ ◆ ◆

We drank our tea and talked about nothing very much. For a while it seemed that Patience had got over her distress at Everett's unkindness, but when the pot was empty and the biscuits she hadn't wanted were gone – she'd eaten three – she excused herself and returned to her room.

Lady Hardcastle stood and looked out of the window. 'Was the argument *that* bad?'

I joined her. 'Honestly, we didn't hear an actual argument. We just caught the tail end of whatever had been going on, and that involved Everett being thoroughly beastly. When we spoke to Clarice she said he talks to her like that quite often.'

'Why doesn't she just leave him?'

'Inertia.'

'Actually, yes, I can understand that. We don't make it easy for a woman to leave her husband.'

'True. But Patience offered to take her in.'

'Did she, indeed? Well, now one wonders if all is entirely well *chez* Sidwell-Plant.'

'How so?'

'She was upset by the bullying—'

'*I* was upset by the bullying. I wanted to slosh him one.'

'And it's to your credit. But one wonders if she has some fellow feeling with the bullied. Her willingness to find room in her home for someone from her broader circle of friends speaks volumes, don't you think? We all like to think we'd move heaven and earth for our closest, most intimate friends. But would we open our homes to mere chums unless . . . ?'

'Unless we were going through the same thing. It's possible, I suppose, but it's a bit of a leap.'

'I specialize in improbable leaps, dear, you know that. I've built an entire career on it.'

'If you can call it that.'

'A career? I suppose that's a bit of a leap, too, isn't it. Still, this is where we find ourselves.'

I sighed. 'In a converted fort on an island a mile off the Devon coast. With the weather closing in.'

'And a thief in our midst, mischievously making things disappear.'

'It's not quite the seaside weekend I was anticipating, I must say. I didn't expect donkey rides and sticks of rock, but I thought we might have a relaxing time at an interesting country retreat in enjoyable company. There might have been some pleasant, sunny strolls along the clifftops.'

'In February? You're an ambitious one, young Flossie.'

'A girl can dream. At this rate we'll be stuck indoors till Monday while our thief-or-prankster hides all our most precious things and laughs at us.'

'And I know how you hate to be laughed at.'

I looked at her. 'Doesn't everyone? I hate practical jokes.'

'As does Dotty B. We shall just have to put our thinking caps on and outwit them. If it's a prank, though, my money's on Granville Bridgewater.'

'He does seem to be the one most likely to find an unfunny joke like that absolutely hilarious. Everett is just vile – I'm not sure he has a sense of humour – but I wouldn't put malicious theft past him. Clarice would be perfectly capable of it if she knew exactly where to find the jewellery, but it would take her considerably more time than she had. Sidwell-Plant is too staid, too proper. George is a little more fun, but he was with us all the time. He's the only one of them who doesn't seem to have had an opportunity so it can't be him . . . Of course, if this were a detective story, that in itself would make him the thief. He'd have some ingenious way of being in two places at the same time.'

'A trained monkey?' suggested Lady Hardcastle. 'We'd have smelled it by now.'

'True. But back in the real world . . . Dotty and Patience might be in it together, of course, but I can't really see it.'

'How about if they weren't working together but against each other?'

'Each stealing the other's prize piece to win their little competition, you mean? It's a possibility, I suppose, but it's a massive coincidence if they both came up with the same idea and each managed to carry out their theft at the same time as the other.'

She shrugged. 'I'm not a great one for coincidences, as you know, but it has an amusing elegance about it.'

'I'm not convinced, either, but those are the only people we have to choose from. Lily wasn't even here.'

'They're not the only ones here. We have to consider the Crawfords as well – do you remember what Everett said about them being up to something? And there's JB, of course. It's all a bit grim, isn't it? Let's hope it's all just a lark, after all, eh?'

A sudden gust of wind made all the windows on the seaward side of the fort rattle. A shriek came from the library next door.

'Sounds like Dotty Dorothy has been spooked by the wind,' I said.

'I thought she was having a nap.'

'As an accredited Master Napper of the Worshipful Company of Dozers and Snoozers, I can affirm that the ideal nap length is about half an hour. She's had plenty of time to refresh herself and rejoin the throng.'

'I forget your many accomplishments, tiny one. But if there's a throng in the library, ought we rejoin it ourselves?'

'It would be the sociable thing to do.'

# Chapter Five

There was, indeed, something of a throng in the library, which had clearly been designed not just as a place to hold a very pleasing selection of books from JB's extensive collection, but as a comfortable, informal gathering place for companionship and conversation.

We first met JB McIntyre sometime around 1906 when he was still trying to find his feet in English society. We were up to some sort of mischief involving a Hungarian spy who had rather skilfully insinuated himself into the company of a member of the cabinet with a view to getting hold of some important state papers. Obviously, we set about putting a stop to that, and it was at a concert at the Albert Hall, where we confronted him and told him his fortune, that we also met JB. He'd been on his way to the bar when he saw Lady Hardcastle, the errant Hungarian, and me emerge from a door marked *Private*.

The Hungarian looked a little the worse for wear and JB asked after his health, but the man scuttled off without answering, leaving Lady Hardcastle to explain in her customary cheerily blithe manner that the poor fellow had taken a tumble on the stairs and we'd been helping to straighten him out. This much was, at least, partially true – he *had* taken a tumble and we had most emphatically 'straightened him out' – but obviously she kept things suitably vague and her explanation contained nothing that would see us fall foul of the Official Secrets Act.

JB was clearly enchanted by Lady Hardcastle – that happened a lot, to be honest – and he invited us to dine with him 'and a few friends'. We'd been part of that ever-widening circle of friends ever since.

So wide was that circle by now that we'd never met any of that weekend's guests before, and if we were to solve the Mystery of the Missing Bijouterie then we would have to get to know them all a lot better.

In that room, at that time, though, we were going to struggle.

I could see no sign of Clarice or Everett, but as far as I could make out, everyone else was present. Or seemed to be, at least; it was difficult to be certain. Dotty and Patience were standing by a window, close to one of the radiators, but the others were in a tight little group, talking in low tones, and I couldn't quickly see who was there.

This was not going to be like mingling at a delightful soirée where guests would flit from group to group like happy bumblebees moving between enticing blooms. If we were going to insinuate ourselves into either of the groups it would be more akin to a military invasion. We would need to establish a forward position and secure our supply lines before attempting any serious incursion.

Instead, I poured us each a cup of tea from the large pot on one of the tables and we stood together, sipping and earwigging.

'. . . and I'd put good money on it being your idiot husband,' said Patience.

'I'd not take the bet, dear,' said Dotty. 'It's exactly the sort of thing he'd find funny.'

'Oh, I didn't mean he's playing a joke, I mean he's going to sell them to fund his extravagant lifestyle.'

'What do you mean by that?'

'I can't believe you don't know exactly what I mean. That house you live in, those clothes you wear, those restaurants you eat in. You're not telling me he can afford all that on his share of the partnership profits at his little solicitors' firm.'

'Well I never. I—'

I'm embarrassed to have to confess that despite my years of experience as a Master Earwigger, a careless lapse of attention led to Dotty noticing that I was looking straight at her and listening intently. She turned slightly away from me and lowered her voice as she continued to argue with her friend.

With a sigh I motioned to Lady Hardcastle that we should move over to the other huddle.

It quickly became apparent that they were crowded tightly around Bridgewater, who was telling one of his jokes – a long, drawn-out yarn I'd heard many times before but which had captivated his small audience. I noticed Lily was among the listeners and was relieved to remember that the story was not a filthy one. I had no idea why I should feel protective of her – I was sure she could look after herself and probably had a repertoire of dirty jokes of her own. Perhaps it was that she was the newcomer to the group and I didn't want her to think badly of the rest of us.

The joke's punch line eventually arrived and was met with genuine laughter. Whatever I might have thought of Bridgewater's addiction to the facetious, he actually did have a gift for joke-telling. If he ever tired of his legal practice I felt sure he could make a passable living in the music halls, perhaps supplementing his income with some after-dinner speaking.

Lily saw us standing in the middle of the room and peeled herself away to join us.

'Hello, again,' she said. 'I really must apologize to you both. When JB ran through the guest list he simply said you were Emily and Florence. I had no idea until just now you were the famous Lady Hardcastle and Miss Armstrong. How very exciting.'

Lady Hardcastle's eyebrows raised comically. 'Gracious. Famous? Us?'

Lily smiled. 'Of course. We see your names in the newspapers all the time. That murder at the theatre a couple of years ago was all my friends and I were talking about for weeks.'

'I'm afraid I can think of nothing more to say than my previous "gracious". We're pals with a local journalist and we feed her titbits when we're able, but one never imagines the stories being of more than mere local interest.'

Lily nodded. 'Well, your pal's local stories have been picked up by newspapers around the country.'

'She'll be delighted. Dinah Caudle is her name.'

'How wonderful. But her name never appears on the stories. They're always presented as though they're written by one of the paper's own reporters.'

'Oh,' said Lady Hardcastle. 'That's a shame. Still, I'm sure her reputation is growing within the newspaper world, if not with the public.'

Lily gave a little shrug. 'That might be the case if she'd had the good sense to be born a man, but . . .'

'Well, quite,' said Lady Hardcastle with a shrug of her own. 'We know from a friend of ours that it's the same in the photographic world. Do you know of Helen Titmus?'

'I'm afraid not, no. I'm just getting started – I've yet to meet any of the big names.'

'She's certain to be a big name one day. If you get the chance to visit Brighton you must drop in and see her. Tell her we sent you.'

'I certainly shall. Thank you.'

'I'm sure you'll both have lots to talk about. It's certainly a treat for me to meet a fellow photographer, I must say. I only dabble, but it's such fun. Florence does, too.'

I nodded. 'My American friend sent me one of the new Vest Pocket Kodak cameras. I take it everywhere now.'

Lily smiled her dazzling smile. 'Snap! Oh, I say. Snap. Clever me. I usually use something altogether more bulky. It gives fine results, but for this weekend I wanted something I could carry in my handbag.'

'What do you usually use?' asked Lady Hardcastle.

'A Graflex Speed Graphic – also American, as it happens. With the f/2.9 lens. It's a marvellous thing but the Vest Pocket is so much more immediate. I'll come back in a few weeks with a larger-format camera but for this weekend's recce it'll be snaps with the little chap.'

'I'll be pestering you for tips,' I said, and then nodded towards Lady Hardcastle. 'I'm getting excellent tuition in the general principles, but we're both struggling with some of the quirks and peculiarities of the Kodak. It would be wonderful to have some advice from a professional.'

'I'll be happy to help in whatever way I can.'

By now, George Wilson had also torn himself away from JB and Bridgewater.

He came over to join us. 'Hello, ladies.'

We offered a fusillade of overlapping greetings.

He grinned. 'I'm feeling a little cooped up in here so I'm going out for a walk round the island.' He indicated his former conversational companions. 'I invited those two but I couldn't get them interested.'

'I can't say I blame them,' said Lady Hardcastle. 'The weather seems to be closing in.'

'Hence my eagerness to get out. I want to clear the cobwebs before we're all confined to barracks.'

Lily and I also indicated our reluctance to venture out into the wind so, with a smile, Wilson went off alone to fetch his coat and,

I hoped, a pair of outdoor boots. The ones he was wearing looked very natty, but I didn't think they'd survive a walk round the island.

'You do know that JB is trying to play matchmaker, don't you, dear?' said Lady Hardcastle when Wilson had gone.

Lily frowned. 'I do. He was very pleased with himself. Does George know?'

'JB mentioned it to him, yes.'

Lily's frown softened to a smile. 'He's a cheeky one, that JB. But I'll make my own matches, thank you very much.'

'Quite right, too. One thinks of JB as a hard-hearted businessman, but he has quite a romantic streak. I think he means well but I thought you ought to be forewarned.'

'Wilson's not really my type, though, I'm afraid,' said Lily. 'And he doesn't seem all that interested in me, anyway. I think we'll be fine.'

Dotty and Patience had noticed Wilson's departure and came over to us.

'Is he going out for a walk?' asked Dotty.

'Apparently so,' said Lady Hardcastle. 'He invited JB and Granville but they turned him down.'

'He didn't bally well invite us,' said Patience. 'I could do with a walk before it gets too unpleasant out there. Anyone coming?'

Once again, Lady Hardcastle, Lily and I politely declined.

Patience tutted. 'What about you, Dots? Fancy a walk before tea?'

'Well, it does look a bit grim out,' said Dotty. 'Perhaps—'

'Nonsense. A bracing stroll round the island will do us a world of good.'

Dotty really didn't look convinced but reluctantly followed her friend to gather their coats and outdoor shoes, their earlier argument apparently forgotten.

JB was still with Bridgewater, who had begun another joke.

'Shall we go back to the sitting room?' asked Lady Hardcastle. 'We can have a natter and leave those two in peace.'

Out in the corridor we could hear Wilson's cheery voice echoing round the hall as he asked the Crawfords if they wouldn't mind him going out through the kitchen.

'It'll save me walking all the way round from the front door,' he said.

Peggy's reply was indistinct but I presumed she'd agreed because Wilson's voice faded as he went further into the kitchen.

Moments later, we heard a 'Wait for us' from Dotty as they raced to catch him up.

Lady Hardcastle and I ambled into the sitting room. I should prefer to say we glid, glode or glided (depending upon your linguistic preferences), but it was definitely more of an amble than any sort of graceful movement. Lily, who was very much a glider, followed but stopped just inside the door.

'I'm so terribly sorry, ladies, but would you mind awfully if I went back to my room? I have the most fearful headache.'

'Of course not, dear,' said Lady Hardcastle. 'Much better to try to rid oneself of a headache than to sit and listen to us two wittering on.'

'I have aspirin if you need it,' I added.

'You're both very kind. I think a little lie-down will do the trick, though. I'll see you at dinner.'

She glided back out into the passageway, leaving us, as so often, on our own.

Lady Hardcastle looked out through the square-leaded windows. 'I'm not in the least bit impressed with this weather.'

'I shall write a sternly worded letter of complaint,' I said as I flopped into an armchair.

'Thank you. I can always count on you. But it's not at all fair. I thought a weekend on a private island would afford opportunities for leisurely walks in the sea air. For birdwatching. Perhaps a game of croquet.'

'Does JB have a croquet lawn?'

'If this wind keeps up we may never get outdoors for long enough to find out.'

'And what birds would we see if we were able to watch them?'

'Herring gulls, for a start.'

'We've seen herring gulls. On the way over on the boat. There was a flock of them following us.'

'Guillemots, gannets, shags—'

I chuckled.

Lady Hardcastle sighed. 'Really? How old are you?'

'Old enough to find shags funny. Great tits, too.'

She shook her head. 'We're too early for the puffins' breeding season, but JB claims there are nests on the eastern end of the island so we could have seen them, as well.'

'On the ground?'

'Yes, they nest in little burrows.'

'So they're floor birds. Did they write *Madame Bovary*?'

This time she sighed. 'If we had a time machine and could hop forwards to spring, we could ask them.'

'If we could do that I'd be satisfied just to hop forwards a couple of days to when this weather has passed through.'

'It doesn't seem to have dented George's enthusiasm for the outdoors, although I suspect the poor chap just wanted to get away from the embarrassment of being shoved in Lily's direction by JB the matchmaker.'

I chuckled again. 'Perhaps. We're all going to crave a little solitude if we're cooped up in here by the weather, though, matchmaking or not.'

'Especially if someone's playing hilarious japes on us all weekend.'

'Well, yes.' I looked about the room. 'If you had the money, would you buy somewhere like this?'

Still standing, she turned and looked out of the window again. 'It has appeal. I mean, I love the sea – even the English Channel in winter has a romantic, white-capped majesty. But would I want to own it? I'm not sure. I think I'd have to have enough money that I shouldn't mind owning a place I only visited a couple of times a year. Which is how it would be – I can't imagine summering here, just the two of us and some staff, waiting for the boat to bring us weekend friends.'

'Weekend friends we'd be stuck with. No escape from the acquaintance who seemed such fun in small doses but who turns out to be an absolute pill when you're confined on an island with them for an entire weekend. At least in a country house you can hop in the car and go to the nearest town for the day.'

She nodded. 'Exactly my thinking. So, no, then. No converted forts for me. It's a lovely place to visit, but I'd rather someone else took care of all the mundane practicalities.'

'A seaside cottage, perhaps?'

'As long as it was within walking distance of a country inn that served decent food and wouldn't mind the likes of us dropping in for a pie and a pint, yes.'

'Please put it on the list after buying the house and getting a flat in London.'

'Shall do. For now, though, I just fancy another cup of tea – this pot's had it.'

We rang the bell again and waited for Crawford.

We passed a pleasant hour in the sitting room reminiscing about the past and speculating about the future. But by four-ish the tea was cold and our limbs were stiff, so we decided we'd be the sort of houseguests who took our dirty crockery back to the kitchen. Such behaviour annoyed and offended some servants, but I had the feeling that Crawford might actually be quite pleased. He was eager but untrained and, without a lifetime's experience to tell him what to expect from the sort of people who employ servants, I didn't think he'd mind if we pitched in and gave a hand.

We trooped down the short flight of steps beyond the hall and found Peggy alone in her kitchen, with no sign of her husband.

She wiped her hands on her apron as we entered and took the tray from us. 'I'm sorry, m'dears. Did that lummox not hear the bell again?'

'No, Mrs—' I began. 'No, Peggy. We needed to stretch our legs so we thought we'd save him the trip.'

'You shouldn't have done that – he'll get ideas above his station.' She gave us a wink, then called out, 'Jago, you lazy lump. We got guests doin' your job for you 'ere.'

There was a rustle of newspaper from the open door of the butler's pantry, then Crawford arrived, putting his reading glasses into the breast pocket of his jacket.

'Oh, I'm so sorry,' he said. 'I must've not heard the bell.'

'Don't worry,' said Lady Hardcastle, 'your wife is teasing you. We needed a little walk round the fort so we brought the tray with us.'

'I wouldn't have minded fetching it.'

'It really wasn't any trouble,' I said. 'As Lady Hardcastle said, we needed a little walk round. It's too windy to go out, so we're getting our exercise indoors.'

'Ar,' said Crawford. 'There's a proper storm coming, you mark my words.'

Peggy rolled her eyes. 'Your lumbago playin' up again, is it? He always says he can tell when the weather's goin' to be bad cos his back starts givin' him gyp.'

'It don't take no mystic signs to tell this one's going to be bad,' said Crawford. 'You only has to look out the window. Anyone could tell we's in for a bad'n.'

I remembered something. 'Is everyone back from their walks? If it's going to get rough out there, do you think we should look for them?'

''T'i'n't so bad yet, but it'll get worse afore it gets better. Mrs Bridgewater and Mrs Sidwell-Plant came back in a while since, but now you mentions it, I a'n't seen Mr Wilson at all. You seen him, Peg?'

'Not since he left. More'n an hour ago now, that was. I 'spect he came back in through the front door.'

'We've been in the sitting room,' I said. 'I'm sure we'd have heard the front door from there.'

'Ar,' said Crawford, 'you would've. Makes a fearful noise that front door. I keeps meaning to oil them hinges, but part of me likes that they makes such a racket – lets me know someone's come in.'

'Should we be worried?' I asked.

'What about?' said a voice from the doorway.

I turned to see Dotty Bridgewater standing there with Clarice on her arm.

'Oh, hello Dotty,' said Lady Hardcastle. 'We're wondering whether to be worried about Wilson. Did he come back with you?'

Dotty gave us a rueful smile. 'No, Speedy and I turned back after about five minutes and came back indoors. It's dreadful out there. Dear George gave us a tut and a smile and strode off without us.'

Lady Hardcastle frowned. 'You all went out before three but he hasn't returned.'

'He must have found the grotto,' said Dotty. 'We found the ruins of some sort of watchtower at the far end of the island when I was making plans for the garden, and I thought it would be rather jolly to use the stones to make a little grotto. A sheltered spot where guests could sit and while away an hour or two in quiet contemplation of the majesty of the sea.'

Clarice gave a derisive snort. 'The majesty of the sea?'

Dotty was unfazed by the mockery. 'Oh, yes. JB takes a very romantic view of the sea. We put a lovely wooden bench out there and I planted some robust little rock-loving plants to give it a bit of life. It's a delightful spot and quite shielded from the wind. If he found it, George could easily spend an hour without even noticing the time passing.'

'Well, I don't blame him for wanting to get away,' said Clarice. 'The atmosphere in here hasn't been exactly festive.'

Most people would be wary of expressing such thoughts in front of the servants, but Clarice was refreshingly unconcerned.

Dotty, it seemed, was less comfortable. 'Oh, I don't know about that, dear. I think it's all been rather fun, actually.'

Clarice gave an impatient *pfft*. Evidently she was over her earlier upset and was back to her usual, abrasive self.

With a clunk and a clatter, the back door opened and a grinning George Wilson entered. The wind followed him in and ruffled our skirts and blew a puff of flour from Peggy's mixing bowl before he managed to slam it shut.

'Oh,' he said. 'A welcoming committee. How nice. Hello, ladies.'

There were murmured greetings.

'We were just getting worried about you,' I said.

'Why on earth . . . ?'

'The weather's foul and you've been out there quite a while. Dotty and Patience have been back for ages, apparently.'

He smoothed his tousled hair. 'Just a little wind – nothing to worry about. Although it'll be raining soon, I'd wager.'

'Told you,' said Crawford.

'But not yet,' said Wilson. 'I'm sorry to have worried you all, though. I found a lovely little grotto thing over by the cliffs to the west.'

'Told you,' said a beaming Dotty.

'I wasn't worried about you,' said Clarice with a sniff.

Wilson gave a delighted bark of laughter. 'Ha. Of course not. I'd have thought there was something amiss if you had been. Never change, my dearest Clarice.'

She offered another *pfft* but said nothing further.

'Well then,' said Lady Hardcastle, 'now that everyone is safely gathered in, I think I shall go and have a rest before changing for dinner. Cocktails at six, Jago?'

Crawford nodded. 'That's the way Mr McIntyre likes it, m'lady, yes.'

'Splendid. And will you be playing for us again, Clarice?'

'Of course,' said Clarice. 'I can't imagine a day without playing.'

We said our farewells and I followed Lady Hardcastle up to the first floor. We exchanged a promise to meet in her room at around a quarter to six so that we could go down together, and I retired to my room.

I looked out of the window. I was only on the first floor, but with the fort perched on its craggy plateau, the sea was far below me. I could just about see the crenelations of the old gun emplacement to my left and the sheer, forbidding walls as they dropped away beneath the platform. Amid the modern comforts of the soon-to-be hotel, it was easy to forget that we were in an actual fortress.

But the comforts were abundant, and I felt my soft mattress calling to me.

I flolloped on the bed and within minutes I was fast asleep.

# Chapter Six

I was awakened by urgent knocking on my bedroom door. I was trying to find the words to say something in response – it would have been something unforgivably rude had I managed – when the door burst open.

'Flo? Are you all right?'

It was Lady Hardcastle.

Full consciousness still eluded me but I was at least able to reply. 'Of course I'm all right, you ninny. What's the matter with *you*?'

'It's five to six. You were supposed to be at my door ten minutes ago in your best frock.'

I struggled to vertical. 'I just dozed off, that's all. We don't have to arrive on time – you always complain about people who arrive for cocktails on time.'

'Well, yes, I suppose I do. But you always fetch me on time and then I shilly-shally so as not to be too early. I was worried about you. You never oversleep – you claim to be the queen of the half-hour nap.'

'I just had a little bit more of a snooze than usual. It must be the sea air.'

She began rummaging in my wardrobe. 'This rose one will look lovely. Do you have shoes to go with it?'

I sighed and stood. 'At the bottom of the wardrobe there. I'm just going for a quick wash.' I walked towards the door.

'There's no time for that. You have to hurry and get yourself changed.'

'I'm going for a quick wash, and we'll be no more than a quarter of an hour late. Keep your drawers on. And even if it takes me longer than that, we'll certainly be in plenty of time for dinner at seven.'

She harrumphed but relented.

Refreshed and re-dressed, we arrived in the library on the ground floor at twenty past six and almost everyone was already there, with Edgar Everett the only absentee. Conversational groups had coalesced, but Robert Sidwell-Plant stood alone and he beckoned us over.

'Good evening, ladies. I was beginning to worry that you might not be joining us.'

'Worry?' said Lady Hardcastle. 'How lovely to be missed.'

He laughed. 'You're both delightful company, of course, but you'd have been missed even if you turned out to be absolute stodgers. JB collects friends and acquaintances with the same enthusiasm he exhibits for his . . . exhibits.' He smiled to himself. 'But he tends to classify us into groups just as he does with his physical collection, and keeps us all separate. It's a rare treat to meet someone from one of the other classifications.'

'And how does he classify you?' I asked.

'We're the "business" group. The boring ones.'

'Certainly not boring,' said Lady Hardcastle. 'But I always get my professions muddled – Bridgewater is the solicitor and you're the accountant, yes?'

'For my sins.'

She smiled again. 'I should have thought it must be very exciting at the moment with all the work you're doing to set up the hotel.'

He laughed. 'I suppose "exciting" is one word for it. I'd steer more towards "stressful" if anyone were to ask me.'

'Stressful?' I said. 'You must have worked on dozens of deals like this. How is this one different?'

Sidwell-Plant paused for the slightest moment before answering. 'Obviously, as his accountant, I can't betray any trust, but let's just say there's an awful lot riding on it. It has to work perfectly.'

'Oh?' said Lady Hardcastle. 'Why's that?'

'It's not my place to say more, I'm afraid.'

She smiled again. 'Fair dos. Let's get back to safer topics, then. We were talking about JB's classifications, weren't we? What about Clarice? Why is she part of this set? Surely she should be in the "artists and musicians" group.'

He laughed again. 'True, true. But she studied at the Royal Academy of Music with my nephew, so she's part of our group by default – a friend of the family, as it were. To be honest, I strongly suspect she gets roped in to a lot of groups. No point in knowing a world-renowned violinist and then not showing her off at every opportunity.'

'What does your nephew play?' I asked.

'Cello and piano, but he's a conductor now.'

'How wonderful,' said Lady Hardcastle. 'I should love to learn to conduct.'

His eyes widened in apparent delight. 'You're another musician?'

'I dabble. Piano.'

'But you're not part of the musicians group?'

Lady Hardcastle smiled. 'Good heavens, no. Although JB did meet us at the Albert Hall.'

If he noticed this inelegant swerve in the conversation he didn't show it. 'That's it. Gran Bridgewater and I have been friends for years and he was doing some work for JB just about the time JB needed an English accountant. Gran recommended me and . . . well, here I am.'

'It must be nice to be able to work with your friend,' I said.

He glanced over to where Bridgewater was telling another of his interminably lengthy jokes. 'I suppose so, yes.'

So much for my clumsy fishing attempt. I'd noticed one or two instances of frostiness between the two men and wanted to know more. It was a bit much to hope he'd suddenly tell all to a new acquaintance, but I thought it might be worth a try. Time for my own inelegant swerve to get us away from this potentially dodgy ground. 'Has there been any sign of Everett since this afternoon?'

'Since his bullying attack on Clarice, you mean?' He looked over towards where Clarice was talking to JB.

'You heard about that?' asked Lady Hardcastle.

'My wife told me. He treats that lovely woman abominably. One day someone will settle his hash. I might have done it myself if I'd been there.'

'It's not a new thing, then?' I said.

'He's been like it for as long as we've known them.' He paused for a moment in thought. 'I always assumed he resented playing second fiddle to one of the world's greatest fiddlers, but perhaps he's just a blackguard. No one likes him, but we put up with him so we can see more of Clarice. Actually, that's not quite true,' he added, bitterly. 'My darling wife seems to be somewhat taken with him. At least I thought so. She seems to have her eye on young George Wilson this weekend, too.'

*Everett and Patience?* I thought. That wasn't the impression I'd got earlier, but I didn't know her well enough to be able to comment.

It was Sidwell-Plant's turn for an inelegant swerve. 'You two were looking for my wife's missing whatnot, weren't you? Any luck?'

'Her diamond brooch,' said Lady Hardcastle. 'No luck so far, I'm afraid.'

'Brooch, that was it. She has so much blasted jewellery I can't keep up. Costs me a fortune. I mean, really, an absolute fortune. It would be much appreciated if you could track it down. You've really no idea what's happened to it?'

'We began with the working assumption that both the brooch and Dotty's necklace had been dropped somewhere and, perhaps, accidentally moved. Kicked along the floor, caught up in someone's clothing, that sort of thing.'

He smiled. 'Do you really think that's likely? Sounds more than a little far-fetched to me. One item, perhaps, but both?'

'Well, quite. Obviously it's more likely that someone took them both deliberately. But who? And why? I'd love to believe that it's some sort of merry jape. We gather there's rivalry over who wears the most extravagant jewels. Perhaps the thief decided that it took enough of the group's attention during these soirees and wanted to teach them both a lesson? The joker would deprive them of their game and then reveal their whereabouts at what he considers to be the funniest moment. Comedy's all in the timing, you see. The alternative is that someone among us is a thief and I really prefer the merry-jape hypothesis.'

'An expensive bloody jape. Mind you, I can think of one person who'd imagine it was hilarious.' He glanced again at his old pal Bridgewater.

'Is it the sort of thing he'd do?' I said.

'Schoolboy pranks are his speciality. Although . . .'

'Yes?' prompted Lady Hardcastle.

'No, nothing. It's probably a joke, as you say. I can't imagine anyone actually stealing them.'

Bridgewater's story finally ended. His small audience groaned at the corny punch line and this seemed to delight him more than any laughter could have.

JB beckoned us over. 'Come over here, you three. We need someone to save us from Gran's terrible gags. He wouldn't dare try it in the presence of a professional.'

Bridgewater looked at us questioningly.

We said nothing.

'Florence here was born in a circus,' said JB when he realized we didn't understand what he meant. 'Her father was a professional knife thrower. She knows a clown when she sees one.'

'Circus, eh?' said Bridgewater. 'Have you heard the one about . . .'

I had, but I let him continue. To be fair, he was quite the gifted raconteur and I could think of worse ways to pass the time before dinner. The large gin and tonic JB pressed into my hand helped, too.

◆ ◆ ◆

By the time the dinner gong sounded and we gathered ourselves together to troop upstairs to the dining room, Everett was still absent.

'Have you any idea where he might be?' said Dotty to Clarice as we sat down.

'None whatsoever,' said Clarice. 'I'm trying to work out if it would be possible for me to care less, but it's a struggle.'

'When did you last see him?'

I couldn't recall whether I'd heard Clarice laugh before, but it was warm and joyful when it came. 'Pause a while and contemplate what you just asked me.'

Dotty dutifully paused. 'When did you last—' Realization dawned. 'Oh, my dear Clarice. I didn't think. I'm so sorry.'

Clarice, though, was still amused. 'Please don't worry, Dotty dear – I was just teasing you. It's a perfectly commonplace phrase and you should never feel you have to police your language around me. But I haven't "seen" Edgar since he stomped off after lunch.'

'Since . . .'

'Since then, yes. Did you hear that?'

'I heard *about* it.'

'Oh lord. So everyone knows? How humiliating.'

'Everyone's on your side, dear. Even the gentlemen.'

Clarice sighed. 'That's all I need – more sympathy.'

She was unable to see Dotty's crestfallen expression.

I decided to step in. 'Have you decided what you'll be playing for us this evening?'

Clarice turned abruptly towards me. 'Not yet, no. It might have to be something I can play without piano accompaniment if his lordship doesn't stop sulking.'

Sidwell-Plant was listening in. 'Lady Hardcastle was telling us she plays the piano.'

All eyes now turned to Lady Hardcastle, who affected an attitude of what I hoped only I knew to be entirely fake humility. 'Well . . . you know . . . one dabbles.'

'She's actually rather good,' I said, playing my part in the social charade. 'She has quite the reputation round our way.'

'Interesting,' said Clarice. 'And how's your sight-reading?'

'Well . . . I mean . . .'

They were going to see through this faux modesty if she laid it on any more thickly, but we all knew how the social game must be played.

Once more, my role in the game was to speak up for her. 'I've seen her open the music for a brand-new piece and play it as though she's been practising for months.'

Clarice smiled. 'Would you mind sitting in as my accompanist, then? There's no money in it, I'm afraid, but it might be a lark.'

'It would be a pleasure,' said Lady Hardcastle. 'And if Edgar reappears, perhaps we might play together some other time. I'd like that very much.'

'It's always nice to have someone new to practise with. Whether tonight or tomorrow, we shall play something together. I say, do you know any ragtime pieces? I'd love to have a go at some of those, but . . . well, he won't let me. But if he's not there . . .'

They began talking earnestly about Lady Hardcastle's favourite ragtime composers. It wasn't long before she'd moved on to how ragtime had even influenced Claude Debussy, and I turned my attention instead to Lily and Wilson, who were sitting the other side of me.

'Was JB telling tall tales earlier?' asked Wilson.

'About what?' I said, though I suspected I knew.

'About you being born in a circus.'

'Ah, yes, that,' I said. 'No, he wasn't – that's entirely true.'

'It is *not*,' said Lily, delightedly. 'How marvellous.'

'No, really. My birth certificate says I'm Welsh, and I certainly spent a decent part of my childhood in the Valleys with my mother's family, but my twin sister, Gwen, and I were born in a circus wagon in England. My mother designed and made the costumes. Talented she was. No one's ever properly explained why she was touring with them when she was almost due, but somehow she was. But as soon as we were born they put the three of us on a train back to Aberdare and she registered our births there. As soon as we were all fit to travel we were all back on the road, and that's where I did most of my growing up.'

She seemed thrilled by this news. 'And your father really was a knife thrower?'

'He really was. He taught me and Gwen, too.'

Wilson laughed. 'Never mind Clarice's beautiful playing – I want to see you do some knife tricks.'

I smiled. 'If you can track down a decently weighted dagger, I'm sure I can do something.'

JB had been listening. 'I have one or two knives in my collection here. I'm pretty certain I can find one that would suit.'

'It doesn't have to be a proper throwing knife,' I said. 'It's not hard to throw a table knife if the need arises, but something with a bit better balance would allow some more impressive tricks.'

I wasn't used to being the centre of attention at occasions like this and I found I was rather enjoying myself. I confess that as dinner wore on, I might have begun to show off a little with my tales, though I was careful never to lie, or even exaggerate. I really did pin that fellow to a wall in Budapest by his coat sleeve. And I really did use a fruit knife to do it.

◆ ◆ ◆

As before, we retired to the library after dinner, where Bridgewater poured Lady Hardcastle and me a large brandy each, and an even larger one for himself.

He saluted us with his balloon glass. 'Chin chin.'

'Here's mud in your eye,' I said, raising my own.

He laughed. 'What in my what?'

'It's an expression my American friend used in one of her recent letters,' I said. 'I thought it might amuse you.'

'It very much does. Mud in your eye, eh? I shall remember that one.' He chuckled a little more. 'I say, that reminds me of a story—'

'We were talking to Sidwell-Plant a little while ago,' interrupted Lady Hardcastle.

'Were you, indeed? What nonsense has that old scoundrel been spouting now?'

'I'm not sure it was nonsense. He was just saying that the two of you have been working for JB for a long time. You were JB's solicitor when he needed an accountant and you recommended your pal.'

Bridgewater relaxed. 'Oh, that. Yes, we've been friends for years, he and I. Dotty and I introduced him to the current Mrs Sidwell-P, don't you know.'

'Was there a previous Mrs Sidwell-Plant?' I asked.

'No, no,' he said. 'Just a figure of speech – Patience is his one and only wife. Our Bobby's too lucky to lose a spouse to accident or illness, and too proud to divorce one. Quite the stickler, old RVSP. Not one to break the law, nor even the conventions of polite society.'

'RVSP?' I said.

'Robert Victor Sidwell-Plant. I can't believe his parents didn't do it on purpose. Too close to RSVP, what?'

'Ah, of course.'

'It must be handy when you're working on a deal for JB,' said Lady Hardcastle. 'It's like having the legal side and the money side all under one roof.'

'Like some sort of business services firm, what?' said Bridgewater with another chuckle. 'It's making everything we need to do for the hotel so much simpler with us both working together, that's for certain. And a good thing, too, if I might say. There's a lot riding on it – we all need the hotel to be a roaring success. More brandy?'

I held up my hand. 'Not for me, thank you – I've only just started this one.'

Lady Hardcastle shook her head, too.

'I'll just have a little one,' said Bridgewater as he helped himself to another large one. 'JB won't mind.'

'He's a generous host,' I said.

'Thank goodness. I'm not sure I could live this high on the hog without him. Keeps the bills down at home if a chap can spend every weekend with his generous benefactor, what?'

Before Lady Hardcastle or I could respond, the host himself joined us.

'Please forgive the interruption,' said JB, 'but I wonder if I might have a word with you, Emily.'

'Of course, JB dear. What can I do for you?'

JB led her out of earshot and I looked around. Sidwell-Plant was having a laughter-filled conversation with Wilson and Lily on one side of the room, while Dotty and Patience were engaged in some heads-together seriousness on the other. Clarice had already gone to prepare for the evening recital and Edgar still hadn't reappeared.

'What was the story you were going to tell?' I said.

Bridgewater was a little distracted. 'The what?'

'When I said, "Here's mud in your eye," you said it reminded you of a story, but Lady Hardcastle interrupted and set us off talking about you and Mr Sidwell-Plant instead.'

'Ohh, yes. Well, now, you see, this chap – tall johnny, d'you see? Lanky, some might say, though never to his face – he's a well-liked sort of a fella. But this chap is out walking in the countryside with his dogs. Lovely creatures. Sharp as tacks, and devotedly obedient. And he passes a gloomy-looking young boy sitting beside the road, and he thinks, "Hallo, this young shaver looks a bit downhearted, I'll try to cheer him up." So he goes over and—'

'You'll never guess who's going to be accompanying Clarice Everett on the piano this evening,' said a grinning Lady Hardcastle as she rejoined us.

I smiled. 'Well, if it's not you it's going to be a very disappointing revelation. Or a very exciting one. Is Patience Sidwell-Plant secretly a world-renowned concert pianist?'

'She may very well be for all I know,' she said.

'She's not bad, actually,' said Bridgewater. 'Robert bought her a new piano for Christmas. Bösendorfer. Seemed like some sort of bribe to me, but a chap doesn't like to interfere in another chap's domestic matters.'

'I had no idea,' said Lady Hardcastle. 'But it's not Patience, it's me.' She beamed.

'Wonderful news,' I said. 'I seldom envy your talents, but I'd give almost anything to be able to play with someone as sublime as Clarice.'

'I had to pinch myself. I say, could you turn the music for me? It would be a massive help and it would almost be as though you were part of the performance.'

I laughed. 'A piano player's mate. I'd love to. Thank you.'

'Now that reminds me of a little ditty I heard recently,' said Bridgewater. 'I'm not the pheasant pl—'

Lady Hardcastle touched his arm. 'I'm sorry, dear, but I ought to nip upstairs to the drawing room. I told Clarice my sight reading was good, but I'd still like to give the pieces a once-over before everyone sits down.'

'There's still no sign of Everett, I take it?' said Bridgewater.

Lady Hardcastle shook her head. 'No one's seen hide or hair of him since before lunch.'

'Can't say I miss the blighter, but it's dashed odd that he could manage to completely disappear like that. I mean to say, it's not a small place, Guardians Rock, but . . .'

'He'll turn up, I'm sure. But I really must dash. See you both in a few minutes.'

She bustled off and I dutifully listened to Bridgewater's joke.

The atmosphere in the drawing room was hard to define. There was excitement – or anticipation, at least – about another performance from Clarice Everett, but also a hard-to-pin-down unease at the absence of her accompanist husband.

Dotty was whispering to Bridgewater. Patience had turned slightly away from Sidwell-Plant and was talking to Wilson in hushed tones, to the evident displeasure of her husband. Lily was sitting with JB and pointing to features in the room as though describing the photographs she intended to take.

I was sitting on the piano stool, feeling slightly awkward and wishing the performers would come in so that I'd have something to do. I looked at the ceiling. The electric chandelier needed dusting. I looked down at the floor. There was a grey smudge on the carpet. Cigar ash? Sherlock Holmes would know. He'd also know exactly where the cigar had been made. And sold. And the names and addresses of all the people who had bought cigars like it. Though he wouldn't need to know because he'd be able to identify them by the smell of the tobacco on their clothes. It had been more than a year since the last story had appeared in *The Strand*. I wondered if there would be any more. A spider walked across the stone floor by the window. Where had it come from? How *did* spiders get to islands a mile offshore? Did they cadge a lift on passing boats? Did they ride on the backs of seagulls? And what did they eat at this time of year? There were no flies to speak of. And—

Lady Hardcastle entered the room with Clarice on her arm. The quiet conversations stopped. I got up and stood beside the stool, ready to carry out my page-turning duties.

Clarice was carrying her violin and bow in her free hand and Lady Hardcastle led her to a spot in front of the piano where she faced her tiny audience. Lady Hardcastle sat at the keyboard and gave me a grin as she arranged the music on the stand for the first piece.

She began to play. And then Clarice began to play and I was once more transported to whatever mystical place it is we go when we're moved by what we prosaically call the 'creative arts'. How did we come up with such a mundane name for something so magical? Why—

A jab from Lady Hardcastle's elbow prompted me to turn the page.

They played several pieces, each more wonderful than the last, and when Clarice finally put up her bow and took her bow, the seven seated friends clapped like a concert hall audience.

'Thank you,' said Clarice, smiling. 'And thank you, Emily – your playing was wonderful. I found things in those familiar pieces I'd never heard before. I—'

With a clatter of the latch, the far door of the drawing room burst open and we turned as one to see Crawford standing there, his face white, his hands trembling.

'Beggin' your pardon for the interruption, ladies and gents, but I need to speak to Mr McIntyre in private. Urgent, like.'

'What is it, Crawford?' said JB, affably. 'I'm sure my guests won't mind a little housekeeping discussion.'

'No, sir, I really have to insist.'

JB smiled and gave a little shake of the head. 'OK, Crawford. I'm sure we can sort it out.'

They left the room and we all looked about, curious and slightly embarrassed.

Clarice was aware of the atmosphere. 'What about some of that ragtime we were talking about?'

'Oh, yes, of course,' said Lady Hardcastle. 'A splendid idea. What about this? It's in E major.'

She began playing. On the second time through the main refrain, Clarice joined in, improvising her own variation as Lady Hardcastle kept up the syncopated accompaniment. By the next repeat I was beginning to wish I'd brought my banjo – what a treat it would be to play with these two.

The others were enjoying themselves, as well. Dotty was almost dancing in her seat. Patience was tapping her feet. Sidwell-Plant was gazing at Clarice with open admiration.

JB returned to the room and walked quickly over to Clarice. She jumped when he gently touched her arm but didn't stop playing. He leaned close and whispered something in her ear. And then she stopped playing.

Lady Hardcastle stopped, too.

JB turned to face the room. 'Friends, I have some terrible news. I have to tell you that our friend Edgar Everett is dead.'

# Chapter Seven

I've talked before about 'uproar' when deaths are announced and, usually, that's the case. The reaction of the other eight people in the room, though, was more difficult to describe. There were shocked gasps, of course, and Dotty's hand flew to her mouth, but no one seemed especially upset. Curiously, Bridgewater and Sidwell-Plant seemed to be more affected than their wives – once you allowed for their instinct towards stiff-upper-lippedness, at least – though perhaps they were considering the legal and financial implications of a sudden death at their client's weekend retreat.

Strangest of all was that Clarice, though obviously jolted, didn't appear to be in any great distress. Then again, given her relationship with her late husband, maybe it wasn't strange at all. I'd have been glad to be rid of him if he were my husband.

Patience rose and helped Clarice to an empty chair.

'How did he die?' asked Bridgewater.

'I'm not entirely certain,' said JB. 'Emily? Florence? I wonder if you'd be good enough to come with me while I check on the . . . while I—'

'Of course, JB,' said Lady Hardcastle, quickly.

'Why them?' said Sidwell-Plant. 'Shouldn't we leave it for the authorities? Send your man Crawford ashore to fetch a doctor so we can do things properly.'

'Robert makes a good point,' said Bridgewater. 'One doesn't like to be indelicate in the presence of the ladies, but in the case of sudden death we should also inform the police. As he says, we need to do things properly.'

JB held up his hands. 'I understand your concerns, gentlemen, but there's nothing to worry about. The ladies have some experience with sudden deaths and I'd appreciate their advice before we involve the authorities. I'm a little out of my depth and I want to be certain of a few things, so that when we bring the doctor and the constable out here in the boat I can have most of my i's dotted and my t's already crossed.'

Lady Hardcastle and I crossed the room together. The two professionals shrugged in an as-you-wish sort of way and JB led us out of the drawing room.

He headed for the stairs and took us up to the second floor.

'Crawford says he's in one of the empty rooms up here on the third floor. We use it as a storeroom.'

'There's a third floor?' I said. 'We only searched three floors when we were looking for the missing jewels.'

'That's right. First, second and third floors.' He paused a moment and then gave a dry chuckle. 'I forget you Brits do things differently. You call this the second floor, don't you?'

'We do,' said Lady Hardcastle. 'And we've been doing it that way since at least the fifteenth century, so I don't suppose there's much chance of us changing. A more interesting question for students of language would be why *you* choose to do things differently. Your early settlers took the language with them along with their goods and chattels – one wonders what made them change this little detail.'

'Makes more sense, I guess.'

'Well, yes, but when did good sense ever have any influence on language. This one?' She indicated an open door.

'This one. I warn you, if what Crawford says is correct, it's not going to be a pretty sight.'

Lady Hardcastle and I exchanged puzzled glances and followed JB through the door. He turned on the electric light.

We had searched the room earlier when we were looking for the missing jewels and almost nothing had changed since then. Dining chairs, rugs and a couple of occasional tables competed for space with tea chests and packing cases in the medium-sized room. But now, sticking out from behind a stack of boxes was a pair of trousered legs. We moved further into the room to investigate.

Everett, it became quickly apparent, had not died from natural causes. His shirt front was stained with blood, which had come from a large wound in his chest. The cause of the wound was lying beside him: JB's prized narwhal tusk.

'You neglected to mention he'd been murdered,' said Lady Hardcastle as she knelt to inspect the wound.

'I didn't want to alarm the others,' said JB. 'It's like I said to them: you deal with this sort of thing all the time.'

'In a manner of speaking. But they'll have to know.'

'I disagree. I think we can keep this from them until the police get here. No need to alarm anyone – it's bad enough that the ladies have lost those expensive pieces of jewellery. I overheard you talking about that as though you think it's a practical joke, so if you see no need to make them think there's a thief in their midst, I reckon there's even less need to make them think there's a murderer in their midst. And if we tell them, we'll alert the killer, too. Best to keep it all low-key.'

'The killer will know that we know,' I said, pointing to the tusk. 'It's not as though we could mistake the damage that thing did for a heart attack.'

'One wonders why they left it with the body,' said Lady Hardcastle. 'Actually, if it comes to that, one wonders why they didn't do a better job of concealing the body itself. They must have known someone would find it.'

'How often does anyone need to come in here?' I asked.

'Hardly ever,' said JB. 'It was just chance that I sent Crawford up to grab something tonight, otherwise we might not have come in here for weeks. Months, maybe.'

'Which would have given the killer time to make a better job of disposing of both poor old Everett and the murder weapon.'

Lady Hardcastle checked her watch and then continued with her examination of the body. She untucked his shirt and inspected the skin around his torso, lifting him slightly to look at his back.

'One of our dear friends is a police surgeon,' she said as she neatened him up. 'He's taught me a few things over the years. From the progress of rigor mortis and livor mortis I'd say he died sometime around three o'clock. There's still a tiny bit of flexibility in the limbs, do you see? And the blood hasn't pooled completely – you see there's still some pinkness here?' She indicated his side. 'Things would look very different if he'd died sooner. Although . . .'

JB raised an eyebrow. 'Although?'

'Well, the other thing Dr Gosling – Simeon – taught me was that none of this is exact. It's more of an estimate, but if one bases that estimate on two or more of the indicators it becomes a little more reliable.'

'What other indicators are there?'

'Body temperature is a good one. It has problems of its own, of course, but if one uses it in conjunction with the others, one can get a reasonably precise idea of the time of death. I don't suppose you have a thermometer?'

'I'm sorry, no. I've never had much use for one.'

'Well, quite – who does? So for now we'll work on the assumption that he was killed at three this afternoon and work from there.'

'But not here,' said JB. 'There's no blood on the floor.'

'I agree that he wasn't killed here,' I said. 'There's no sign of a struggle and the body is very neatly laid out – he's obviously been moved.'

'But the lack of blood doesn't tell us anything. The tusk would have stopped his heart immediately. If the heart's not beating, there's no bleeding. Some would seep out through the wound, but that's been soaked up by his shirt.'

'I see,' said JB. 'But the other things say he was killed someplace else, right?'

'Agreed,' said Lady Hardcastle. 'Given the choice of murder weapon, I'd suggest we start in the long gallery.'

As we left the storeroom, JB produced a key from the pocket of his dinner jacket and locked the door. He caught Lady Hardcastle's puzzled expression. 'Crawford gave it to me. I wasn't carrying it on the off chance.'

We went down to the first floor and into the long gallery, whose main door was opposite the bottom of the stairs.

Inside, all seemed in reasonable order as we made our way to the end, where the narwhal tusk had been on display until earlier in the afternoon.

'Is anything amiss?' asked Lady Hardcastle.

JB looked around. 'I'm not sure. It looks a little . . . off, I gotta say. Like things have been moved and not put back exactly right.'

My eye was caught by the carpet near one of the wingback chairs. There were dents clearly marking where the chair usually stood, but the feet were now a few inches away.

'That chair's been moved, certainly,' I said. 'Give me a hand?'

JB helped me lift the chair out of the way and we found that it had been carefully placed to cover a small bloodstain at the very edge of the carpet. Closer examination revealed that what must have been a much larger stain had been wiped from the stone floor. The killer had made a reasonable job of cleaning up, but there were still faint traces.

'From the way it's smeared,' I said, 'I'd say Everett's body was dragged through his own blood before the killer picked him up. Did you look at the back of his jacket?'

'I confess I didn't,' said Lady Hardcastle. 'I'd warrant there wasn't a great deal of blood, though. The tusk punctured his heart, as far as I could tell, so he'd have died very quickly – not enough time for him to bleed very much.'

'How did he miss these stains on the floor?' asked JB. 'He took pains to mop up, but he didn't do a very good job.'

I pointed towards the window. 'The weather was quite gloomy all afternoon, so if the lights weren't on in here, the floor would have been illuminated only by the limp light coming in through the windows. The killer probably couldn't see the floor well enough to see what they'd left behind.'

'They'd have got blood on their own clothes,' said Lady Hardcastle. 'And there'll be a rag or cloth somewhere that they used to wipe the floor.'

I nodded. 'Incriminating. If we find them.'

'You keep saying "they" and "them", like you don't know whether it's a man or a woman,' said JB. 'But surely none of the ladies here could have carried his dead body upstairs. It must be one of the men.'

I shrugged. 'I could carry him – it's as much technique as brute strength. But you're right – a woman on her own might not have managed it. Two working together, though . . .'

'That doesn't bear thinking about,' he said.

'It's something we *must* think about,' said Lady Hardcastle. 'We need to consider all possibilities.'

'In that case,' I said, 'is it possible that we're not alone on the island?'

An odd hope dawned in JB's eyes. 'You mean it might not be one of my guests after all? That would be a relief.'

'But is it possible?'

'Sure. There are plenty of places to hide on the island. There's a cave on the south side we're pretty sure was used by smugglers early in the last century. You could land a small boat there and hole up without anyone knowing.'

Lady Hardcastle looked less happy. 'That's rather alarming, actually. That would mean there's an unseen killer lurking just out of sight.'

'And you think that's more frightening than a killer right in our midst?' said JB. 'We're in a fortress – we can keep out an invading army if we have to.'

'Unless they're already in here,' I said.

They both sat in silent contemplation for a few moments.

'We'd better get the police out here as quickly as we can,' said Lady Hardcastle.

I nodded. 'As soon as possible. What are we going to tell the others?'

'Nothing,' said JB emphatically. 'We just say Everett's dead and that Crawford will fetch the authorities.'

'And if they ask for details?'

'Evade. Obfuscate. Offer bland reassurances. Comfort Clarice and tell everyone else that everything's going to be just fine.'

By the time we went to find the others, they had retired to the library – everyone's favourite spot, it seemed.

I went at once to Clarice and took her hand. She didn't speak but she gave my own hand a tiny squeeze.

'Well?' said Sidwell-Plant.

Lady Hardcastle's face was impassive. 'Well what, dear?'

'Everett. Is he—?'

'Dead? I'm afraid so. It was quick, though.'

'What was it?'

She paused a moment. 'His heart.'

That wasn't a lie, at least – the tusk had certainly pierced his heart.

'Poor chap,' said Bridgewater. 'Just goes to show, you never know when your time's up. Could happen to any of us at any moment. One minute you're going about your day, minding your own business, the next—'

'Oh, for heaven's sake,' said Dotty. 'Do shut up for once, won't you? Clarice has lost her husband and you're wittering on like . . . like . . . Oh, I don't know. But I do wish you'd stop.'

'The world's a better place without him,' said Sidwell-Plant.

Patience was aghast. 'Robert! You can shut up as well. Think of poor Clarice.'

'You had a soft spot for him, did you? Was he the one? But he was a cad and a bully. Everyone knew it, and Clarice is better off without him.'

Patience gave a *pfft* and crossed her arms.

'It's a shock, I know,' said Lady Hardcastle, 'but we'll send for a doctor and the local constable at once and—'

I'd noticed a flash outside the window a second or two before, and now the thunder sounded with a loud bang and a sound like ripping canvas. Dotty shrieked. Sudden, fierce wind threw rain against the glass like a child throwing handfuls of gravel.

'I'm not sure anyone's going to make it out of the door in this,' said Wilson, 'much less sail to the mainland and back.'

Everyone started talking at once.

JB held up his hands for quiet. 'It's just an Atlantic storm. We get 'em all the time. Nothing to worry about. They blow up wild and then pass through just as quick. By morning it'll be calm as a millpond and we'll send Crawford ashore then.'

It would take a day or two for the sea to become properly calm, I knew, but the idea was sound: sit tight and it'll soon be over. What I didn't know, though, was whether we could keep everyone ignorant of the truth, nor what the killer might do next. I didn't really believe my own suggestion that it might be a mysterious stranger and was actually convinced that someone in that room had killed Everett. This was not a safe place for any of us to be overnight.

'Can we at least telephone the police?' I said. 'The sooner we report the matter, the fewer questions we'll have to answer.'

'No can do,' said JB. 'No phone line, remember? Your GPO have been dragging their heels. "We can't lay a cable under the sea, Mr McIntyre." There's cables all the way to North America, I told 'em. But they insist they can't do it.'

'Radio?' suggested Lady Hardcastle.

'Don't have a radio set, no. But who would be listening, anyway? Look, the storm will be gone by morning and we can do everything the old-fashioned way with a pen and paper and a loyal messenger on a boat. Until then, how about some games to keep our spirits up?'

'I'm not in the mood for games,' said Sidwell-Plant. 'I think I'll retire.'

'Me, too, actually,' said Lily, who hadn't said anything up to this point and seemed to be the most shaken of the group.

One by one, the rest of them expressed a desire to take themselves off to bed, with Sidwell-Plant offering to help Clarice.

'I hardly think it's proper for you to be accompanying a woman to her bedroom,' said Patience.

Sidwell-Plant looked at his wife coldly and was about to reply when Dotty spoke up.

'I'll take you, dear,' she said. 'Nothing improper in dotty Dorothy showing a pal to her room.'

A brief flurry of activity followed as the guests said their good-nights and made their way up to their bedrooms. Lady Hardcastle had another quick word with JB before grabbing two brandy glasses and ushering me out the door.

◆ ◆ ◆

I sat in the armchair in Lady Hardcastle's room while she sat cross-legged on the bed with her notebook and mechanical pencil.

I sipped my cognac. 'How sure are you about Everett dying at three o'clock?'

'Not nearly as sure as I tried to convince JB I am. From what Sim says it's all a bit general and vague, and whenever we press him on time of death he always gives a window of a couple of hours. But we have both blood pooling and rigor to go on, so I'm going to stick to three-ish as the centre of our window, at least, but it could be an hour or so either side, really.'

I nodded.

'I'd be a little more certain if I could have taken his temperature, but even that would have been an estimate with him lying there on that cold stone floor all afternoon.'

'Out of curiosity, why did you tell JB it was definitely three o'clock?'

'People don't want their experts to be equivocal, dear. They want firm answers. They don't want "it could have happened any time between two and four but we can't even say that for certain because the methods we've used are inexact". They want "it was three o'clock on the dot and I'd stake my reputation on it".'

'Fair dos,' I said. 'So can we plot everyone's movements after Everett's row with Clarice?'

'When was that? About half past one, would you say?'

'About then.'

'So that's the opening of our time-of-death window.'

'You were with JB when Patience, Lily and I overheard Everett and Clarice, weren't you?'

'And George Wilson, yes. We were in the long gallery talking about JB's maritime collection.'

I was ticking people off on my fingers. 'Dotty went off for her nap. Sidwell-Plant and Bridgewater went off to the drawing room to play billiards. Then Lily, Patience and I tried to go to the sitting room, and that was when we overheard Everett and Clarice.'

Lady Hardcastle was making notes. 'So that's where everyone was at the moment of the row. I presume Everett stalked off afterwards?'

'He did. Then Lily took Clarice off to her room—'

'Clarice's room or Lily's room?'

'I don't know. Clarice's, I assumed, but I can't say for certain. But Patience and I stayed in the sitting room until you arrived.'

Lady Hardcastle made a note. 'For my part, I have to assume that Wilson and JB went straight to the library, but I can't be certain, either. Then you and I had some tea with Patience, but she left . . . when? About two-ish?'

'Something like that. Maybe a little later. And then you and I went to the library to be sociable. Dotty and Patience were there, heads together – I remember that.'

'JB was there, too. And Bridgewater was telling his interminable jokes to Lily and Wilson.'

'Do you recall seeing Sidwell-Plant?'

'Not at all, no. Then Wilson went out for a walk. Patience and Dotty left to go with him and we gave up and went back to the sitting room with Lily.'

'That was at about three,' I said. 'I remember hearing the hall clock striking while Wilson was talking to Peggy Crawford on his way out through the kitchen door.'

'Lily left us almost immediately,' said Lady Hardcastle, 'and we saw no one until we took our teacups back to the kitchen at four.'

'When Dotty and Clarice turned up in time to meet Wilson coming back in from his walk.'

'And we're sure he didn't sneak back in before that?' I asked.

'We can't be absolutely sure. Dotty said he strode off into the distance when she and Patience turned back, so he was definitely out at that point. And there are only two ways in and out: the front door and the kitchen door. The front door squeals – Crawford told us that – and Peggy didn't move from the kitchen. If he came back and went out again, he'd have been seen or heard. He was definitely outside for the whole period.'

'So, we have Everett available to be murdered from about half past one until your time-of-death window closes at four.'

'Yes. Any earlier and . . . well, we'd all have noticed someone stabbing him with a narwhal tusk at the dining table, wouldn't we? Any later and rigor mortis would have been much less advanced by the time we examined him.'

I started ticking people off on my fingers again. 'We have Dotty going off for a nap at half past one. Lily and Clarice go off shortly after that. Patience is with Lily and me but leaves at about two. Sidwell-Plant is unaccounted for after his billiards game, but both Lily and Dotty are back in the library by the time we join them before three.'

'I think that's right, yes.'

'Then we leave them all in the library, but we know that Wilson goes for his walk, Dotty and Patience briefly join him, and Lily goes for a lie-down. We still have no idea where Sidwell-Plant is. We don't see Clarice until she turns up in the kitchen with Dotty, and then Wilson comes in from his walk. That's around four.'

Lady Hardcastle consulted the notes she'd been taking. 'So by my reckoning, we're reasonably sure where JB, Bridgewater and Wilson were for the two hours in question, but Dotty, Patience, Clarice, Lily and Sidwell-Plant are all unaccounted for at various points.'

'Sidwell-Plant is a reasonably vigorous chap – he could move a body on his own. And he definitely has a thing for Clarice.'

'All the men have a thing for Clarice, dear,' she said. 'She's a beautiful, talented woman. Add the blindness and their "manly" instincts take over. They all want to protect her, to keep her safe from the dangerous, wicked world. I don't think it's occurred to any of them that she's perfectly capable of looking after herself.'

'Well, yes,' I said. 'But only Sidwell-Plant had the opportunity to do Edgar in, no matter how much the others might have wanted to.'

'True. But I'm still not ruling out two or more of the women working together. With help from Dotty, Patience or Lily, even dear, beautiful, vulnerable Clarice could have put an end to the cruelty.'

'You've said yourself more than once that women are more inclined to poison their victims.'

She shrugged. 'You wouldn't. You'd have broken his neck or stabbed him with the knife no one but me knows you keep strapped to your forearm.'

'Of course. But that's because I have certain skills. Even I wouldn't take down an ornamental narwhal tusk and run someone through with it.'

'You might if there were a sudden altercation and you needed to defend yourself.'

I sighed. 'Very well. Yes, in that specific circumstance I might grab whatever was close at hand, even if it was a whale's tooth.'

'And so what if Clarice was in the long gallery with Dotty, or Patience, or Lily – or all three of them, come to that – and in comes Everett, all swagger and sneer? What if he started another argument, calling her names – calling the others names? What if they argue back and he loses his temper and raises a hand to one of them?'

'If all of that happened, then perhaps one of them would grab the tusk in a fit of rage and run him through,' I conceded.

'And then they'd clean up and hide the body. The clean-up was very proficient – can you imagine Robert Sidwell-Plant putting everything back in its place and mopping the floor?'

'But if they were so careful and efficient,' I said, 'would they really do such a shabby job of hiding the body and the murder weapon?'

'They ran out of time. We've all agreed that moving the body would be arduous, so they had to do the best they could without being away for ages. Both were hidden well enough for the time being – perhaps they intended to make a better job of it later.'

I hmm'd. 'Perhaps. But what's your William of Occam thing again? Fewest assumptions?'

'If we're going for the solution with the fewest assumptions, then it has to be Sidwell-Plant. Means, motive and, probably, opportunity. We need to find out where he was after the billiards game.'

I nodded. 'We need to find out exactly where everyone was.'

'Indeed. But first we need another little glug of this excellent cognac.'

# Chapter Eight

Before we finally turned in, Lady Hardcastle and I had arranged to be first down to breakfast on Saturday morning, and so we were both up, washed, dressed and ready for the day well before eight o'clock.

We were the first ones into the dining room, but breakfast was already waiting on the sideboard.

Lady Hardcastle helped herself to toast and a cup of coffee. 'I miss my starter breakfast when we're away from home, but if we're going to have to be here for a while, I think I can indulge myself. It won't be the same as having you rudely awaken me and shove it under my nose, but it might suffice.'

'I can rudely shove it under your nose if you think that will enhance the experience,' I said.

'You're very kind, but I shall content myself with simply sitting at the table and eating it. What are you having?'

'I agree with you – we're going to have to pace ourselves if we intend to linger. I think I'll have some toast, too. That marmalade looks nice.'

We sat at the table together and started munching.

'JB was right about the storm,' I said. 'It's not exactly bright and sunny out there but the rain has stopped and the wind has died right down. Crawford should be able to get to the mainland this morning.'

'I was thinking the same thing. We can hand everything over to the Devon County Constabulary and . . . I was going to say get back to a relaxing weekend, but we're not going to go back to anything like normality even once everything is in the hands of the authorities and everyone finds out Everett was murdered. Do you think it's us?'

I spooned an overly generous dollop of marmalade on to my toast. 'Do I think *what's* us? Did we kill Everett, do you mean? I think we'd have noticed.'

'Well, quite. But that's not what I meant. What I meant was that wherever we go, someone always seems to get murdered.'

I laughed. 'Maybe it is something to do with us, then. Perhaps we're *cursed*.'

'We did upset that woman in the hut in the Bavarian Alps that time. She definitely threatened to put some sort of hex on us for walking through her vegetable patch.'

'It would be an oddly specific hex, though, don't you think? "Wherever thou dost go, murder shall there be, but never thine own. Thou shalt be doomed forever to solve the deaths of others." Only in old-fashioned German. Obviously.'

'Obviously. But it is odd, isn't it?'

'What's the phrase you use? Statistically improbable.'

JB had entered the room. 'What's statistically improbable?'

'That Bristol City will win the second division,' said Lady Hardcastle without missing a beat. 'Actually, at this point I think it might be mathematically impossible unless half the other teams are disqualified. And that *is* statistically improbable. They did beat Stockport County 7–2 a few weeks ago, but Stockport are doing poorly, too, so it wasn't quite the achievement it might have been.'

'I have to tell you I don't understand football at all. Half the rules don't make sense. "Offside"? I mean, surely getting behind the *de*fence is what it's all about. And then after all that effort you can still end a game with a tie—'

'A draw, dear.'

'There you are, you see? I can't even get the language right.'

'What's your favoured sport, then?' I asked.

'Baseball. The Philadelphia Phillies are my team. Been cheering for them since they were founded back in '83. Of course, last season they didn't do much better than your Bristol City, but we have high hopes for 1913. Not that it means anything – everyone starts every season with high hopes.'

Sidwell-Plant strolled in. 'Fair warning, ladies: don't get him started on baseball – you'll be here all morning.'

'I think it's good for people to have a passion,' I said. 'Are you a sporting man?'

'I rowed a bit at Oxford. Played a little rugger.'

'That's rugby, right?' said JB as he sat down with a heaped plate.

'It is. Like your football but without obstruction—'

'Interference,' said JB with a wink to Lady Hardcastle.

'Really? That makes it sound worse. One can't pass the ball forwards, either. Or wear padding.'

JB chuckled. 'Sounds like you're intentionally making things difficult for yourselves. But at my age I'm going to stick to billiards. Maybe a little golf.'

Lady Hardcastle turned to Sidwell-Plant. 'How did you get on yesterday afternoon?' she asked. 'Didn't you and Bridgewater have a game?'

'We did. Although we actually played snooker – he prefers it. He used to play in India so he knows he can beat me.'

'And did he?' I asked.

'Absolutely thrashed me. Good thing we weren't playing for money or I'd be broke by now.'

'I thought he looked kinda pleased with himself when he joined us in the library,' said JB. 'Is that why we didn't see you? Off licking your wounds?'

Sidwell-Plant gave a rueful smile. 'Something like that, yes.'

For one hopeful moment I thought JB was going to do our job for us and establish Sidwell-Plant's movements during the two hours when Everett was murdered. No such luck. But how to proceed? Should we press him or was that vague 'something like that' all anyone was going to get?

Lady Hardcastle was keen to keep going. 'I find a good walk eases my melancholy when Florence beats me at cards. Or at anything – she's rather good at most things, to be honest. And if it's too late for a walk, I find brandy always numbs the pain.'

'It wasn't really the afternoon for a walk,' said Sidwell-Plant. 'I don't know what pleasure Wilson got from it, but I certainly wasn't going to go out in that. Patience tells me it was ghastly out.'

'Brandy, then?' I asked.

He laughed. 'I'm more of a scotch chap, but in truth I just went back to my room and had a manly sulk.'

'What did Patience think of that?' said Lady Hardcastle.

'She wasn't there. I sulked alone.'

Interesting. So his uncorroborated alibi was that he was alone in his room. Meanwhile, Patience's whereabouts remained unknown after she'd returned from her aborted walk.

Wilson came in next, talking earnestly with Bridgewater.

'. . . put you in touch with a chap who has one if you're serious.'

'Would that I were, dear boy. If I had deeper pockets and much longer arms I might take you up on it, but I fear that sort of thing is a little out of my price range.' Bridgewater seemed to notice the rest of us for the first time. 'Ah, good morning, ladies and gents. Did you sleep well? Wasn't the storm frightful?'

'I guess I'm getting used to it,' said JB. 'Like I tried to explain last night: we get storms like that out here quite a lot. Most don't amount to nothing.'

'Well, it kept me awake, I can tell you. We don't get that sort of weather in Belgravia.'

They helped themselves to platefuls of food and joined us at the table.

Lily arrived next, looking a little bleary, and the gentlemen all rose.

'Someone else didn't get much sleep,' said Bridgewater, dabbing his mouth with a napkin.

'It was that storm,' said Lily. 'I might have managed to sleep through it but I rather foolishly fell asleep yesterday afternoon so I wasn't tired enough to ignore it.'

Bridgewater nodded. 'That's why I avoid afternoon naps. The memsahib swears by them, but no matter how drowsy I get in the afternoon, I try not to give in. If I sleep in the daytime, I'll never manage to sleep at night.'

'I just couldn't stay awake. I'd been travelling all morning, then there was that business with' – she looked around to check who else was present – 'with Clarice and Everett. It was all rather exhausting. I wish I'd taken your route and stayed awake, though – I might have missed the storm.'

'You'll have to speak to Mrs B,' said Bridgewater. 'She might have some expert tips.'

'Expert tips on what, dear?' said Dotty, who had just entered with Clarice on her arm.

'Afternoon naps,' said Bridgewater as he resumed his seat once more. 'They don't seem to take the same toll on you as on everyone else. Young Lily here didn't manage to sleep through the storm because she slept all afternoon.'

Dotty was already helping herself from the silver warming dishes on the sideboard. 'Ah, well, now, you see, that's where you're going wrong, dear. The professional napper never sleeps for more than half an hour.'

I gave Lady Hardcastle a grin, and her smiling nod acknowledged that I'd said the same thing myself the day before.

'I slept like a log,' said Clarice.

I thought that this was almost certainly an occasion where her blindness was actually an advantage. No one said anything, but the shocked expressions on their faces would have given her pause if she had been able to see them.

'And here comes my own darling wife,' said Sidwell-Plant as, once again, the gentlemen all rose.

Patience just shook her head and made her way to the sideboard.

'How did you sleep, dear?' asked Dotty.

Patience carried on spooning kedgeree on to her plate. 'On my side, mostly.'

Dotty gave her a puzzled frown. 'No, I meant—'

'I know what you meant, Dotty darling. It was a joke—'

'Not a very good one,' muttered Sidwell-Plant.

She ignored him. 'You wanted to know whether I was affected by the storm. I slept through most of it. Honestly, if I can sleep through Robert's snoring, I can sleep through anything.'

Bridgewater laughed, oblivious to the atmosphere. 'You didn't make young Lily's error and sleep the afternoon away.'

Patience sat at the table looking slightly puzzled. 'I didn't, no.'

*Well done, JB*, I thought. For the life of me I hadn't been able to fathom out how we might discreetly ask about everyone's whereabouts between two and four the previous afternoon, but he'd managed to make it all sound like a pleasant, natural conversation. Pleasant-ish, at any rate – I didn't feel the Sidwell-Plants would have been happy rays of sunshine even in less distressing circumstances.

◆ ◆ ◆

With everyone now present, Lady Hardcastle and I felt it was at last safe to eat properly, and by the time we rejoined everyone at the table we both had substantial plates of food to work through.

Despite Everett's sudden death and the odd atmosphere between the Sidwell-Plants, breakfast was surprisingly convivial. There was the usual amount of small talk, and even a little teasing of Wilson and Lily, who seemed to be taking JB's ham-fisted matchmaking in good spirit.

Sidwell-Plant asked about the progress being made on finding the stolen jewellery.

'We're pursuing a few lines of inquiry,' said Lady Hardcastle. 'We have a couple of leads, but we need to check a few more things before we can say anything for certain.'

I knew this to be something of a fib – we had absolutely no idea what had happened – but from the many nods around the table it seemed that the others were satisfied with this empty response.

'Good show,' said Bridgewater. 'Worth a fortune.'

Another nod from Sidwell-Plant confirmed that he, too, was concerned about the value of the missing pieces.

Conversation returned to less sensitive matters for a while.

Inevitably, though, the subject of Everett's death was eventually raised and talk turned to the urgency of sending Crawford ashore to fetch the authorities.

'Have you sent him yet?' asked Wilson.

'It's only been properly light for about an hour,' said JB. 'I had him help with breakfast first, but I sent him down to the boat about twenty minutes ago. He should be well underway by now.

Give him ten minutes to get going, a quarter of an hour or so to get to shore, say half an hour to an hour to get the constable and a doctor, then half an hour to get them both up here. I'd say he'll be back around eleven.'

There was a knock on the dining room door and a diffident *ahem*. 'Beggin' your pardon, sir, but can I have a word?'

It was Crawford, his cap scrunched in both hands.

'What is it, man? I was just telling everyone you were on your way to shore.'

'That's just it, sir. I can't.'

'Why ever not?'

'It's the boat, sir. Seems she broke loose from her moorin's in the storm. As far as I can tell, she smashed up against the rocks and damaged her hull.'

'How badly damaged is she?'

'Bad enough that she's at the bottom of the inlet, sir. Just her funnel showin' above the swell.'

'So we're stranded here?' said Lily. 'We've no boat, no telephone, no nothing.'

'Just for a couple days,' said JB. 'Vickerman will come out with the mail Tuesday.'

'Who's Vickerman?' asked Wilson.

'Vickerman the Fisherman,' said Bridgewater. 'Chap we saw at the quay on Thursday.'

Wilson shook his head. 'So we're waiting for the postman.'

'I guess you could put it like that,' said JB. 'But we'll be fine. Nothing to worry about.'

'You've forgotten that Edgar Everett is dead, I suppose?' said Sidwell-Plant.

'No, I'm well aware of that. But Crawford, could you move Mr Everett to the outside storeroom, please? It'll be cold enough out there.'

Crawford nodded.

'The doctor can examine him out there, too. The police won't quibble over the delay in reporting things, given the circumstances.'

'Aren't you forgetting Clarice?' said Patience. 'She needs—'

'I do hope you're not going to be a frightful bore and speak for me as though I'm not here,' interrupted Clarice. 'I'm perfectly capable of expressing my own needs, thank you.'

'Yes . . . Well . . .'

JB raised a placatory hand. 'Like I say, we'll be fine. We've plenty to eat, plenty to do—'

'Nowhere to go,' said Sidwell-Plant. He looked at Patience. 'No one to spend a quiet moment with.'

She gave a *pfft* in response but said nothing.

'I know we've suffered a tragedy,' said JB, 'but we have to make the best of it. We were planning to be here anyway, so let's just carry on as best we can and wait for Vickerman to come out as usual.'

Sidwell-Plant gave a *pfft* of his own. 'He'd better not forget. I was rather depending on getting away on Monday – I have to be back in London.'

'Everyone has places to be,' said JB. 'At the risk of repeating myself one too many times: we'll be fine.'

The grumbling and mumbling that followed this assertion very much seemed to indicate that the others didn't believe him, but he was unfazed. He got up from the table and came round to lean down between Lady Hardcastle and me. He spoke softly. 'Would you two ladies mind coming with me, please? I'd like a word away from these guys.'

We got up and followed as discreetly as we could. We needn't have bothered – by now they were all so busy arguing with each other about whose appointments were the most important that they didn't even notice we'd gone.

◆ ◆ ◆

JB led us upstairs to what turned out to be his own private suite of rooms, and into his study. He closed the door.

He leaned against his desk and gestured for us to sit in the two armchairs opposite him. 'Am I lying to my friends?'

Lady Hardcastle frowned. 'Of course you are. You knew that.'

'Oh, I don't mean about Everett – that's just an expedient misrepresentation of certain details. I mean about whether we'll all be OK.'

'Ah, I see. Well, you're being optimistic, certainly. Only one among us can be certain whether the killer will strike again, and if Everett's murder was a crime of – shall we use your word? – *expedience*, then even he won't know whether circumstances might conspire to require him to murder someone else.'

'How does a murder become a matter of expedience?'

'As I understand it, there are only three principal motives for committing murder: passion, money, and to cover up another crime. If Everett were killed out of jealousy, or, say, revenge over his treatment of his wife, then there seems no reason to kill anyone else. With the object of his rage out of the way, the passion is spent.'

'So you agree it's a he.'

'In truth, no, not yet. I just didn't want to get into another discussion about the sex of the killer.'

JB smiled but didn't respond.

'I can't quickly think of a financial motive for bumping off Everett,' continued Lady Hardcastle, 'but if there is one, it's also likely that no one else needs to die. On the other hand, if he had knowledge of some other crime and had to be silenced, any of your guests might have similar knowledge and might also be in danger.'

'So the key is knowing the motive.'

'It so often is. Let's start with passion. Everyone, I think, knows about Everett's appalling treatment of his wife. I gather yesterday's wasn't an isolated incident.'

'No, we've all known about him for a while.'

'But none of you have tried to stop him.'

JB bridled. 'Of course we have. Each of us have – how do you Brits put it? – "had a go at him" over the years. Sometimes he laughed it off, sometimes he angrily denied it, sometimes he told us it was none of our damned business how he treated his own wife, but he never stopped. Patience has been trying to get her to leave him. Dotty has . . . well, you know Dotty by now. Not the most forthright or practical lady, but she's been offering comfort and support.'

'So you all have a motive for killing him, to save Clarice.'

'I suppose we do, yes.'

It might take us off at a tangent, but there was something else I wanted to know. 'What did Sidwell-Plant mean just now when he made that remark about us having no one to spend a quiet moment with? It seemed to be directed at Patience.'

JB sighed. 'They're a far from happy couple. Patience wants him to divorce her, but he refuses. She's been quite open about her affair to try to force his hand, but still he won't budge. He believes that while he stays clear of the divorce courts he can dismiss her infidelity as gossip and rumour. But if he divorces her, he makes the cuckoldry official, and he doesn't want the scandal.'

'I see. I think. Who else knows?'

'Patience has made sure we all know. Like I say, she wants her divorce so she can marry her new man.'

'And who's the new man?'

'Well, now that one, no one knows. She's trying to protect him, I suppose. There have been rumours, of course, but no one knows for sure.'

'Could it have been Everett?'

'I can't see why she'd have fallen for a rat like him, and no one else thinks so, except . . .'

'Except Sidwell-Plant?' suggested Lady Hardcastle.

'Yup, except him. We keep telling him Everett's the last person she'd want to be with, but he's as dogged in his belief that it's a possibility as he is in his refusal to grant her a divorce.'

'So he might have finally decided to bump off his supposed rival.' I thought for a moment before taking us off in yet another direction. 'We're saying we can't see how Everett's death might have benefitted anyone financially, but surely Clarice is better off now? She inherits his estate.'

JB nodded. 'And it's not a bad one, either. Musicians don't earn vast fortunes but he comes from money – he inherited property and a decent stock portfolio when his father died.'

'So that gives her two motives,' I said. 'Revenge and money.'

'She'd need help,' said Lady Hardcastle.

I shrugged. 'She'd not be short of offers – it seems everyone hated Everett.'

JB shook his head furiously. 'Absolutely not. I love that girl like she was my own daughter. I'll not have you speaking ill of her. She's not involved in this in any way.'

'Very well,' said Lady Hardcastle. 'But what of your other guests? What do Lily and Wilson think of Everett?'

'As far as I know, they just met him this weekend. I don't reckon it ever took anyone more than a weekend to take a dislike to Edgar Everett, but I wouldn't say either of them has had long enough to develop a hatred strong enough to inspire murder.'

'That's all very helpful,' said Lady Hardcastle. 'Thank you. So that just leaves us with covering up another crime. Do you have any ideas?'

JB shook his head. 'Not unless it's the missing jewellery. But you seem to think that's a prank.'

'It could still be a prank, of course, but now there's been a murder I think we ought to at least entertain the possibility that it's a genuine theft.'

'I guess. But who'd murder someone over a couple baubles? I mean, even if Everett were on to the thief, are a few gems worth swinging for? A pragmatic man would just try to make a deal and give them back.'

'True,' I said. 'But men have been murdered over a few pennies – pragmatism can evaporate in the heat of the moment. But the truth is, they're not just a "couple of baubles". From what we understand, the combined value of the two pieces would buy a decent house in one of the swankier parts of London.' I remembered something else I'd been wanting to ask. 'Is Granville Bridgewater having financial problems?'

'What makes you ask that?'

'He's said one or two things that made me wonder, that's all.'

'You're very perceptive – I could have made good use of someone like you when I was running my business. Good judge of people. Yes, Granville has always lived beyond his means. He works with wealthy folk and wishes to live as they do, but his income never quite matches his outgoings. It's not that he's a foolish spendthrift or a wastrel, but his tastes have always been those of a man worth a great deal more than he actually is.'

'Would he stoop to theft?'

'Outright theft? I don't know, but I wouldn't say so, no.'

'How about insurance fraud? If Dotty's ruby necklace went missing in the presence of some unimpeachable witnesses, he could make an apparently valid claim. Taking Patience's brooch would add a touch of authenticity by making it look as though both wealthy ladies had been targeted.'

'Again, I don't see it,' said JB. 'Not bumbling old Bridgewater. He's the affable fool with the after-dinner stories, not a scheming crook. He might live in a house he can't afford, but that kind of thing isn't his style. Nor is murder.'

'Fair dos,' I said. 'What about the others? Could Wilson be a jewel thief?'

'I guess anyone could be a jewel thief. I've not known him long but he seems like a trustworthy guy.'

'He was with us all evening when the gems went missing,' said Lady Hardcastle.

'Actually, yes, he was,' I conceded. 'How well do you know your staff, JB?'

'Well enough. I'd vouch for them, certainly. Salt of the earth, as they say.'

'Everett seemed to think they were up to something.'

'He said something to that effect, yes. But he was a snob, among his many other failings. I didn't read anything into it.'

I shrugged. 'So where are we now?'

JB chuckled. 'Pretty much nowhere, as far as I can tell. And I'm still no nearer to an answer to the question I brought you in here for: will we be OK?'

Lady Hardcastle smiled. 'We'll make sure of it, dear. We'll find out what's going on and everything will be fine. Although . . .'

He raised an eyebrow. 'Although?'

'Well, we have a pretty decent record for working these things out, but it can take time. If our killer has more murder in mind, we might not be able to stop them before they kill again.'

◆ ◆ ◆

The guests had dispersed by the time we got back to the dining room, but there was still food on the sideboard and I made myself one last sausage sandwich.

I waved it at Lady Hardcastle. 'You know what this could do with? Some tomato ketchup. It's an American thing – you'd think JB would have some for his guests.'

'Or some HP if he wanted to appear to have been properly anglicized and use one of our own mass-produced table sauces.'

'Either way, it would be greatly enhanced. Nice sausages, though. I think you can judge a host or a hotel by the quality of their sausages.'

'Just a moment while I indulge myself with a music hall snigger.'

'Hoist by my own petard. What are we up to next?'

'I thought we might try to track down Clarice and have a quiet word. I think we should offer our sympathies—'

'Carefully – she has a low threshold for condescension.'

'Indeed. And then just as carefully try to find out a little more about Everett and her relationship with him.'

It didn't take us long to find her – we just followed the sound of the piano coming from the drawing room next door – and I was still finishing my mouthful of sandwich and brushing the crumbs from my dress as Lady Hardcastle announced our presence.

Clarice carried on playing to the end of the phrase and left the final chord ringing. 'Come to join me? I'd love to duet if you have a minute or two to spare. Oh, how rude of me – I'm sorry. Do you play, Florence?'

'She's tried to teach me, but I never stuck at the practice, I'm afraid. I'll make myself comfortable and listen, if you don't mind.'

Clarice released the loud pedal and the ghost of the chord fled the room.

Lady Hardcastle sat on the right-hand side of the stool. 'Budge up.'

They made themselves comfortable somehow, both of them on a seat built for one, and Clarice began vamping some melancholy chords. Lady Hardcastle improvised a suitably wistful melody over the top. They played like this for a few minutes, occasionally swapping roles, until the extemporized piece came to a natural end.

'We should play that this evening,' said Clarice.

'It's certainly lovely – you play very well, dear – but it's a touch gloomy, don't you think?'

'Ah, but it would suit the circumstances perfectly – they expect me to be gloomy.'

'Are you not?'

Clarice paused a moment. 'I've only known you since Thursday, but I get the sense you're not the sort to be bound by society's petty rules. I think I can be honest with you about this . . . No, I'm not gloomy. There's a touch of genuine sadness, I confess. We were married for nearly fifteen years, after all – I'm bound to miss him. But mostly there's relief. It struck me this morning when I woke and realized I'd not have to pay attention to his mood, not have to watch what I said, be careful how I reacted. I'll mourn his loss as I would anyone who leaves my life, but I can't bring myself to weep, wail, or gnash my teeth. Overall, the world's a brighter place without Edgar Everett in it.'

'To echo your own words of a few moments ago,' said Lady Hardcastle, 'I'd only known him since Thursday, but I can't say I'm terribly disappointed I'll not be seeing him again. He wasn't sparkling company.'

Clarice nodded. 'He was not. What do you think, Florence?'

'Me?' I said. 'I would never have admitted it in public if you hadn't said what you just said, but I couldn't stand the man. After the incident in the sitting room yesterday I was ready to knock his lights out. If Patience hadn't stopped me, I might have.'

Clarice laughed. 'He had that effect on people. But you're quite small—'

'How can you tell?'

'Your voice comes from lower down than everyone else's. Either you're always crouching or you're little.'

'I am, indeed, pleasingly petite.'

She laughed again. 'So it's a good thing you didn't try to slosh him one. He wasn't a violent man, but he was surprisingly strong.'

'Our Flo is something of a dab hand at the fighting arts,' said Lady Hardcastle. 'I'd always bet on her in a scuffle.'

Clarice beamed. 'I say, you're not one of those suffrajitsus they talk about in the newspapers, are you?'

It was my turn to laugh. 'No, but I have taught some of the Bristol suffragettes how to look after themselves if things cut up rough.'

'How very marvellous.'

'How did you and Edgar meet?' asked Lady Hardcastle.

'At a concert, naturally. My elder sister used to be my guide and chaperone, and we were backstage at a recital in Cheltenham one evening in the summer of '98 when a man barged into me. My sister began to berate him, he began to berate me, and I just stood there with what I'm told was a stupid smile on my face.'

'Why were you smiling?' I asked.

'He smelled divine. I couldn't have described it, but there was something about his . . . his presence, I suppose, that made me grin. He had a lovely voice, too.'

'Actually, he did, didn't he. I didn't get close enough to smell him, though.'

'You'd have been disappointed – he smelled very ordinary thereafter. I think it was something he'd come into contact with backstage at the theatre. Honestly, I could have ended up marrying a stagehand if I'd got close enough to one to sniff him. Anyway, we sorted out the misunderstanding and introduced ourselves. My regular accompanist had missed his train so the theatre had booked Edgar at the last minute. We played wonderfully together and I managed to arrange to work with him again a week later in Birmingham. Things just sort of went from there. Within a few months my sister was no longer needed and Edgar accompanied me to the theatres as well as when I played. We were married in October.'

'A charming story,' said Lady Hardcastle. 'It's a pity he turned out to be . . . well, to be Edgar, I suppose. Still, it's a shame your last interaction was a disagreeable one.'

'Actually, yes. I really am glad we've finally parted, but I think I should have preferred we part on better terms.'

'So you didn't . . . see him again after your row.'

Another laugh. 'Everyone has to get over that – we all use "see" figuratively like that. Is it figurative? But you know what I mean, don't you. But no, I didn't see him again in either sense – I neither perceived him with my sightless eyes, nor was I in his company. I'm not sure I'd have said goodbye, though, so it would probably have made no difference.' She sat silent for a while. 'You said it was his heart?'

'As far as we could tell,' said Lady Hardcastle. 'But we've no medical training.'

'I hope it was quick. He was a beast, but I still hope he didn't suffer.'

Neither Lady Hardcastle nor I had an answer to that.

# Chapter Nine

We offered to help Clarice find her way to her next location, but she said she was on her way back to her room. It was on the same corridor as the dining room so she was confident she could find her own way without any trouble.

We left her playing and started to walk towards the long gallery, where we might, we thought, see something in the wan morning light that we'd missed in the evening gloom.

As we neared the stairs we could hear voices coming from inside the Bridgewaters' room. It was Patience and Dotty and, though their voices weren't raised, they were definitely not happy.

'. . . you and I both know he did it,' said Patience. 'Robert knows, too, and he's going to go to JB unless Gran comes clean and gives it back.'

'He wouldn't. Oh, Speedy, he couldn't.'

'He can and he will. Can't you intercede? I don't want to see Gran fall from favour any more than you do, and God knows I can't bear to see Robert getting the upper hand in anything. Can't you just persuade him to give it back?'

There was movement within the room and it sounded as though one or both of them might be heading for the door, so we hurried on.

As we entered the long gallery, we saw Wilson, bending forwards and examining a chronometer in its polished wooden case.

He looked up as we entered. 'Hello again, ladies. Have you seen this?'

We moved closer and I tried my best to feign interest in the clock.

Lady Hardcastle's interest appeared to be genuine. 'I was hoping JB might talk about it when we were in here yesterday.'

'Me, too – that's why I came back. This one is British. 1861. One of only twenty made by this company to this specification. It was accurate to within a second a month. Can you imagine? When it was new, a captain could sail from Liverpool to New York and his chronometer would only be out by one second. I can't do the navigational calculations, but I'd bet his reckoning of his position would be out by yards rather than miles.'

Suddenly I wasn't having to feign interest. 'It's an important instrument, then?'

'One might argue that John Harrison's invention of the marine chronometer in the 1700s was what enabled Britannia to rule the waves,' said Lady Hardcastle. 'That and a complete disregard for anyone else's rights and sovereignty, obviously.'

Wilson gave a puzzled frown. 'I suppose when you put it like that . . .'

'It's a beautiful thing, though,' I said. 'The clock, not the Empire.'

He was on safer ground. 'Beautiful indeed. I had a client asking about one last year but we couldn't find one for sale. I wish I'd known JB then – we might have been able to do a deal.'

'Does he sell his pieces?' asked Lady Hardcastle. 'I got the feeling he wasn't that sort of collector. He seems to be building the collection with a purpose – selling items off after he'd taken such pains to acquire them doesn't seem like him at all.'

'No, you're probably right. So many of my clients are interested only in the monetary value of their collections. I forget that some of them actually want the pieces for their own sake. I confess I'm a bit baffled by posh people. No offence.'

'None taken, dear. I'm a bit baffled by many of us, too.'

'I mean, it's wonderful that there are people about with money to burn – I depend on them for my living – but so many of them are so . . . odd. I suppose once you have that much money you struggle to find things to spend it on. Now you've said it, though, JB really is a proper enthusiast. These things, these hundreds – maybe thousands – of pounds' worth of things all mean something to him.'

Lady Hardcastle nodded. 'I think they do. It's a very focused collection.'

'What's his obsession with the sea?'

'He told us once over dinner at his London home. It seems he read *Moby-Dick* as a young man and it very much captured his imagination. When he found out he was born the day the book was published in America, he decided they must be linked in some way. He developed a fascination with anything to do with whaling, and then with maritime history generally.'

'Then I'd never have persuaded him to part with the chronometer even if I had known him. This one was owned by the captain of a steamship that *almost* took the record for the fastest Atlantic crossing three years running. Oddly, I think there's something rather romantic about being an almost record holder.'

'I agree. We British do love an underdog.'

We all looked at the chronometer a little more. I was still a tiny bit uncertain what more we could learn from staring at it, but the other two seemed to be enjoying themselves.

'Do you have a hankering for the sea?' I asked Wilson.

He gave that puzzled frown again. 'How do you mean?'

'Well, you went out all afternoon to stare at it yesterday, even though it was getting a bit blowy. It seems like the sort of thing someone who shared JB's romantic notions of seafaring might do.'

'Ah, yes, I see what you mean. But no, I don't. I have an Englishman's sentimental idea of our scepter'd isle and all that – a precious stone set in the silver sea – but I have no desire to set sail. I just wanted some time to think, away from that ghastly tick Everett. He'd created such a poisonous atmosphere and I needed to clear my head. I'm trying to secure something for JB and I needed to think my plan through without any distractions.'

'How exciting,' said Lady Hardcastle. 'Have you been JB's antiquities consultant long?'

'Not long, no. We met last October. A pal of mine introduced us. JB heard that some charts once owned by a Nantucket whaling captain had come on the market and my pal suggested I might be the man to get hold of them for him. We missed the boat on that one, as it were, but I did find him a couple of diaries and a rather nice telescope, so we kept in touch and I look out for things he might like. I've let him know about a few but he's not been interested. Now, though, I have a lead on a ship's bell salvaged from a trading ship that sank in the Gulf of Maine in 1782 during the War of Independence, so he invited me to join him this weekend. Fingers crossed, eh?'

'Fingers crossed, indeed,' I said.

'At least, that's what I thought I was here for until I found out he'd also invited Miss Thacker.'

'Ah,' said Lady Hardcastle, 'the fair Lily. I can't see why he wouldn't want to mix business with a little mischief. A man who built an entire collection inspired by his love of a book must have some romance in his soul.'

'I'm sure he means well, but I could do without being thrown into the company of random women.'

'I think she's rather charming,' I said.

'She's delightful, but I'd much prefer to make my own matches. I'm quite capable of meeting suitable women without help, no matter how well-meaning the helper might be.'

'I don't believe JB will mess you about,' said Lady Hardcastle. 'His matchmaking is just a little fun, I think – Lily is here to do some research for the photographs JB wants, after all. He might be a romantic mischief-maker, but he's a barely reformed robber baron at heart.'

Wilson smiled. 'I need all the robber barons and capitalist exploiters of the bourgeoisie I can get my hands on – they pay my rent. But I do wonder what blackness lurks in their souls. No one ever got rich by being kind and selfless. If you ask me, there's always something wicked lurking beneath their oh-so-proper façades. Present company excepted, of course.'

Lady Hardcastle grinned. 'Oh, you have no idea of the wickedness and depravity that lurks beneath my façade, dear. I terrify even myself, sometimes.'

◆ ◆ ◆

Secrets had been my stock in trade for my entire adult life, and I liked to imagine I had learned to handle them with suitable professionalism. Despite my professed facility for keeping and managing secrets, there remained an odd feeling of disconnection when dealing with people who were involved in something but were not privy to the full details, as though we were living in two separate worlds with two separate versions of the same events.

And so it was an odd experience to be among a group of friends who had suffered a loss – even if the lost one wasn't someone who would be greatly missed – and who thought his death was a medical tragedy, when we knew he had been murdered.

To them it was sad but was 'just one of those things'.

Death comes to us all in the end.

To us it was a wicked crime whose perpetrator was in our midst. Like us, that perpetrator was in on the secret and we were living in that separate world where that one tiny piece of knowledge changed everything.

All of them, including – we presumed – the killer, had made it to lunch. The 'heigh ho, what can one do?' mood of the breakfast table was fading in favour of a certain snippy impatience.

It was Sidwell-Plant who gave voice to the reason for the change of atmosphere. 'I mean, it's not as though we weren't expecting to stay until Monday morning anyway, and an extra day would ordinarily be a treat. I, for one, could do with a long weekend away from the office. But we *have* to stay. That blasted storm destroyed the boat and now we're stranded on the island rather than idly passing a few pleasant days here by choice.'

I couldn't help but think that a more mature response would have been simply to accept that things couldn't be changed and to try to make the best of it. Perhaps that was the Stoic in me.

'Could be worse, old chap,' said Bridgewater. 'Could be you lying dead in the storeroom rather than Dreadful Edgar.'

'Granville!' said Dorothy. 'Do at least try to show a little respect. Think of poor Clarice.'

'Don't worry about me,' said Clarice. 'I've called him worse and I'm not sorry to be shot of him.'

Patience was sitting next to me. Under her breath, she said, 'I'd be just as happy if it were either of them.'

I didn't think any of the others had heard.

Bridgewater was impervious to criticism. 'But if it's getting you down, old bean, we ought to play a game of some sort. D'you have any golf clubs, JB? Tennis rackets? A football?'

'Sadly not,' said JB. 'Maybe I'll bring some sports gear out in the summer. For now it's still a little blustery for outdoor games, though. There's a parlour croquet set in the cupboard in the drawing room. A tournament, maybe?'

I could almost hear the grinding of mental gears as half the guests tried to work out if it would be acceptable to voice their enthusiasm, while the other half tried to work out how to politely say that they'd rather join Edgar, dead in the outside storeroom. Was it all right to be excited by a silly game in these sad circumstances? Was it all right to be a killjoy when people so obviously needed cheering up?

They settled, as groups so often do, for the middle ground, and the consensus around the table was that it wasn't a terrible idea and perhaps that was the sort of thing we ought to do.

The mood picked up thereafter and became positively buoyant when lots were drawn to find out who would be paired with whom. Paper and a pencil were found so that Sidwell-Plant, the accountant, could draw up the score charts and league table.

◆ ◆ ◆

With lunch polished off, we retired to the drawing room, but not before I'd visited the kitchen to instruct Jago Crawford in the noble art of making a rum punch. Under my expert tutelage he produced a very large jug of the sustaining beverage and brought it up to where the room had been prepared for the Great Croquet Tournament.

For the first round, I was paired with Lily, who turned out to be competitive but inept – a deadly combination – but remained pleasant company.

Clarice had insisted on playing and had, most fortunately, been drawn with Lady Hardcastle, who was a hopeless parlour croquet player but a patient tutor. Between them they seemed to be having more fun than the rest of us put together.

Conversation with Lily was effortless and relaxed. Perhaps it was the closeness in our ages, but I found her very easy to get on with. I knew I had to try to establish her movements on the previous afternoon, but I hadn't wanted to bring up the subject of Everett's death for fear of spoiling the otherwise jolly mood.

Bless her little heart, she brought it up for me. 'It's odd to think of poor Everett lying dead somewhere while we were all going about our business yesterday afternoon. Where did Crawford find him?'

'In one of the empty rooms upstairs,' I said.

'I wonder what he was doing up there. Snooping about, I expect. I fancied a little snooping myself, I have to say, but time ran away from me. After I'd taken Clarice back to her room I had a lovely chat with Dotty in the library. I was going to have a wander after that, but by the time I'd listened to yet another one of Bridgewater's interminable stories, I was absolutely pooped. I almost joined you in the sitting room, didn't I, but I simply had to have a snooze.'

I realized that I knew all that already, but I couldn't find a non-accusatory way of asking her if she'd *really* been for a snooze. It's easy when you have a suspect tied to a chair, but it's a great deal more difficult to casually slip that sort of thing into a friendly chat.

She missed the hoop but managed to strike Patience's ball.

'Oops,' she said with a charming giggle. 'Silly me.'

Patience grumbled good-naturedly.

Lily played her croquet shot, knocking Patience's ball again to send it awkwardly behind a chair leg. 'I wonder if he suffered. Everett, I mean. I was absolutely furious with him after that business in the sitting room with Clarice, and I'm ashamed to say I wished him dead right there and then. But I wouldn't have wanted him to suffer. Not *too* much anyway.' She giggled again. 'It was his heart, you said? I hope he wasn't too frightened.'

Play progressed amiably, and at the end of the first round Sidwell-Plant withdrew to a windowsill, where he performed whatever arcane calculations were required in order to establish our rankings. I was third out of the ten of us, with Lady Hardcastle in last place behind Clarice.

Sidwell-Plant's impenetrable rules required that we change partners for the second round, and this time I found myself partnered with fourth-placed Granville Bridgewater.

'Aha,' he said. 'Lucky me. I've been watching you. I fancy you're rather better at this than the current standings would seem to show. Perhaps we can elevate each other out of the mid-table doldrums.'

'Is that how it works?' I asked. 'I confess I don't completely understand the scoring system.'

'Ha! No one does, m'dear. No one but RVSP. And that's the way he likes it. Loves to be in control, our Robert Victor. Loves to be the one who knows what's going on. He's in his element, look.'

I glanced over and saw Sidwell-Plant smiling happily as he made more calculations on his many sheets of paper.

'That's accountants for you,' I said. 'They do love to count things.'

Bridgewater gave another bark of a laugh. 'They do indeed. And reconciling the books. Knows where every penny's gone, that one. Have you met many accountants? Strange chaps.'

'I've known my fair share.'

'*Unfair* share, what?'

'But most of them have been decent enough. If a bit odd.'

'Ha. Odd is right. Still, I suppose you have to be a little odd to want to spend your days keeping track of other chaps' money. You come across any wrong 'uns in your murder investigations?'

'Any dodgy accountants? No, I don't think so.'

'Solicitors?'

'No, nor them. Bankers, property developers, publicans, actors . . . but no accountants or solicitors.'

He smiled and played his shot.

◆ ◆ ◆

Despite my misgivings about Sidwell-Plant's impenetrable scoring system, I was forced to accept its accuracy in the end when he totted up the final scores and declared me the winner. All, I felt, was finally right with the world.

With the mood of the fort suitably lifted, we all dispersed to our rooms for a preprandial break. I opted for a bath and a nap, while Lady Hardcastle said she might go to the drawing room to practise her piano part for the evening recital.

By a quarter past six I was rested, clean and dressed for dinner. I went to call on Lady Hardcastle in case she needed any help.

She didn't, so we went down early for cocktails. There was no one there.

It was about ten to seven by the time everyone showed up, almost as if it was some sort of coordinated plan in which we'd not been included. Drinks were hurriedly mixed and then sipped to the accompaniment of bland, superficial chit-chat. Hearts, I felt, were not in it.

Things started to liven up over dinner, though. Once the cocktails had taken effect and the first glasses of wine had been downed, tongues loosened and things became a little more animated.

As usual, Sidwell-Plant and Bridgewater were vying for conversational supremacy.

'Wait, wait,' said Bridgewater, 'I've got one. You see, there was a farmer, living out in the wilds. Cumbria, it was, miles from the nearest village. And he had a daughter. And one day—'

Sidwell-Plant held up his hand. 'Got to stop you there, my friend. If this is the yarn I think it is, it's the sort of thing we'll appreciate more with a few drinks inside us. Heaven knows I'm no prude, but it's a bit racy for the dinner table. Save it for brandies and port.'

Clarice was sitting next to him. 'In that case, I think he should carry on – I like a racy tale.'

Sidwell-Plant leaned close to her and whispered in her ear for a few moments.

She guffawed. 'No, fair enough, that's not one for the dinner table. But do tell it later, Gran – I think everyone will enjoy it. How do you come up with these things?'

Bridgewater was beaming. 'Can't really take credit for any of them, I'm afraid. All . . . shall we say, "borrowed" from other chaps. I just take 'em and make them my own.'

'That's very much your style, isn't it, old mate?' said Sidwell-Plant. 'Taking things that aren't yours and making them your own.' I wasn't sure, but I thought he winked.

Bridgewater's mouth smiled, but his eyes did not. 'Ha! Yes. Never been all that talented at making up stories – much better at telling them. Sometimes one chap owns a thing but it's left to another chap to take the best care of it.'

Did *he* wink this time?

Whatever had just happened, Sidwell-Plant was scowling.

JB decided to step in. 'Tell you what, fellas, why don't we do as Robert says and leave it till we've got some cognac inside us.'

'Sounds fair to me,' said Sidwell-Plant. 'You've laid in a good stock, I noticed.'

JB looked puzzled. 'I have? Just a normal amount for a weekend with friends.'

'Do we really get through four cases of the stuff?'

'Four cases? I didn't buy four cases – just a few bottles.'

'My mistake. Sorry. I thought I saw four cases of French brandy in the kitchen when I was down there yesterday morning looking for my wife's blessed brooch.'

JB was still looking puzzled but said no more.

Lily broke the awkward silence. 'Are you and Emily going to play for us again tonight, Clarice?'

'I think so, yes. If you don't mind, Emily.'

'Not at all – it's a pleasure and a privilege to play with you, dear.'

'Splendid. We might even do a piano duet. We were messing about this morning and it seemed to go rather well.'

Dotty looked uncomfortable. 'Are you sure you ought to? You know, under the circumstances.'

'Play a piano duet?' said Clarice, innocently.

'Play at all, Clarice dear.'

'The only good thing Edgar ever did was make music. I think it's what he would have wanted.'

'I think he might have wanted not to die of a heart attack on a desert island,' said Bridgewater, 'but point taken.'

'Granville!' said Dotty.

'I think we ought to be honest about it,' said Patience. 'None of us liked the man, and Clarice had more reason than all of us to despise him. Good riddance to the awful monster, I say. We're better off without him and we should definitely enjoy ourselves as best we can.'

This, I believed, was something they needed to hear, something they'd all been thinking but none dared say. The mood of the room lifted immediately and conversation flowed once more, as did the wine. A convivial meal ensued.

The good humour continued through brandies in the library, where Bridgewater's story was as old as I feared, but as filthy and funny as Clarice had promised. He really was a natural raconteur.

It was in the drawing room, as Clarice and Lady Hardcastle played, that the rancour returned. I couldn't hear what was being said from the front of the room, but between page-turns I could see Sidwell-Plant having whispered arguments first with Bridgewater, then with Patience. Dotty tried to intervene but was snapped at for her troubles.

All of this made Wilson and Lily, who had been rather quiet all evening, look somewhat uncomfortable.

Only JB seemed to be enjoying himself. Either he was oblivious to the atmosphere or he didn't care. He was just there for the music.

◆ ◆ ◆

Lady Hardcastle had neglected to return the Louis XIII she'd 'borrowed' from the library and we were sitting in her room once more, cradling our brandy balloons and trying to make sense of the day's events.

'We got absolutely nowhere on alibis,' I said.

'Indeed. Everyone we spoke to just confirmed what we'd already surmised.'

'True. I thought it was interesting that Lily provided one without being prompted, though.'

'She did?'

'She did. She just rattled off a list of her movements, completely unbidden. It's very much the sort of thing you expect a guilty person might do.'

Lady Hardcastle shrugged. 'Or a determined chatterbox. She *might* have been making sure you thought she was nowhere near Everett, but she might just as easily have been chuntering on because she can't stop herself.'

'True. What's going on with Bridgewater and Sidwell-Plant?'

'All that stuff about stealing stories, you mean? After that argument we overheard between Patience and Dotty, I'm beginning to wonder if Bridgewater stole the jewels.'

I nodded. 'Exactly my thinking. Did you see Sidwell-Plant wink or did I imagine it?'

'I'm afraid I was looking at Wilson and Lily. They do make a lovely couple, no matter how much they might protest.'

'You incorrigible softy. Well, I thought I saw a wink, as though he was taunting Bridgewater about something.'

'I say, you don't think Bridgewater's the one Patience is having it away with?'

I laughed. 'Seriously? She's a fine-looking woman and stiletto sharp, and he's . . . well, he's Granville Bridgewater, amiable buffoon and plodding solicitor. What do you suppose she might see in him?'

'He could be a wizard at the old bedchamber fun-time shenanigans.'

I laughed again. 'Can you imagine? No, he's not her paramour. But I wonder from his retort to Sidwell-Plant if he knows who is.'

'Or was.'

'You're back to Everett, then?'

'I know JB said it was unlikely, but he did say Sidwell-Plant suspected him. Perhaps Bridgewater was goading him back.'

I shrugged. 'Perhaps. It makes Sidwell-Plant an extremely likely suspect, wouldn't you say?'

'If he really did think it was Everett, then yes. He remains unaccounted for during our time-of-death window, but then again, so do half the people here.' She made more notes in her little notebook. 'So if he doesn't think Bridgewater is tupping Patience, what *does* he think he's "stealing" apart from comic anecdotes? Does this back up what we were saying this morning when we were talking to JB? Could it be straightforward theft, or is it a boring insurance fraud?'

'It very well could be either,' I said. 'But would Bridgewater kill if he were found out?'

'As we always say: anyone might kill. But Bridgewater had no opportunity – we know exactly where he was during those two hours.'

'You know who we haven't considered, don't you?'

She nodded. 'The Crawfords. I was thinking that over dinner. We searched their rooms, but only in a perfunctory, embarrassed, sorry-to-bother-you sort of way. We didn't take a look in the storeroom because we were afraid of it appearing that we were accusing them of something.'

'For my part it was because I was a bit bored of the whole thing and had convinced myself it was all a prank.'

She smiled. 'Well, there's that, too. But what if Jago Crawford had seen these women showing off their jewellery before and thought he might liberate a couple of items for his retirement fund?'

'We can't rule it out. And he'd be out of a job if he were found out – that would give him a motive for killing Everett if he knew what he was up to – which he sort of hinted he did. But . . .'

She was still writing. 'But what, dear?'

'But I think the Crawfords have another dodge on the go. I think they're smuggling.'

'The four cases of brandy, you mean?'

'Indeed. This is an ideal spot for it, don't you think? His Majesty's Customs and Excise will be watching the big ports, as always. They might even keep an eye on a few smaller fishing harbours or beaches with easy access, but they wouldn't pay any attention to a private island a mile out to sea. Smugglers could drop off their contraband at that smuggling beach on the south side of the island, and then Vickerman the Fisherman could take it ashore when he comes to deliver the supplies. No one would be any the wiser.'

'It sounds like a workable scheme, but we only have Sidwell-Plant's word for it that there was any brandy in the kitchen in the first place. I certainly didn't notice any, and I have a nose for these things.'

I shrugged. 'So why would Sidwell-Plant mention it?'

'Magician's misdirection. He's trying to get us to look at the Crawfords to stop us looking at him. So far only you and I, JB,

Jago Crawford and the murderer know Everett didn't die of a heart attack, so whoever it is is going to be working hard to make sure we're not paying them any attention.'

I took a sip of my brandy. 'Sounds as though we're talking ourselves into thinking of Sidwell-Plant as the main suspect.'

'For the murder, at least – I still can't rule out Bridgewater for the jewel thefts. But for now it makes more sense for Sidwell-Plant to have killed Everett than the four women. The only people who had the time to kill him are Sidwell-Plant, Dotty, Patience, Clarice and Lily. Bridgewater, Wilson and JB are accounted for. I love to daydream about a world where women are equal in all things, but I'm struggling to imagine any of those four running Everett through with a narwhal tusk and carrying the body upstairs. Even working together it seems a stretch. I think we should definitely start trying to find out more about Sidwell-Plant and see if we can't properly pin down his movements on Friday afternoon.'

# Chapter Ten

I woke on Sunday to the sound of gulls. Devonshire herring gulls are the size of small sheep and spend most of their waking hours shouting at each other at the top of their great sea-air-filled lungs. They are no respecters of human traditions like the Sunday Morning Lie-In and will make any amount of noise they like outside your window while you're trying to sleep. They're a menace once you're awake, too, and many a trip to the seaside has been spoiled by aggressive gulls pinching holidaymakers' chips while they're strolling along the prom.

I would never wish a fellow creature dead, but I did wish they'd bugger off and give me a few more minutes' peace before the day began.

Ordinarily I'd be full of up-and-at-'em spirit on a weekend away, but this one had stopped being fun as soon as we saw Everett's murdered body and, like our fellow guests, I was very much ready to go home. But unlike all but one of the others, I knew it was murder – which meant that Lady Hardcastle and I couldn't just mope about and wait for the boat to come.

We had to solve the murder.

But why did we? Why did we have to spend our time asking questions and verifying alibis? Why did we have to hunt for clues and try to imagine motives? Despite the fevered fantasies of hundreds of mystery authors scribbling away in their garrets, there was no such thing as an amateur detective, so why weren't we relaxing and taking it easy with our fellow weekend guests while we waited for the rozzers to arrive?

Because we were the famous Emily, Lady Hardcastle, and her redoubtable sidekick Florence Armstrong, that's why. Of course I was going to get up and get washed and dressed so I could shake Herself from her pit. Of course we were going to dig and delve into the lives of our fellow guests. Of course we were going to solve the murder. Of course the local rozzers would be condescending and doubt our word. Of course we would travel home and pretend we'd had a lovely weekend away when our friends in the village asked us what we'd been up to.

I leapt out of bed with renewed enthusiasm and stubbed my toe on the corner of the chest of drawers as I went to throw open the curtain. I swore loud and long in Welsh, because Lady Hardcastle said that swearing helped in those sorts of circumstances.

I was still limping a little as I hobbled along the corridor to Lady Hardcastle's room and knocked on the door.

'Who is it?' came the sing-song reply from within.

'It's the RSPCA, madam. We've had reports that there's an old bat in this room, though we might have misunderstood.'

'Just bloody well come in, you idiot.'

'The door's locked.'

I could hear her *harrumph* from outside as she got out of bed and stumbled across the room. A long stream of colourful expletives suggested that she, too, had found something to stub her toe on.

The door opened.

'Get in. I've hurt my foot because of you.'

'I didn't lock your door.'

'I was worried about prowlers.'

'You didn't warn *me* about prowlers and tell *me* to lock *my* door.'

'You can look after yourself, dear. As I keep saying: I'd not back anyone here in a straight fight with my Flossie. But I am but a frail and delicate flower. I need the protection of a locked door.'

I entered. 'Have you been burgled?' I indicated the mess of clothes, shoes and books strewn across her floor.

'Very droll. Can you help me find something to wear? I'm starving and I want to get to breakfast immediately if not sooner.'

◆ ◆ ◆

The dining room was crowded by the time we arrived, but to our surprise, obvious lines had been drawn between the groups.

The Sidwell-Plants, though still not on especially good terms with each other, were very pointedly nowhere near the Bridgewaters.

For their part, the Bridgewaters seemed to be keeping their distance from JB as they chatted to Clarice.

Wilson and Lily, though, to JB's evident pleasure, were getting on like the proverbial house on fire and seemed oblivious to the tension around them.

'Good morning, one and all,' said Lady Hardcastle, breezily, as she began to investigate the warming dishes on the sideboard.

The assembled breakfasters tried to balance the competing desires to warmly welcome us and to not appear too friendly towards anyone else.

It was going to be a long day.

Hunger and a delicious spread saw us through the awkwardness of breakfast, but as soon as we could we beetled downstairs to the library.

I plucked a random volume from the shelves – an account of an eighteenth-century gentleman's attempt to sail across the Atlantic in a three-masted schooner of his own design – and we settled in two of the comfortable wingback chairs with the cups of coffee we'd brought with us from the dining room.

'Well, that was simply lovely,' I said. 'What's up with everybody this morning?'

Lady Hardcastle sipped her coffee. 'I'd thought things were brightening up after the croquet match yesterday, but it seems the circumstances really are getting to people. And under pressure, they fall back on old alliances and enmities.'

'Or on new ones,' I said. 'I thought they all got on, but the Sidwell-Plants and the Bridgewaters definitely don't seem to be pals at the moment. That would make sense if our hypothesis is true: that Sidwell-Plant believes Bridgewater is the one having an affair with Patience. But—'

'But it was very obviously the Bridgewaters who were shunning the Sidwell-Plants and not the other way round.'

'Exactly. And I'm still struggling with the idea that Patience and Bridgewater make anything even vaguely like a perfect couple, your prurient speculation about his amorous prowess notwithstanding.'

She laughed. 'Me, too, to be honest. Which means the Bs have some other reason to be cross with the S-Ps.'

'And whatever it is, it's brought the S-Ps together.'

'It's all very peculiar. I wonder—'

'Hello, ladies,' said Wilson from the doorway. 'I'm not interrupting anything, am I? I was looking for somewhere quiet to sit, away from . . . from—'

'Away from the poisonous atmosphere between the accountant and the solicitor?' I suggested.

'You noticed it, too, then.'

'We couldn't miss it, dear,' said Lady Hardcastle. 'Come and join us; we're atmosphere-free. Although Florence does seem to have a dreary-looking book with which she might attempt to bore us in due course.'

I held it up. '*A Schooner to Nova Scotia*, the gripping tale of a Regency idiot and his attempt to sail the wrong ocean at the wrong time of year in the wrong type of boat. It has all the hallmarks of a bestseller.'

Wilson grinned. 'Does he make it?'

'I've not read it yet, but I'm going to go out on a limb and say no. I rather think we'd know more about Aloicius Fitzroy-Denman if he'd accomplished something so extraordinary. We'd talk of nothing but the Fitzroy-Denman Shipping Company and its world-beating range of ocean-going schooners.' I quickly riffled through the book. 'Ah, here we are. "Chapter 24, in which my beloved *Sea Spirit* sinks off the Scilly Isles". That's a shame. Still, it's nice for a person to have a hobby.'

He laughed. 'It is. Do you have any hobbies, Miss Armstrong?'

'I'm not sure whether I do,' I said. 'I can always fill my spare time with *something*, but I'm not sure I have any passions.'

'I see. What about you, Lady Hardcastle? Do you have any passions?'

Lady Hardcastle smiled. 'One or two. You've seen one already: I love to play the piano. And I share one with your new paramour: photography. Although my interest there is in moving pictures. I make animated films.'

'Animated?'

'I make small models – usually animals – with a wire armature so I can pose them. If one shoots a series of still images with the models moving slightly between each shot, it gives the appearance of motion. It makes it look as though the tiny models are alive and moving of their own volition. It's great fun.'

Wilson's mouth was open in surprise. 'Really? You can really do that?'

'I really can. It takes forever, though, and it needs good light, a commodity we often lack in Gloucestershire. I wish we had electricity so I could have some consistent lighting.'

'You should speak to JB – he has his own generator in an adapted outbuilding. It wasn't too much of a monster to install and it runs on diesel oil. It needed a reinforced floor, but a decent structural engineer could sort that out for you. You could generate enough electricity to run your whole house if you wanted.'

'I shall definitely look into it,' said Lady Hardcastle with a smile. 'Florence often talks about how convenient life would be with electricity.'

'I do, it's true. But what about you, Mr Wilson? Do you have any hobbies?'

'I'm most fortunate in that my hobby is also my living. I don't have the money to collect the wonderful old objects my clients buy, but at least I get a chance to see them, to handle them, before they go to their new homes.'

'And sometimes you get the chance to see them in their new homes as well,' said Lady Hardcastle.

He smiled. 'Actually, that's true, yes.'

'With added matchmaking,' I said with a wink.

He groaned. 'Don't keep reminding me. Although I must say that it's been something of a relief to have an ally during all the frostiness. While the Montagues and Capulets are drawing daggers against each other it's pleasant to have someone to talk to who isn't part of all the ancient grudges and new mutinies.'

'And, as you said yesterday, she *is* delightful.'

'And very easy on the eye,' he said with a smile. 'Perhaps I need to rethink my irritation with JB's meddling.'

'A man doesn't have the sort of business success JB's had without knowing a thing or two about people,' said Lady Hardcastle.

Wilson laughed. 'Curse him.'

'Or wonder at his perspicacity. Perhaps you should just give in to it and try to get to know her.'

'Perhaps I should. Whatever I do, though, I should leave you in peace – I'm sorry for interrupting. Good luck with your book, Miss Armstrong. I hope no one is hurt in the sinking.'

With a cheery wave, he left us to ourselves.

Lady Hardcastle prowled the library shelves looking for . . . actually, I hadn't the foggiest idea what she was looking for. Her reading tastes were broad and she was curious about absolutely everything so she should, I felt, have been able to find *something* to divert her for a few minutes, but she just prowled. She prodded books. She took them down. She put them back.

I couldn't concentrate on Aloicius and his schooner. 'Is there nothing there to your taste?'

'Plenty I could sink my teeth into were I not distracted by Certain Things,' she said.

'Do you want to talk about it?'

'Not in a public place – someone could come in at any minute.'

Patience arrived at exactly that moment, perfectly proving her point.

'Hello, ladies. Do you mind if I join you? I'm not interrupting anything, am I?'

'Not at all,' I said. This time I decided not to try to extol the dubious virtues of *A Schooner to Nova Scotia*. 'We're not really doing anything. She's prowling. I'm sitting.'

Lady Hardcastle returned a large volume to the shelf. 'And if I sit, we can all sit together. Shall I ring for tea?'

She pressed the bell and helped Patience haul two more of the wingback chairs around the low table where I had made myself comfortable.

'There,' said Lady Hardcastle. 'Nice and cosy. Are weekends with JB always like this?'

Patience frowned. 'Like what?'

'Like—'

She was interrupted by the unusually prompt arrival of Crawford. We ordered tea and biscuits and he took our empty coffee cups away.

'The atmosphere, dear,' continued Lady Hardcastle when he'd gone. 'One tries to avoid clichés like the plague, but I venture it might be possible to cut the atmosphere here with one of JB's many seafarers' knives.'

Patience smiled. 'Things certainly used to be a good deal more jolly, but people change, don't they? Relationships move on. Friendships falter. Love fades.'

'Very true,' said Lady Hardcastle. 'Do you mind my asking what's going on?'

Patience thought for a moment. 'Actually, we probably owe you some sort of explanation. It's hardly fair for us to bring you both into the middle of our nonsense – it's supposed to be a relaxing weekend among friends, after all. Oh, and heaven knows what Wilson and Lily must think of us all. You, at least, have known JB for a while – they've only recently met him through their work. The fact is that mine and Robert's marriage is not a happy one. I want him to divorce me but he refuses.'

Lady Hardcastle nodded. 'That much we knew, I'm afraid. JB told us.'

'Really? I ought to be troubled by his indiscretion but I suppose Americans have different standards for that sort of thing, so I can't really hold it against him. But indiscreet or not, he's right: I do want

Robert to divorce me. I've destroyed my own reputation giving him grounds but he won't budge. I used to imagine we could just bump along, pretending everything was all right for the sake of appearances, but now I can't bear the sight of him. I swear there are days when I could happily plunge one of those knives you mentioned into the wretched man's heart.'

'You don't feel like that all the time, though, surely,' I said. 'You were allies this morning in whatever feud it is you have with the Bridgewaters.'

'Oh, that was just me trying to keep out of the way as best I could, darling. Lord alone knows what Robert and Gran are arguing about. Robert's never told me and I'll be damned if I'm going to give him the satisfaction of asking. It has something to do with work – that much I've surmised – but exactly what remains a mystery.'

We paused again when Crawford arrived, and talked to him about the weather as he poured the tea.

When he was gone, Patience spoke up again. 'But enough about us miserable lot. What about you two? You've been very cagey every time anyone's pressed you for details of the cases we read about in the newspapers. So, come on – I've opened my private life to you; share something.'

'I'm not sure we're nearly as exciting as you think we are,' I said. 'Most of the details are in the newspapers. The national press picks up the stories from the *Bristol News,* where they're written by a good friend of ours: Dinah Caudle. She's careful to get everything correct and we trust her with more information than we'd share with some bloke from a London paper.'

'Your modesty ill becomes you. What about that business with the wild animals in Gloucestershire, for instance? Or the stolen Shakespeare book? And that time you were in the theatre and saw an actual body on the stage?'

Together, Lady Hardcastle and I led Patience through some of the previously undisclosed details of the cases she had mentioned, as well as a few she hadn't. It occurred to me as we talked that I should probably write some of those stories down at some point, but I struggled to imagine that anyone would be interested.

We were just finishing what I have to admit I thought was a particularly exciting retelling of the events surrounding our murder-filled holiday at Weston-super-Mare – although we omitted any mention of our involvement in the world of espionage – when JB poked his head round the door.

'Ah, there you are. I'm sorry, Patience, but might I borrow Emily and Florence for a few minutes?'

Patience gave us a curious look. 'Of course you can, JB darling. We can return to their yarns when you're done with them.'

We put down our teacups and followed him.

◆ ◆ ◆

JB led us once more to his private suite and into his office.

'Just wanted to catch up,' he said, gesturing to the armchairs opposite his desk. 'Where do we stand?'

'Frustratingly, in much the same place as when we last spoke,' said Lady Hardcastle. 'We ran with the idea that Bridgewater had stolen the jewellery as part of an insurance fraud, and then killed Everett when he found out and threatened to expose the scheme. But Bridgewater does appear to have an alibi for the murder.'

I nodded. 'Lily also appears to have an alibi—'

'Lily?' interrupted JB. 'What in the hell could Lily possibly have to do with it all? She wasn't even here when the jewels went missing.'

'But she was here for the murder,' I said. 'There are only twelve people on the island. If we assume it wasn't any of the three of us, that still leaves nine suspects. We have to suspect them all and rule them out one by one.'

'Sure. I guess. But nine? There are only seven of us by my reckoning.'

'And your staff, dear,' said Lady Hardcastle.

'Do you know, I never even considered it might be them.'

'We overlooked them at first, too, but we'll be considering them as we go on.'

'For now, though,' I said, 'we're chasing the idea that Sidwell-Plant believes Everett was the man having an affair with Patience. We still can't link that to the jewellery but they're such wildly different crimes—'

'If the missing jewellery even is a crime,' said Lady Hardcastle.

'Well, yes. But they're such wildly different . . . events that they might not be linked anyway.'

'I've got to agree with you there,' said JB. 'So what about the others, before we go accusing Robert?'

'Clarice's account of her own movements holds up,' I said. 'And her questions about his death seemed genuine. We can't rule out Patience yet, but the rumour of her affair with Everett makes it seem unlikely.'

JB shrugged. 'Unless she'd tired of him and wanted to get rid of him.'

'That's possible, one supposes,' said Lady Hardcastle, 'but improbable, don't you think?'

He shrugged again.

'We've not spoken to Dotty Bridgewater,' I said, 'but I'd put her quite low on the list anyway. George Wilson has a solid alibi and has no real connection with Everett. And that leaves only the Crawfords. What do you know about them?'

'Not a great deal. They were recommended to me by a village parson, of all people. We got to talking one day and I happened to mention that I was in need of staff for the fort – both now, when it's just me, and in the future when we open as a hotel. He said he knew just the couple. Parishioners of his, he said, down on their luck since they lost their pub. A bit rough round the edges with no training as domestics, but honest enough—'

'How honest is "honest enough"?' asked Lady Hardcastle.

He laughed. 'Well, now that's the question, isn't it? Seems that like most publicans they had a bit of a reputation for not-quite-legal transactions – a little smuggled booze here, fencing a few stolen items there – but he reassured me they were good people. I talked to them and they seemed like they'd be up to the job so I hired them.'

'Do you think they're still smuggling?' I asked.

'The cognac RVSP thinks he saw? I wouldn't put it past them.'

'Doesn't that bother you?' asked Lady Hardcastle.

'I guess it should, but I'd rather they were cheating the government out of some excise duty than stealing from me, so I'm happy to turn a blind eye.'

'But wouldn't you rather know?'

'It's better if I don't. If they get caught and I know nothing about it, it's nothing to do with me. They're adults acting on their own initiative. They might happen to be breaking the law, but how am I supposed to know what they get up to? I can't watch them all the time.'

'It makes sense when you put it like that. But I'd want to know, all the same. If men from HM Customs and Excise were going to come knocking on my door, I'd like to be as well informed as possible.'

'One of the things I learned in business was that you can't manage every little detail. Sometimes you just have to let people get on with it.' He turned and looked out of the window for a moment. 'Murder, though . . . well, you just can't let people get on with that. How are you going to catch RVSP?'

'If it's him,' I said.

'Sure. Assuming it's him, how're you going to prove it?'

'That's going to take a little more thought,' said Lady Hardcastle. 'Until we have a clearer picture of exactly how things played out on Friday, we're just groping around in the dark hoping someone will let something slip. We'll not be able to prove anything until we have a decent idea of what there is to be proven.'

'It'd be nice to hand this over to the flatties with a pretty bow on top. I don't want them stomping round the place if I can avoid it. This is supposed to be my bolthole, my island sanctuary. I don't want my image of it tarnished by clumsy police investigations.'

I frowned at the idea that his image of the place wouldn't be tarnished by the fact that one of his guests had been violently murdered there, but I decided not to pursue it.

We wrapped things up with a few more only-slightly-insincere reassurances and left him to brood.

On our way back down the stairs, I said, 'We didn't ask if he knew anything about the Bridgewater/Sidwell-Plant animosity.'

'We didn't, you're right. Blast. On the other hand, though, would he know anything about it? Would he want to know, I mean? If he's disinclined to take an interest in his domestic staff possibly smuggling finest French jack-a-dandy, he's not going to concern himself with personal squabbles between two of his advisers.'

'I suppose so. I still feel stupid for not asking.'

'I'm sure it's not important. Or at least, not relevant. How would their squabble lead to the death of Edgar Everett?'

'True, true. How shall we pass the time until lunch?'

By now we were back in the library.

She looked out of the window. 'The weather's not too bad. Shall we take a turn around the island? We can take a look at Smugglers' Cove.'

'Is that what it's called? I've not heard anyone say that.'

'They're always called Smugglers' Cove down here. There's a local by-law.'

And so we donned warm coats and stout boots and clomped through the kitchen on the way to the great outdoors.

◆ ◆ ◆

As we clomped down the kitchen steps I was struck by the rich aroma of roasting meat. There were vegetables, peeled, chopped and in bowls, waiting to be cooked. There were knives, ladles, wooden spoons, pots, pans and even a rolling pin. What there was not, however, was a cook.

Lady Hardcastle and I exchanged shrugs and carried on towards the back door. As we passed the door to the butler's pantry, we heard raised voices from within.

'. . . I thought we'd had the last of all that nonsense when we left the pub,' said Peggy.

Jago huffed. 'Well, if his American lordship was payin' us, we would have. But we haven't seen a penny of his so-called vast fortune since afore Christmas. We can't live on thin air, Peg, my love.'

'We've a roof over our heads and more than enough to eat. What more do we need?'

'And what about when he turfs us out on our ears because the whole thing's gone down the pan? What then? We can't call on our fancy friends to help us out. We can't get our pal the bank manager to give us no loan. We gots to take care of ourselves. We'll just sell this lot and see what we gets. We might not have to do no more.'

'But what if we get caught? That was how we lost the pub in the first place.'

'No one will find out. They's all got their own problems . . .'

Their voices faded as the conversation moved into their private flat.

Lady Hardcastle and I exchanged astonished glances but resumed our march to the door.

◆ ◆ ◆

The walk was . . . 'bracing', I think is the euphemism we use for 'absolutely, miserably freezing'.

The island, though, despite the frigid weather, was beautiful. Beyond Dotty's cleverly designed almost-but-not-quite-ornamental walled garden the landscape retained its natural, rugged state. Clumps of gorse shared the uneven, rocky ground with thick tufts of wind-swept grass.

As we approached the grotto at the western end of the island, the ground evened out a little and the grass became more lush as the soil improved. Lady Hardcastle pointed out the remnants of the puffin burrows and we both expressed our disappointment at not being able to see the bright-beaked little charmers as they bumbled about.

'The chicks are called pufflings,' she said.

'They absolutely are not. You're definitely making that one up.'

'Not this time. I say, look at that.'

The grotto itself was utterly charming – Dotty had a good eye for whimsical design – though perhaps not as charming as dozens of pufflings might have been. It was much more sheltered than I had imagined. I could well believe that Wilson had spent a happy hour there on Friday. I, for one, was certainly glad of the chance to sit for a while out of the wind.

We walked on.

The cave in the cove was next, and was much less impressive than the grotto or the fort. When I hear of smugglers' caves, I always imagine deep caverns, perhaps with multiple chambers where contraband might be stacked, ready for onward transit.

Ideally there would be a skeleton with a dagger between its teeth, resting a bony arm on a small keg of smuggled rum. There was none of that. This cave was a single, large hollow in the rock, well above the high-water mark. It would be fine for the temporary storage of a few smuggled crates or barrels, and would serve as a shelter for the night in a pinch, but it was no use as a hideout for a gang of ruthless contrabandists. At least there was no sign of the stranger we'd worried might be lurking on the island.

We passed the outbuilding housing the island's electricity generator that Wilson had told us about, and skirted once more round Dotty's garden. Between that and the grotto, the island was going to be a wonderful summer retreat once her plants were established.

We'd gone out through the kitchen and we planned to return the same way, having realized that it was all but impossible to reach the front door from where we were without following a track all the way down to the jetty and then coming back up the path we'd originally followed when we'd arrived on Thursday.

As we passed the stout door to the outside storeroom, I tried the handle.

It opened.

'Fancy a look?' I asked.

'Of course.'

There was a light switch just inside the door and I flicked it on to reveal . . . a big, surprisingly cold storeroom full of wooden boxes of food and drink. There were four cases of cognac – presumably the ones Sidwell-Plant had seen and about which JB was blithely unconcerned. Wooden cupboards had been built into the rear wall against the solid rock and there were shelves along the other walls. It was unremarkable in almost every regard, with the almost-certainly-smuggled brandy the only remarkable feature.

The second most remarkable feature, of course: Everett's body, wrapped in a tarpaulin, lay in one corner.

We closed the door behind us as we left.

The kitchen, by contrast, was a wealth of sensory treats. Peggy – who, we had to assume, knew full well that Everett had been murdered – was nevertheless pressing cheerfully ahead with the planned Sunday roast.

We let ourselves in and apologized for getting in the way as we bustled through. I thought of offering to help but decided Peggy would probably be insulted.

Up the steps and out in the hall, we bumped into Patience and Clarice, who were making their way from the library–sitting room corridor to the stairs.

'It's Emily and Florence,' said Patience.

Clarice sniffed. 'Hello, ladies. What's it like out?'

'Bracing,' said Lady Hardcastle.

'Bloody freezing,' I added.

Clarice laughed. 'We're on our way to the drawing room. Everyone else is in the library and we don't want to be. Join us?'

'I don't like to speak for Florence—' began Lady Hardcastle.

'You speak for me all the time,' I interrupted.

'Actually, yes, that's true. So . . . ah . . . I shouldn't speak for Florence but I'm going to anyway: we'd love to, but we need to get changed for lunch. Can you smell the deliciousness coming from the kitchen?'

'It does smell rather yummy,' said Clarice. 'But you go and do what you need to do. Obviously I don't care how you're dressed, but I know it makes a difference to you stupid sighties.' She grinned.

We walked up the stairs together and went our separate ways on the first-floor landing.

# Chapter Eleven

Lunch, as the kitchen aromas had promised, was magnificent. Talented chefs can work wonders with sauces and delicate, fussy ingredients. But a country house cook, with nothing more than a joint of beef, some roast potatoes and a few vegetables, can conjure up a meal so thrillingly spectacular that men will offer their entire fortunes for just one more bite of gravy-soaked Yorkshire pudding.

Despite the impression I'd gained from Patience and Clarice's urgent desire to leave the others in the library, the assembled guests were in quite good form. Conversation was light and bright, and hatchets, if not buried, had at least been laid to one side for the time being.

JB seemed to have been waiting until Lady Hardcastle and I both had our mouths full. 'I gather you two ventured outside. Did you enjoy your walk?'

I struggled to swallow my food. 'Enjoyable but extremely blowy. The grotto is pleasantly sheltered, though.'

'Isn't it?' said Wilson. 'The way it sits in that natural little bowl seems to protect it from all but the very worst of the weather.'

'It was surprisingly comfortable. Oh, and we found Smugglers' Cove, too.'

JB smiled. 'I think that's actually called the South Landing on the official charts.'

'Which just goes to show how boring the Admiralty can be,' said Lady Hardcastle. 'Not an ounce of romance in their souls. You'd think sailors would be a sentimental lot – all that concertina music and yearning to return to their sweethearts – but they've not an ounce of imagination between them. Military intelligence, on the other hand—'

'Oxymoron, what?' said Bridgewater.

'Well, quite. But they come up with some wonderful codenames. Operation Bunny Rabbit was one of my favourites. And they once recruited an agent in Cairo who played for the embassy cricket team. Absolute duffer. His codename was W. G. Graceless.'

'How on earth do you know that?' asked Patience.

'Oh, one picks up little titbits here and there. It's astonishing how indiscreet people can be.'

'She knows quite a lot about indiscretion, our Speedy,' said Bridgewater with a wink.

Patience scowled. 'Oh, do shut up, Gran, there's a good boy.'

'If you can't take the heat, dear girl, stay out of strange men's bedrooms.'

'You need to be careful, *dear boy*, or I might indiscreetly let slip something I learned about you from Robert.'

And with that, the atmosphere reverted to its earlier frosty state. Bridgewater went white, Patience went red, Dotty looked absolutely terrified, and I realized Patience had lied to us earlier: she did know what was going on between the solicitor and the accountant.

The silence lasted for almost a minute before conversation resumed, but this time with people talking only to their neighbours and not to the whole table.

Honestly, if the roast hadn't been one of the best I'd eaten in a long while, I'd have made my excuses and returned to my room, but it's surprising how strong the pull of hearty nosh can be.

◆ ◆ ◆

The spotted dick and custard kept me at the table for a little longer but, as soon as it was seemly, I gave Lady Hardcastle the signal and we made a polite exit.

The library had become our preferred sanctuary. Its size made it eminently suitable for large groups, and the large group was avoiding it, presumably in an effort to keep to themselves.

Once more we'd taken our coffees with us, but this time Lady Hardcastle managed to sit rather than prowl and I managed not to burden myself with a tedious book.

'How are we going to approach Sidwell-Plant?' I asked. 'We need to pin him down and find out once and for all what he's been up to.'

'And, just as importantly, what he knows about what Bridgewater has been up to.'

There was an *ahem* from the doorway. It was Dotty. 'I think I might be able to help you there.'

'Dear Dotty,' said Lady Hardcastle. 'Come and join us. I do apologize for my indiscretion. I shouldn't be gossiping.'

The third chair was still in place around the little table and she came to sit with us.

'It's not gossip if it's true, dear. Or is it? Am I thinking of slander? Whatever it is, Gran is up to something and I just don't know how to deal with it any more. My poor nerves.'

'And do you want to tell us?' asked Lady Hardcastle. 'You really don't have to.'

*No, you really do*, I thought. *Not knowing is doing* my *nerves in*.

'You know he's JB's English solicitor?'

'We do.'

'He has control over certain aspects of JB's companies and trusts – he's responsible for various accounts, and deals with all the payments. For the past few years he's been . . . he's been . . . he's been—'

'He's been making payments to an account of his own?' suggested Lady Hardcastle.

Dotty nodded. 'Just a few pounds at first. We needed to have the roof repaired. But then there was some plumbing work in the kitchen and he took a little more to cover that. And then a little more for a few other items of household maintenance. And it was all so easy. He could barely believe he got away with it. So he took a little more to pay for some wine. And more for dresses for me and suits for him. And more for a new dinner service. And a little more to restock the wine cellar. And it went on and on. I dread to think how much he's . . . used. No, stolen. He stole it and it's driving me mad. I can barely sleep for the worry. He doesn't care, of course. He's always been one for the finer things and he resents having to live a life where he can't have them. He reasons that it's not as if he's stealing from charities – he's stealing from a man so rich he doesn't know what to do with all his wealth.' She stopped for a moment. 'Good heavens, it's a relief to say all that out loud. You have no idea how hard it's been.'

'Guilt is a terrible burden,' I said. 'Even when the misdeeds are not your own. Would we be right in assuming that Sidwell-Plant knows? He's an accountant so putting two and two together is very much his forte. When he saw all those unusual disbursements to an account he didn't recognize, it wouldn't have taken him long to work out where the money was going.'

'He knows. And he's given Gran an ultimatum: give the money back or he'll tell JB. He's so damnably proper. He won't divorce Speedy, and he can't turn a blind eye to Gran's embezzlement. There's no such thing as a grey area where Robert's concerned.'

I wasn't entirely convinced there was anything even vaguely grey about misappropriating funds from a client, but I didn't like to say.

Dotty sighed. 'A good part of my guilt comes from the fact that I enjoy it all so much. I love living in a nice house and having nice things. But he's never satisfied. He spends and spends and there's nothing left to pay back. If JB finds out, we'll be destitute. I simply can't bear to think about it.'

'Is there really nothing left?' asked Lady Hardcastle.

'Barely a shilling. We'd have to sell the house, but even that's mortgaged. And then what would we do? If the Law Society found out, he'd never work again.'

'JB's not a vindictive man. He won't be happy to learn that his trusted adviser has been stealing from him and he'll definitely want the money back, but one doubts he'd behave unreasonably.'

'It's a terrible thing to have dangling over us, though, isn't it? I could swing for that stupid Patience and her big mouth. I thought she was my friend but she had to try to score points at dinner.'

'To be fair,' I said, 'Mr Bridgewater had been extremely insulting. If he'd said that to a man he might expect a fat lip at the very least.'

Dotty sighed again. 'Keeping his mouth shut has never been one of Gran's talents.' After another moment's silence, she said, 'I don't suppose you could intercede with Robert on Gran's behalf? You're a neutral observer, after all. Do you think you could?'

Lady Hardcastle raised an eyebrow. 'Well . . .'

'Please? Everyone is in awe of you. I'm sure if you explained the situation you might be able to persuade Robert to at least delay his snitching.'

'In awe of me?'

'Of both of you, darling. Dear Clarice might be a world-renowned violinist, but she hasn't fought villains and dodged bullets. To my knowledge she hasn't solved a single murder. You live lives of glamour and excitement that we can only dream of.'

'Well,' said Lady Hardcastle, 'when you put it like that . . .'

I knew well the speed at which Lady Hardcastle's mind worked, but I couldn't be certain that she was going to seize this perfect opportunity. We needed an excuse to talk openly to Sidwell-Plant, and Dorothy was handing it to us on a decorated plate with whipped cream and a strawberry on top.

'Of course we shall,' I said. 'We can't guarantee the results, but we can certainly talk to him and try to persuade him to follow a more generous course.'

Dotty smiled for the first time since she'd entered the room.

◆ ◆ ◆

With a proper excuse to question Sidwell-Plant, we finally felt justified in tracking him down and probing him for proper details of his actions over the past couple of days.

We eventually found him, in the drawing room, playing a solo game of snooker.

'Good afternoon, ladies. Care to join me?'

'I'll not, thank you,' said Lady Hardcastle with a smile. 'I'm something of a duffer at that sort of thing. Florence, on the other hand, is an absolute wiz at anything that involves aiming.' She turned to me. 'I always thought you should have studied applied mathematics, dear – you have an instinctive understanding of ballistics, and of elastic collisions.'

'I can't fire a gun,' I said.

'You *won't* fire a gun, dear. There's a difference. On the vanishingly small number of occasions when you've been compelled by circumstance to use firearms, you've proven yourself to be a remarkably good shot.'

I bowed my head in acknowledgement.

'Ha!' barked Sidwell-Plant. 'So what do you say, Miss Armstrong? Honestly, I'm such a duffer myself I don't mind how good or bad my opponent is – I just want to play. One day I'm going to beat that idiot Bridgewater, and the only way I'm going to manage that is to practise.'

I bowed again. 'Oh, well, in that case, how could I say no? Set up the table and I'll find a stool to stand on.'

There were footstools at the other end of the room that people had been using during the recitals, and by the time I returned to the snooker table Sidwell-Plant had already replaced the coloured balls on their spots and was dropping the last of the reds into the triangle. He fussed with it briefly, getting it into exactly the right place, and then hung the wooden triangle at the end of the table.

Lady Hardcastle handed me a cue. 'Your snooker bat, m'lady.'

Sidwell-Plant barked again. 'Ha! Would you care to start, Miss Armstrong? I'm rather afraid I've been set up here and I'd like to see how bad it's going to get for me.'

I fussed about with the stool and then made a performance out of getting the cue ready before playing a perfect opening shot that left Sidwell-Plant trapped behind the reds.

'Ah. I see. It's going to be like that, is it? Well, I suppose I ought to be used to losing by now.'

'To your good pal Granville Bridgewater,' said Lady Hardcastle.

'Well, to everyone, actually. But especially Gran, yes.'

He took his shot and opened up the pack.

Lady Hardcastle watched. 'Is Bridgewater really an idiot?'

'Depends who you talk to,' said Sidwell-Plant. 'JB thinks the sun shines out of his fundament.'

'But you know different? We've just been talking to Dotty, and she—'

'Don't tell me, she wants you to have a word with me to see if you can persuade me not to go to JB with what I know.'

'She does. And what is it that you know?'

'Didn't she tell you?'

I took my shot and potted one of the loose reds.

Lady Hardcastle stepped out of my way as I rounded the table with my stool to line up on the black. 'She did, but I wanted to hear your version.'

He shook his head as I potted the black and lined myself up perfectly for another red. 'For some while, dear Mr Bridgewater has been embezzling money from JB's various private trusts. In truth he wasn't an idiot about it, and he'd covered his tracks rather well. It was only by chance that I queried one of the payments and uncovered a pattern of systematic theft going back a couple of years. The theft was bad enough, but he had betrayed a trust. As JB's legal representative he had been given control over several accounts and had been trusted to look after a fair amount of JB's British interests.'

'And is that why you intend to go to JB?' asked Lady Hardcastle. 'Because he betrayed his trust?'

My turn at the table continued.

'It's my duty as JB's accountant to advise him of any discrepancies, but, yes, I find myself particularly enraged that a fellow professional could do such a thing to his client. It's an outrage that cannot be tolerated.'

'You're not prepared to give him time to repay the money he stole?'

'I wonder if Dotty Dorothy told you quite how much money is involved. I wonder if the poor woman even knows. It would take him years to repay it, even were he inclined so to do.'

'I take it he isn't.'

'He is not.'

I potted the black again. 'Did you take Dotty's necklace as a down payment?'

He laughed. 'No, that wasn't me. I assumed Gran was setting up some sort of insurance fraud. I certainly wouldn't put it past him.'

I was back on to a nicely placed red. 'Is it your sense of propriety that's stopping you from divorcing your wife?'

'I *beg* your pardon?'

'She tells everyone she meets that she has a lover and wants you to divorce her, but you won't.'

'I expect you'd rather kill him,' said Lady Hardcastle.

'I can't say I hadn't thought of it, but fate rather solved that one for me when he died on Friday.'

I potted another red. 'So it was Everett?'

'Who else could it have been? She's always cosying up to him on weekends like this. It must have been him. So good riddance. Perhaps she'll stop her foolishness and get back to a normal married life now.'

'She wasn't exactly cosying up to him this weekend,' said Lady Hardcastle. 'She was positively furious with him when he verbally attacked Clarice.'

'That's Speedy's standard reaction to everything. She's a furious lady. But I know she was tupping him and I'm not sad the vile little man is gone.'

The last red went down and I lined up for one more go at the black before clearing the table. 'It makes sense. There's a definite likeness between the two of you.'

He laughed. 'There is not.'

'No,' said Lady Hardcastle. 'I can see it. Similar height, similar colouring.'

'Except that he was a complete cad,' said Sidwell-Plant.

I put down the yellow. 'Oh, you're as different in character as two men could possibly be, but physically, she definitely has a type.'

'I don't have to worry about that now, though – the bounder's dead. Hopefully she's got it out of her system, and she and I can get on with married life, as I said.'

With the green and brown already potted, I was on to the blue. 'So you didn't see Everett before he died?'

'I didn't see him at all after lunch. I played snooker with Bridgewater – who isn't even a tenth as good as you, by the way – then went to my room.'

'Was Patience there?' asked Lady Hardcastle.

'No. She was probably with *him*.'

The pink went down easily and I was positioned nicely on the black to finish the game. 'But, as you say, his death seems to resolve one of your problems. Is there nothing we can do to persuade you to come to some arrangement with Bridgewater?'

'Nothing whatsoever.'

'I believe that makes my score 147,' I said, handing my cue to Lady Hardcastle so she could put it back in the rack. 'Good game. Thank you.'

We left him brooding.

◆ ◆ ◆

Back downstairs, we could hear the sound of conversation coming from the sitting room so we headed down the corridor.

Patience was coming out. 'Hello, ladies. It's a peculiar atmosphere in there. Again. I'm off to find somewhere quiet to sit. I might play the piano for a while.'

Lady Hardcastle put her hand on Patience's arm. 'Your husband is in the drawing room, dear. He's sulking over the snooker table after Florence thrashed him.'

Patience laughed. 'Couldn't happen to a nicer chap. But thank you for the warning – I'll find another spot.'

'One thing before you go,' I said. 'We were talking to him while I annihilated him and he's absolutely insistent that you were having an affair with Everett.'

She laughed. A beautiful, ringing, genuine laugh. 'As if. I'm deeply in love with my doctor, darling. Dr Darcy Lamkin, and he really is an absolute lambkin. Everett, indeed. Can you imagine?'

She walked off, still chuckling.

We entered the sitting room and found two groups. The Bridgewaters were with Clarice, while Lily and Wilson sat at the other end of the room on either side of another of the low tables.

Wilson beckoned us over.

'Come and join us. We have tea.' He indicated two empty chairs and then the large teapot on the table. 'Unless you fancy yet another interminable yarn,' he added in a low voice.

We sat.

'Thank you, dear,' said Lady Hardcastle.

I helped everyone to tea. 'Patience said there was an atmosphere in here. It seems fine to me.'

'I think Patience was the cause,' said Lily. 'She was sitting here with us and the Bridgewaters were looking daggers at her. I'm not surprised she left. Have you any idea what's going between them?'

'Not a clue,' said Lady Hardcastle. 'It'll be some silly feud, I'm sure. Things will simmer in the background between old friends for years until a chance word brings them explosively to the fore. I'm sure it will pass.'

Lily shrugged. 'Perhaps. I could do without it, though.'

Wilson nodded. 'I've been wondering what I let myself in for. I like JB and I thought a weekend at the fort with his pals would be a hoot.'

'Under other circumstances, I'm sure it would have been.'

'Perhaps,' said Lily again. She looked at Wilson. 'But there's one consolation, at least.' She grinned.

He grinned back.

I don't know how Lady Hardcastle was feeling, but even though they'd invited us to sit with them I was feeling decidedly gooseberry-like. I'll happily play many roles in life, but I didn't feel that 'fake chaperone' was the best use of my many skills. If they wanted to canoodle, they should just go off and canoodle.

I was trying to think of a diverting topic for conversation when polite laughter from Dotty and Clarice signalled the end of Bridgewater's story. Bridgewater's own hearty guffaw indicated that he'd been much more pleased with it than they had been.

He stood. 'And on that note, dear ladies, I shall leave you. I have one or two things to attend to.'

We watched him go.

Wilson grinned at Lily again and then turned to Lady Hardcastle and me. 'I say, would you care to come out for a walk with us?'

I gave Lady Hardcastle my 'not if you paid me' look.

'No, dear,' she said. 'You don't want us hanging around getting in your way.'

'Are you sure?' said Lily. 'We could explore the island together.'

'We went out there this morning,' I said. 'You go. Have some fun while you can. But wrap up warm – it's absolutely perishing.'

More grinning followed before they both got up and disappeared.

A few minutes later we heard Wilson's loud, echoing voice from the hall as he greeted Peggy Crawford and asked if she minded them using her kitchen to get to the outside.

Dotty and Clarice were deep in conversation about something or other to do with gardens. I didn't fancy that so I motioned to Lady Hardcastle that we should leave.

# Chapter Twelve

Time passed pleasantly, and by five o'clock there was still no one in the library. We'd brought fresh cups of tea from the sitting room and made ourselves comfortable in our favourite chairs. The day's main meal had been Peggy Crawford's spectacular Sunday roast so supper was to be light, and much later. No recital was planned.

All of which meant that there was no urgent need to change, and no need to work ourselves into the right frame of mind to be sparkling company at cocktails. But it also meant that the evening sprawled intimidatingly ahead of us with no routine to fill it.

At home we might have read, played games or, in Lady Hardcastle's case, made music. If that failed to enchant us, we could stroll into the village for a drink at the pub with our friends. Here, though, there was no escape.

We could read, of course, but further perusal of the shelves had revealed that the dreary *A Schooner to Nova Scotia* was one of the livelier books in JB's collection.

Music had been a major part of the weekend so far, but Lady Hardcastle wasn't in the mood for more, and it would have required us to trudge up the stairs to the drawing room, anyway.

There was a rather lovely scrimshaw chess set with pieces inspired by JB's favourite book, *Moby-Dick*, but neither of us was in the mood for that, either. I wondered, briefly, why there was no copy of *Moby-Dick* on the shelves, but then remembered seeing one in JB's office.

This left cards or conversation. Or, preferably, cards *and* conversation. There were several packs in most rooms, along with notepads and pencils for scoring, so we had found two sets and prepared them for a game of bezique. There was a card table by the window, but we were too comfortable in the wingbacks so we decided to make do with the low table that held our teacups.

We had been playing for some time and I had been winning convincingly.

'What do you want for your birthday?' asked Lady Hardcastle as she arranged her newly dealt hand.

'Oh, I have everything I need, thank you.'

'Of course you do. But do you have everything you want?'

'I do hope not. Can you imagine how empty life would be if we had nothing left to want?' I fiddled with my cards. 'A trip to London to see Gwen and the baby? It's her birthday, too, after all.'

'With dinner and a show?'

'I'm not sure my niece is ready for the theatre. To judge from Gwen's letters, she's quite advanced for a seven-week-old, but I don't think little Meg should be going to West End shows quite yet.'

She tutted and rolled her eyes. 'We'll bring Gwen, Dai and Marged up to Harry's house and leave the baby with their nanny while we all go out together. My brother won't mind.'

Lady Hardcastle's brother, Harry, lived in Bloomsbury, so it was handy for the theatre and a number of good restaurants. My twin sister and her husband got on well with Harry and his wife – everyone got on with Harry and Lady Lavinia – so this actually seemed like a good idea. And Lady Hardcastle, I knew, already harboured a daydream that one day our nieces would take over where we left off, so she was keen to introduce Meg to her own niece, Addie, as soon as possible.

'That sounds wonderful, actually,' I said. 'Shall I write to Gwen and set things up?'

'No, dear, leave it all to me. You shouldn't have to arrange your own birthday treat. Just choose the show you wish to see and I'll sort everything out.'

'Thank you. My birthday's on a Monday so the theatres will be shut, but there's an American comedy I want to see and it'll be on at the Queen's on Shaftesbury Avenue. *Get-Rich-Quick Wallingford*. They say it's hilarious.'

'Then I shall secure half a dozen tickets and book a table for dinner on the Saturday evening. Leave everything to me.'

We played on, making more plans for my birthday weekend in late March, and I was soon wishing we were playing for money.

JB came in. 'Ah, there you are, ladies. We were all wondering where you'd gotten to.'

'We've not been hiding, dear,' said Lady Hardcastle. 'We've been sitting here playing cards and chattering.'

'So I see.'

'Ah, there you are.' This time it was Patience.

'They've been in here the whole time,' said JB.

'It's not as though there are many places we could be,' said Lady Hardcastle. 'Are we required for something?'

'No, no,' said Patience. 'But your company always lightens the mood, both of you.'

'Ah, here they are,' said Bridgewater. 'I say, Clarice, it's Ebb and Flow.'

Clarice smiled. 'Super.'

'Join us, do,' said Lady Hardcastle. 'It's flattering to have so many people so pleased to find us. I'd offer tea, but we don't have any.'

'It's after five,' said JB. 'I think it's time we opened up the liquor cabinet. Who's for a drink?'

Orders were enthusiastically given and just as enthusiastically whipped up by JB, the 'bartender'.

Lady Hardcastle declared me the winner – principally because I had a squillion more points than her – and I set about sorting the cards back into two separate packs.

Conversations sparked up. Bridgewater started telling a story.

'Gran, darling?' said Patience. 'Do give it a rest, there's a good boy. Let someone else have the floor for a change.'

'Right you are, Speedy, old thing. So who knows a good joke?'

'Matter of fact,' said JB, 'I heard one a little while ago. There's a one-horse town out West. You know the sort of place – just a general store, a saloon and a jailhouse. And one day this fella rides in. He's dusty from the trail, burned by the sun, and he hitches his horse outside the saloon and steps inside. There's a piano playin' in the corner. There's a couple fellas playing cards at a table near the window. And he walks across the room, boot heels clomping on the floor, spurs jingling. He bellies up to the bar and says to the bartender—'

'Ah, there you all are.'

There was a slight groan from the small throng at the interruption, followed by cheerful greetings as Wilson and Lily returned from their walk looking windswept and more than a little pleased with themselves.

'Come on in, you two,' said JB. 'Let me get you a drink and I'll carry on with my tale.'

The joke was an old one, but either JB had learned from Bridgewater or he, too, had a knack for adding colour and detail to make an ordinary joke into something special. And somehow, because those details were a little alien to us, it had an exotic flavour that made even the entirely predictable punch line seem funnier than it ought.

In spite of everything, it looked like it might be a pleasant evening after all.

By the time JB started mixing up the second round of drinks, the atmosphere in the library was positively festive. More jokes had been told, more reminiscences shared, and the mood was about as far from the tension of lunchtime as it was possible to get.

A lot of that, I suspected, was probably down to the continuing absence of Sidwell-Plant, but it was still a little odd that both he and Dotty were elsewhere while all the fun was happening in the library.

I took Lady Hardcastle to one side. 'Don't you find it odd that neither Sidwell-Plant nor Dotty is here? Do you think we should go and look for them?'

'It might not be a bad idea, actually. Unless they're—'

'Are you seriously about to suggest that they might be canoodling somewhere?'

'And why shouldn't they be? They're both very attractive people who are at loggerheads with their spouses. Or exasperated by them in Dotty's case, but it amounts to the same thing. Who's to say they haven't found solace in each other's arms?'

'Well, yes. But . . . it doesn't fit Dotty's public persona. She's like the group's mother.'

'Mothers need a little canoodling, too, you know. And perhaps little Bobby needs some mothering.' She chuckled.

'You're incorrigible.'

'And her public face might not match the private one, anyway. We don't know what she's like behind the closed bedroom door.'

'Still,' I said. 'It's hardly the time and place for those sorts of shenanigans.'

'You've been to enough country house weekends to know what's what, dear. They're in and out of each other's beds all day and all night. It's the reason many of them choose to attend.'

'I know, but—'

Suddenly all eyes turned to the doorway, where an ashen-faced Dotty had just burst in.

'Dotty, darling,' said Patience, 'whatever's the matter?'

'It's . . . it's Robert, darling. He's . . . he's dead.' She began crying.

Patience gave JB her drink and went to her friend. 'What do you mean, "dead"?'

'I mean dead. I'm so sorry just to blurt it out like that, but . . . well . . . I mean . . . he's dead.'

'Do you know what happened?' I asked. 'Was it another heart attack?'

Dotty sniffed. 'No. No, he was stabbed. Through the heart. With a long knife.'

Patience fainted.

◆ ◆ ◆

The party atmosphere evaporated at once. JB, Bridgewater, Lady Hardcastle and I rushed to help and comfort the two women. Clarice found the arm of a chair to sit on and waited to be told more about what was going on.

Once he was sure that Dotty and Patience were all right, JB drew Lady Hardcastle and me to one side.

'I need you two to come with me and look at the body again.'

'Where is it, dear?' asked Lady Hardcastle.

'I'm so dumb I never asked.' He turned back to the group. 'Dotty, honey, where did you find Robert?'

'In . . . in our room. I'd been in the drawing room playing the piano and I went back to the room to get changed for dinner. I found poor dear Robert lying on the floor by the washbasin. I can't even begin to imagine what he was doing there.'

'Thank you. Gran, you look after these two. Wilson, you and Lily make sure Clarice is OK. Emily and Florence: with me.'

He strode out and we followed.

In the Bridgewaters' room we found exactly the scene we'd expected. Sprawled on his back between the bed and the washbasin stand was Robert Sidwell-Plant, with a long sailor's knife protruding from his chest.

'He was killed in here this time, right?' said JB.

Lady Hardcastle knelt to examine the body. 'Hard to say. There's no blood on the floor, but once again the weapon pierced the heart. No pulse, no bleeding.'

'Sure, that's what you said. I remember. So either he came in here and met the killer, or he was in here and the killer came in and found him. But why was he in here?'

Lady Hardcastle paused before shaking her head. 'We might never know.'

I was glad she didn't mention her facetious Dotty speculation, but it was clearly on both our minds.

'When did he die?' asked JB. 'Can you tell?'

Lady Hardcastle continued her examination. 'The large muscles are loose.' She gently flexed his arm. 'So rigor mortis hasn't fully set in yet. But look here at his mouth and jaw. You see the stiffness starting to set in? Rigor begins in those small muscles so I'd say he died about two hours ago.'

'Give or take . . . ?'

'Actually, this time I'm a little more certain. Again, it's not an exact science and all bodies differ to some extent, but one would expect to see this sort of reaction only after about two hours in normal conditions. It's too short a time for there to be too much variation.' She looked at her watch. 'So I'd say he was murdered at about four this afternoon.'

'So where was everyone at four?' he asked.

'That, my dear JB, is what we must fathom out.'

'OK. I'm going to go back and get everyone to return to their rooms. I'll have Crawford make up another bed for the Bridgewaters and move their baggage – they can't stay here. We'll serve a light supper in the rooms.'

'Why?' I asked.

'I want to know where everyone is. One of those guys is a killer and I don't want them wandering about at night. Crawford and I will keep an eye on things and make sure they all stay put. You two are free to go wherever you want, of course – I want you to solve this.'

'As you wish, dear,' said Lady Hardcastle. 'Will you put him in the storeroom with Everett?'

'It's good and cold out there. It'll keep him better till the boat arrives Tuesday.'

◆ ◆ ◆

Lady Hardcastle and I retired to my room. We could have sat in her room as usual but I decided that if we were going to eat a carpet picnic, or whatever 'light supper' Peggy prepared, I'd rather not risk food poisoning by eating amid the Hardcastle mess and chaos. Obviously I could have tidied up for her, but I was on holiday so that wasn't going to happen.

She was standing by the window, peering out into the darkness. 'I've no idea how we're going to get through tomorrow now the cat's out of the bag.'

'Are you looking to see if we could swim ashore and leave them to it?'

'I can't deny it; the thought has crossed my mind. Although, in my version, you swam ashore and came back in a boat to pick me up.'

'Naturally – a lady shouldn't have to exert herself unnecessarily. But since that's not going to happen – I don't have my bathing suit, for one thing – what's going on and what are we going to do about it?'

'What's going on is that jewels are missing and two men have been murdered, one of whom was my favoured suspect for the first murder, if not the thefts. The murder weapons were both readily accessible but we've almost no one else whom we think might have committed the first murder who also had the time to do it.'

I thought for a moment. 'Then let's ignore the first murder and the theft and concentrate on the second. You say it happened at four o'clock.'

'I say that, yes, but I'm still nowhere near as certain as I made out. There are so many variables in the calculation that it's impossible to say with quite that much accuracy. But we have to start somewhere, so four it is.'

'Right. So where were we at four?'

'In the sitting room, I think. If I'm right, we left Sidwell-Plant in the drawing room at around three and made our way downstairs. Patience was coming out as we went in.'

'Because she didn't like the atmosphere,' I said. 'Inside, the Bridgewaters were with Clarice and we sat with Wilson and Lily. There was no sign of JB.'

She was making notes. 'Not until around five. But I'm jumping ahead. Bridgewater finished his joke and then left for parts unknown.'

'He did. Then Wilson and Lily went for a "walk" around the island and we heard them leave through the kitchen.'

She looked up from her notebook. 'And we went into the library after that. We were there for ages, but I fancy we'd have heard Dotty and Clarice passing by – dear Dotty's not the quietest of the guests.'

'We were playing cards for ages, then everyone joined us – starting, as you said, with JB at about five. I'd say that by a quarter past, everyone was there, including the canoodlers.'

She totted up the names she'd been listing. 'So four of them are accounted for, while JB, Patience and Bridgewater all had plenty of time to kill Sidwell-Plant.'

'As did the Crawfords,' I said.

'Ah, yes. The smugglers.'

'Or the thieves. What were they talking about when we overheard them this morning? Peg thought they'd left something behind, and it could have been the smuggling, but it could just as easily have been a bit of tea-leavery. If JB hasn't been paying them, they might have to resort to more drastic measures.'

'And it might give either of them a motive for doing away with Everett and Sidwell-Plant if they thought they were on to them.'

'Exactly. And what about JB, Patience or Bridgewater?'

'I should think those three all have a decent motive, too. Bridgewater was afraid Sidwell-Plant was about to expose his embezzlement. Patience wants to marry her doctor and live happily ever after, but Sidwell-Plant wouldn't divorce her.'

'And JB?' I said. 'What motive does he have? I mean, if he's not paying the Crawfords, that might mean he's short of funds, but that would only give him a motive for stealing the jewels.'

'Ah, you have me there, tiny servant – apart from covering up the putative jewel theft there doesn't seem to be any reason for JB to kill Sidwell-Plant. Unless he just doesn't like accountants.'

'There'd be no accountants left if people who didn't like them started bumping them off. I suppose he could be protecting Patience.'

'Actually, yes,' she said. 'And he could have been protecting Clarice, as well, by bumping off Everett. But he had no opportunity for either murder. Bridgewater, on the other hand . . .' She riffled through her notebook. 'Did he have an opportunity to kill Everett? Let me see . . . No, he was in the library when Everett was killed. At least we believed so when we talked about it before.'

There was a knock at the door and I answered it to find Crawford outside with a trolley.

'Good evenin', miss, is Lady Hardcastle in there with you?'

'She is indeed. Is that our supper?'

'It is. I knocked on her door but she weren't there so I thought to myself, I thought, "I bet she's in with Miss Armstrong." And there you both is. Can I bring it in?'

I stood aside and gestured towards the desk by the window.

''T'i'n't nothing special. A cold collation and some bread. Fresh-made piccalilli. Apples. A pork pie.' He was pointing as he listed the items on the trays. 'Peg made some Scotch eggs, an' all. I does love Peg's Scotch eggs so I says, "You put some of your Scotch eggs on there, my darlin', and they'll be happy as a dog with two tails." And there's wine and a couple of bottles of cider. And some fresh water. If you wants anything else, you just ring.'

We both thanked him and he bustled out to make the rest of his deliveries.

'I'm glad Peggy was asked to prepare a *small* supper,' said Lady Hardcastle. 'What are we going to do with this lot?'

'I suggest setting the trays down on the rug, sitting on the floor and stuffing ourselves stupid.'

'You've had worse ideas. Wine or cider?'

'*¿Por qué no los dos*?'

'Why not both, indeed? I like the way you think, young Flossie. You pour and I'll start shovelling things on to plates.'

We tried our best to forget about murder and theft and spent a pleasant evening putting the world to rights.

Lady Hardcastle left before ten and I retired straight away.

# Chapter Thirteen

An early night allowed for an early morning and I was up shortly after six. I knew there was no point in visiting Lady Hardcastle, who would be sound asleep until eight, so I did my Chinese exercises in my nightdress and then clambered back into bed to read the book I'd brought with me.

But there was a lot to do. We had at least one evildoer to catch, possibly as many as three, and we had little more than twenty-four hours to work out who he, she or they might be. I couldn't concentrate on the book so I got washed and dressed – yet another previously unseen outfit because heaven forfend I should be seen twice in the same dress – and set off for Lady Hardcastle's room.

It was still not long past seven by my reckoning, so I braced myself for the inevitable grumbling and knocked.

'Floss?' came the voice from within.

'None other.'

'In you come. We've a lot to do.'

I entered and found her already dressed and sitting at her desk.

'You're up early,' I said as I sat on the end of the bed.

'I know – I surprised even myself. But we've a lot to do so I thought I'd better get a wiggle on. I might need you to work your usual magic on the old barnet, though.' She waved a distracted hand at her not-quite-neat hair. 'It looks all right from the front, but I'm told people care about what one looks like from behind as well, and I fear I might not be making a good impression on that front. Or that back, as it were.'

'It's nothing a garden rake and a decent pair of shears can't fix. I'll make you spick and/or span before you're exposed once more to the vulgar gaze of the populace.'

'I don't know what I'd do without you.'

'I hope you never need to find out. What's our plan?'

'For today?' She consulted her notes. 'Quite a few things, but most of all I want to establish exactly where Granville Bridgewater was during both our murder windows.'

'He's top of your list now?'

'By default, yes. JB would be my number-one suspect, but he really hasn't had the opportunity. Of all of them, he's the one whose whereabouts we best know.'

'Him and Wilson,' I said.

'Wilson, yes. So it can't be him, either. He was with us when the jewels went missing and striding manfully about the island when both men were murdered.'

'And he doesn't have a motive anyway.'

'Well, quite. I'd be more comfortable if I knew where Patience was during both windows, too.'

'Do you think her capable of murder?'

'More than capable, and more than willing, I'd wager – she had reason to hate both men.'

'But not the others?'

'No, I've given it a great deal of thought since we spoke last night.' She began counting off on her fingers. 'It doesn't make sense for it to be Clarice on her own, for obvious reasons. Dotty is just Dotty and she has an alibi for Sidwell-Plant anyway. She could be working with Clarice but that just seems unnecessarily complicated. Lily wasn't here for the jewel theft and has an alibi for Sidwell-Plant, even though we're not completely certain where she was on Friday when Everett was killed. I'm down to Bridgewater or Patience, with the Crawfords as long-odds outsiders. I can't imagine them killing to protect their putative smuggling operation – they don't seem the types – but we've not checked their alibis so it feels foolish to rule them out completely.'

'Bridgewater and Patience it is, then. We'll have to see what we can do.'

◆ ◆ ◆

We were first to the dining room and had our pick of the breakfasty goodness on offer. Whoever JB's butcher was, he deserved full credit for the quality and tastiness of the sausages he made, and I elected once again to make myself a sausage sandwich. There were fried eggs in one of the warmers so I added one to the bangers before slapping a slice of buttered bread on top and sitting down at the table.

'You can take the girl out of . . .' began Lady Hardcastle. 'Actually, I'm never entirely certain where to say you come from. Dear Jane Tetherington introduced you as Welsh, but your official story has it that you were born in parts unknown. Obviously I already knew the thing you told Lily about yours and Gwenith's births being registered in Glamorgan, but does place of birth determine nationality? It does for the Americans – it's in their constitution – but don't we usually go by parentage?'

'I suppose we do. I prefer the idea of a matrilineal heritage, though, so that still makes me Welsh. And I spent my formative years in the Valleys so I feel a strong connection to the place. But your little phrase stumbles in the second half, don't you think? You can take the girl out of Wales, but you can't take the Wales out of the girl? What does that mean? Are you saying that my breakfast choices are uncouth and that the Welsh are ill-bred heathens? Think carefully before you answer. Remember that

I know more than a dozen ways to kill you and that I'd be a good deal cleverer about disposing of your body than our island murderer has been.'

'Well, if you put it like that, I can think of nothing more elegant and sophisticated than shoving a whopping great sausage and egg sandwich into one's face first thing in the morning.'

'That's what I thought.' I reached for the silver coffee pot. 'Coffee?'

She sat down. 'Yes, please.'

I indicated her own heavily laden plate. 'And this is classier than my sandwich? You've enough there to feed a family of six.'

'Nonsense. This is just what a growing girl needs to start the day.'

I bit into my sandwich and let the yolk drip on to the plate.

She shook her head. 'Elegant and sophisticated.'

I swallowed my mouthful. 'Shut your face.'

JB came in. He was clean-shaven and wearing fresh clothes, but didn't look as though he'd slept much, if at all.

'Good heavens, JB, you look dreadful,' said Lady Hardcastle.

He gave her a wan smile. 'Gee, thanks.'

'Oh, you know what I mean. Have you slept?'

'A little.'

'It's perfectly understandable, given the awful circumstances. Nothing can bring them back, but explanations will be forthcoming and justice will prevail. It will help you to come to terms with it.'

'I guess so. I see it's not affected your appetite, though. That's quite a plateful you've got there.'

I made a 'see?' face at Lady Hardcastle.

'Brain food, JB dear,' she said. 'Fuels the synapses and sharpens the whatnots.'

He shook his head and chuckled. 'Is that so? Well, you go ahead and enjoy it.'

He picked up a single round of buttered toast and sat down. I poured him a cup of coffee.

'What we're planning to do today,' I said, 'is to speak to everyone and to try to get a thorough idea of where they all were during the times of both murders.'

'Wait a minute,' said a woman's voice from the doorway. 'Both murders? Who else has died now?' It was Patience.

'No one else,' I said.

'Then why are you talking about *both* murders? You're not saying . . . ? Oh, my goodness. Was Everett murdered? You all said it was his heart.'

'Don't blame them, Speedy,' said JB. 'I asked them to lie. I didn't want to spook anyone.'

'Don't you "Speedy" me, Joseph Brendon. The three of you looked us in the eye and said it was natural causes.'

'To be fair,' said Lady Hardcastle, 'we never actually said those words. We said it was his heart and, in a manner of speaking, it was. At JB's request we omitted the crucial, gruesome fact that his heart stopped because it had been pierced by a narwhal tusk.'

'A narwhal . . . you mean that spear thing in the long gallery?'

'Yes,' I said. 'We didn't want to cause a panic. We thought we'd be able to keep everything under wraps until the police got here, but we hadn't reckoned on the boat being sunk by the storm and us all being stranded here until tomorrow.'

'Instead you just gave the murderer a chance to strike again.'

'To be fair again,' said Lady Hardcastle, 'I don't think that would have made any difference. The murderer is the only one among the rest of you who knows we know what really happened. They know we examined Everett's body and that we couldn't possibly mistake the wound for natural causes. They've been well aware that we'd be trying to find out who they are since we got back to the library on Friday night.'

'But if the rest of us had known, we would have been on our guard. Bobby might still be alive.'

JB finally spoke up. 'It's my fault. I bound the ladies to secrecy. I take full responsibility.'

'No,' I said, 'you shouldn't. It's not your fault either of the men is dead – it's the killer's fault. Nothing you could have said or done would have prevented their deaths.'

'Are you sure?' demanded Patience. 'If Bobby had known, he would never have let anyone get close enough to stab him.'

'Perhaps,' I said. 'But perhaps not. Both he and Everett were killed face to face with very little struggle. Even if they'd known that someone among us was a killer, would that really have helped? We're all friends. Are you suggesting we'd all have turned on each other?'

She looked at me coldly for a moment. 'How do we know it's not you? You both have a reputation for trouble. How do we know you didn't wheedle your way into our little group to do us in?'

I shrugged. 'You don't.'

'But why would we?' asked Lady Hardcastle. 'What possible motive would we have for killing Everett and Robert?'

'What motive does any of us have for the matter of that?' asked Patience, defiantly.

'You were furious at Everett's bullying of Clarice,' I said. 'And your husband wouldn't divorce you even though neither of you wanted to be married any more.'

'Are you suggesting—'

'I'm merely pointing out the dangers of flinging accusations about. You might not agree with JB's decision to keep the news from you, but imagine how terrible things would be by now if you'd all had an extra two days to stew on it. You've just proved my point, haven't you? We'd all have turned on each other.'

She glared but relented. 'So who was it?'

Lady Hardcastle shrugged. 'That, Patience dear, is at the heart of the matter. Who, indeed?'

'Well, it's not me. And you insist it's not you. So that doesn't leave many possibilities.'

'Very few indeed. So think back to Friday afternoon. We estimate Everett was killed sometime around three in the afternoon in the long gallery and then his body was moved to a box room on the second floor. Can you remember where everyone was on Friday afternoon?'

Patience thought for a moment. 'No. I remember Florence, Lily and I overhearing Clarice and Edgar's row. Then . . . I'm not sure. Did I talk to Dotty? Probably – that's mostly what I do at these weekends. I might have had a nap then, so I'm afraid I didn't see anyone else.'

'No sign of Bridgewater?'

'Gran? You're not suggesting—'

'We're not suggesting anything,' I said. 'We just need to know where everyone was.'

Patience looked at JB. 'I thought he was playing snooker with you and Bobby.'

JB shook his head. 'Just Bobby. I was with Wilson and Lady Hardcastle in the long gallery, then Wilson and I went to the library. I don't know where Lady Hardcastle went when she left us and I didn't see Gran or Bobby until later.'

'No, I'm sorry, I just can't believe it's Gran.'

'Very well,' said Lady Hardcastle. 'And who did you see yesterday afternoon around four o'clock?'

'Is that when Bobby was killed?'

Lady Hardcastle nodded.

'I saw you two as I came out of the sitting room but then went straight up for another nap. I didn't see anyone else. Sorry.'

We didn't have a chance to respond – at that moment, Bridgewater and Dotty walked in.

'Good morning, darling,' said Dotty. 'How are you?'

'I don't think it's really sunk in yet,' said Patience. 'I just can't believe he's gone.'

Dotty put her arm around her shoulders. 'It's terrible. Terrible. But if there's anything Gran or I can do, you have only to say.'

'Thank you.'

'I'll miss him,' said Bridgewater. 'We had our differences, of course we did. Who in business doesn't? But he was a good egg.'

Patience gave a half smile. 'That's certainly how everyone thought of him.'

'Honest and loyal,' said Bridgewater with an emphatic nod.

'Do either of you remember who you saw yesterday afternoon at about four?' asked Patience. 'They're trying to get a picture of where everyone was.'

Again both Dotty and Bridgewater told us exactly what we thought we already knew. They did the same when Patience asked them about Friday. None of us mentioned the fact that Everett had been murdered and, for some reason, the Bridgewaters didn't question it.

I feared it was going to be a long, unproductive day.

We left the dining room just as Lily, Wilson and Clarice arrived for breakfast. I wondered about stopping to talk to them but we had twenty-four hours or so before Vickerman arrived with the boat, so I knew we still had plenty of time. I also secretly thought we actually didn't stand much chance of working it out anyway – so what, really, was the point?

We umm'd and ahh'd in the hall for a few moments while we tried to decide whether to settle in the library or the sitting room. We eventually plumped for the sitting room, imagining it would provide a more intimate setting should we need to get some serious interrogation going.

Again, though, I seriously doubted that any amount of questioning, serious or otherwise, was going to get us anywhere. Excluding the two of us, there were only nine other people on the island, and two of those – the Crawfords – could probably be excluded simply on the grounds that they had other criminal enterprises to keep them busy, without the added complication of murder. Yet despite the paucity of suspects, we were still no nearer to finding the culprit. Well, I was, anyway. Lady Hardcastle, as was her habit, was playing her cards close to her ample chest so I had no idea how near she might be.

We rang for Crawford and asked for a large pot of coffee and some biscuits when he arrived, then stood together looking south across the English Channel. There was a ship's compass on the windowsill.

'Where's the nearest land?' I asked. 'I've been meaning to look it up since we got here.'

She glanced at the compass. 'Due south it would be the northern coast of Brittany, I think. Look south-eastish and it's Guernsey, then the Cherbourg peninsula.'

'Nowhere exotic, then.'

'It depends how exotic one finds northern France or the Channel Islands. If France didn't jut out like that it would be Spain. And then Morocco.'

'That's more like it,' I said. 'I'll imagine myself looking towards Morocco. Do you remember chasing that gunrunner through the souk at Tangier?'

'Oh, I do. I'm not completely sure I remember why we became involved, though, to be honest.'

'Don't you? The French and Spanish authorities were so busy arguing between themselves about who should take responsibility that nothing was getting done. You lost your patience with them and stepped in.'

'That certainly does sound like me. What larks, eh?'

'What larks indeed.'

Our coffee arrived and we sat in matching wingback chairs, carefully angled so that we could see anyone walking past the door.

Our first customers were, as I'd hoped, Wilson and Lily.

'What ho, you two,' called Lady Hardcastle.

They stopped and peered in.

'Oh, hello,' said Wilson. 'We were looking for somewhere comfortable to sit. Do you mind if we join you?'

'Not at all, dear. I'll be honest: that's why I hailed you.'

They came in and Wilson drew two more chairs over to our little table.

Lily grinned as she sat down. 'Sick of your own company?'

'You have no idea,' I said. 'She's such a bore.'

Lily laughed. 'Hardly. You're both utterly fascinating.'

'No, really,' said Lady Hardcastle, 'I'm crushingly dull. Whereas you two . . . An antiquities dealer and a photographer? What could be more fascinating than that?'

'Oh, I don't know,' said Wilson. 'I'm not much more than an agent. A go-between. I do very little dealing, I merely find interesting objects and put buyers and sellers together.'

'An antiquities hunter, then,' I said.

He laughed. 'Well, when you put it like that, I'm as glamorous and exciting as they come.'

'I'm not going to protest,' said Lily. 'I mean, I myself am as dreary as the next girl, but my job . . . well. I think being a photographer is absolutely the utterest utter.'

'And rightly so,' said Lady Hardcastle. 'Now, then, I wonder if you can help us with a little something. You know of some of our exploits, so obviously you must suspect that we're trying to fathom out what's been going on here. You're both observant young people with excellent memories. I wonder if you have any memory of seeing anyone at about four o'clock yesterday afternoon?'

Wilson looked at her shrewdly. 'Is that when you think Sidwell-Plant was murdered?'

'There or thereabouts, yes. We're trying to get a picture of where everyone was.'

'I'm afraid that's about the time Lily and I were taking our long walk around the island. There was no one else about. Sorry.'

'No, dear, don't worry, that's what I thought. I just wondered if you'd encountered anyone on your way out or your way back, that's all.'

'No one but Mr and Mrs Crawford in the kitchen,' said Lily. 'Actually, no, that's not quite right. We only saw Peggy on the way out, but they were both there when we came back.'

'I don't suppose you remember the time?' I asked.

Lily shook her head. 'No, sorry. Oh, no, wait. There's a big clock on the kitchen wall. I remember noticing it as we came back in. It was just coming up to ten minutes to five. By then everyone was in the library.'

'Except Sidwell-Plant, obviously,' added Wilson. 'And Dotty – she came in a little later.'

'With the terrible news,' said Lady Hardcastle. 'Yes.'

At JB's insistence, Monday's lunch was an informal, come-as-you-please affair not unlike breakfast. There was a large tureen of stew alongside a warming dish piled high with mashed potato and we were expected to help ourselves.

When Lady Hardcastle and I arrived, JB and the Bridgewaters were quietly discussing Dotty's plans for spring planting in the gardens. At least, JB and Dotty were discussing it – Bridgewater, without a joke to tell or an audience to listen to it, was just staring at his now-empty plate.

He brightened as we entered. 'Afternoon, ladies. Come to save me from gardening talk?'

'I'm always happy to provide an alternative if people are talking about plants,' I said. 'They're a mystery to me.'

'And to me. I'm perfectly at home with the intricacies of the Companies Act but I can't tell a petunia from a begonia and I'll be damned if I know a loamy soil from a lime tree.'

I smiled. 'My feelings exactly. Herself tries to teach me but it goes in one ear and out the other. When she and the gardener get together they might as well be speaking Mandarin. Except that I understand Mandarin.'

'Ha! Well, sit yourself down and we can leave these two to their hardy perennials.'

As it turned out, we weren't able to talk for long before JB and Dotty took themselves off to inspect Dotty's proposed site for a kitchen garden, and Bridgewater, with feigned reluctance, followed.

We sat alone for a short while with our stew.

'This is remarkably tasty,' I said. 'I've had many a bland stew in my time, but Peggy definitely has a way with herbs and seasoning. I'm not sure I would have served it with mash, but it's not unpleasant.'

'JB's always been a fan of the mashed potato, don't forget. I often wondered if it was an American thing or a McIntyre thing.'

'I'm certainly not going to ask. I think he'd much rather we were solving the murders than examining his culinary preferences.'

'Hmm,' she said as she took another forkful of stew.

I gave her a quizzical look. 'Hmm?'

'Yes, hmm. I can't help but keep coming back to the notion that JB is an extremely likely candidate for the role of murderer in this weekend's performance.'

'A great candidate,' I said, 'but one who is excluded from the running by the fact that he had no opportunity to kill Everett. There are minutes here and there when we don't know his whereabouts, but he had no time to kill him *and* move the body.'

'No, I know. But that's at the core of it all, isn't it? No one who had the strength to move Everett also had the opportunity to kill him.'

'In that case, there's something very wrong with our knowledge or our assumptions.'

She thought for a moment. 'That has to be it. Either we don't know what we think we know or our thinking has led us astray.'

I shook my head. 'That's exactly what I just said, only wordier.'

'Indeed it is, dear. But sometimes one has to say these things out loud for oneself.'

Patience appeared at the door. 'Hello, ladies. What's for lunch?'

'Beef stew and mashed potato,' I said.

'No dumplings?'

'Sadly not. Will you join us?'

'I might give it a miss, thank you.' Nevertheless she came in. 'Are you any nearer to finding out who stabbed Robert?'

Lady Hardcastle took a sip of water. 'No, dear. But then again, yes.'

'You'll forgive me for pointing out that that makes no sense.'

'Nothing makes sense any more, dear, but I accept the criticism. What I think I meant was that we're no nearer, but that our frustration is leading us to challenge what we think we know. And that might lead us to the answers that have thus far eluded us.'

'I see. Well, good luck. I shan't miss Robert, but I didn't wish him dead. Well, not often, anyway. His killer needs to be brought to justice.'

'We shall do our utmost.'

# Chapter Fourteen

Patience left us to finish our lunch and we were thereafter uninterrupted, save for a visit from Crawford, who asked if we would like tea or coffee.

Lady Hardcastle gave him her winningest smile. 'I should love a pot of tea, Crawford. Thank you. Florence?'

'Tea would be perfect, thank you.'

'Tea for two, then,' said Lady Hardcastle. 'Would you mind awfully bringing it up to my room? We shall adjourn there to keep out of everyone's way for a while.'

'Very good, m'lady. Would you care for something sweet? Peg makes a lovely Madeira cake.'

'Oh, that would be delicious, I'm sure. Tea and cake, please.'

He left, and a few moments later we made our way down the hall and round the corridor to Lady Hardcastle's room.

She sat on the bed with her notebook and I sat in the comfy chair, wishing it were higher up so I could look out of the window.

By the time Crawford arrived with the tea tray, Lady Hardcastle had reviewed most of her notes and I was standing to get a better view of the now calm sea.

'Thank you,' I said. 'Just pop it on the desk and I'll take care of it.'

With a 'Very good, miss' and a little bob of the head, Crawford was gone.

I poured two cups of tea and handed one to Lady Hardcastle.

'What assumptions need challenging, then?' I asked.

'All of them, I think.'

I tried not to sigh. 'Starting with . . . ?'

'Means, motive and opportunity.'

'No, that's three things. Pick one.'

She didn't try not to sigh. 'Means, then.'

'Everyone had the means. Even us. The two murder weapons were on display in the long gallery and we all had access to them all the time.'

'That's fair, I suppose. So we can accept our assumption that everyone had easy access to a weapon.'

I nodded.

'Motive next,' she said.

'JB has no obvious motive for killing Everett. But Sidwell-Plant was intent on exposing Bridgewater's embezzlement and that would cause a scandal that would harm his financial interests. By killing him he avoids the ruinous revelation, leaving him to deal with Bridgewater privately.'

'Very well. Clarice?'

'She has a clear motive for getting rid of her awful husband, but no reason I can think of for killing Sidwell-Plant. I can think of problems with opportunity, too, but we haven't got to that part, yet.'

'Indeed. Bridgewater?'

'Similar to JB,' I said. 'Other than Everett's general awfulness, he has no clear motive there. But killing his old friend Sidwell-Plant might save him from doing bird for fraud. Risky, though – a few years in the clink would always be preferable to a few seconds at the end of a rope.'

'Quite. Dotty?'

'Ignoring whether I think it's likely that she'd do anything of the sort, her motives are the same as her husband's: none, and keeping the fraud secret.'

'Agreed. Patience?'

'Of them all, she was the most furious at Everett's treatment of Clarice. She offered her a place to stay if she left him and said she could set her up with a new manager. I could easily see Patience losing her rag and running Everett through if he taunted her in the long gallery. And of all of them she also has a strong motive for killing the husband who was effectively holding her captive in a marriage she was no longer committed to.'

Lady Hardcastle nodded. 'On motive alone, she's the strongest candidate so far. What about Wilson?'

'I can't see he has any motive at all. He barely knows any of them so he hasn't had time to foster any grudges. He seems like an honourable sort of bloke so he might have wanted to free Clarice and Patience from their awful husbands, I suppose.'

'We've seen people kill for flimsier reasons. And last of all, Lily.'

'We're excluding the Crawfords?'

'Actually, you're right – we're challenging assumptions. But Lily first.'

'I can't imagine any real motive for either murder. She witnessed the incident in the sitting room and she was shaken by it, so that might count, I suppose. But she had no reason to kill Sidwell-Plant, as far as I know.'

'Fair enough. Crawford?'

'None that I can think of. There's the smuggling, but I don't know what harm either man could do to that. And the same goes for Peggy – she just doesn't have a reason.'

Lady Hardcastle reviewed her notes. 'Patience has a strong motive for both, and Wilson has a possible motive for both, but the rest either have no motive at all or a motive just for one. And that leaves opportunity.'

'Which we've been chasing since Friday. No one seems to have had a proper chance to kill both men except Patience. Do you think she actually could be the killer?'

'As we always say: anyone could be a killer. Oh, and she'd also have benefitted from the jewellery thefts on Thursday evening. I see practical difficulties, mind you. Moving Everett's body wouldn't have been easy for her, but she's resourceful and I'd imagine she's quite strong, too. I just don't see it. I mean, why here? Why now?'

'It doesn't make a huge amount of sense.'

We lapsed into silence for a while as she stared at her notes and I munched on another slice of Madeira cake.

At length she spoke up. 'The simplest thing is to assume that our assessment of motive is broadly correct, and that our error is in our belief that no one apart from Patience had the opportunity. There's something we're missing – some infuriatingly simple thing we've overlooked – but I'm blowed if I can think what it might be.'

'You know there's someone we haven't talked to about everyone's whereabouts.'

'There is?'

'Of course. Thanks to a dim-witted assumption on our part, we haven't asked Clarice what she noticed on both days. We thought – well, I thought, at least – that because she can't see anyone, she wouldn't be able to tell us anything. But we know that Clarice notices things without having to see them. We should go and talk to her.'

'As soon as I've finished my cake and nipped to the WC.'

◆ ◆ ◆

We decided to begin our search for Clarice in the most obvious place: her room.

Lady Hardcastle knocked.

'Oh, do push off, JB, there's a good chap,' said a familiar voice.

'It's not JB, dear, it's us,' said Lady Hardcastle.

There were sounds of movement from within, then a key turned in the lock and the door opened.

'Friendly faces at last. Well, I assume you have friendly faces. You might be old boots for all I know, but you have friendly voices at least.'

We entered.

'She's an old boot,' I said, 'but I have a beguiling Celtic beauty.'

'She's not wrong,' agreed Lady Hardcastle. 'Has JB been bothering you?'

Clarice shut the door behind us. 'He's been fussing over me ever since Edgar died. It's just avuncular concern – nothing sinister – but it's getting on my nerves a tad. Do tell me you haven't come to fuss.'

'We have not,' I said. 'We've come to ask you for help.'

'Me? You need a violinist for your ragtime band?'

'Actually, that would be a splendid idea,' said Lady Hardcastle. 'Flo plays the banjo, you know. We could take the nightclub circuit by storm. But no, it's not that. We're looking for witnesses.'

Clarice laughed. 'And how do you think I might be able to help there?'

'You observe more in other ways than most people see with their fully operational eyes. We thought you might have noticed things that completely passed everyone else by.'

Clarice paced carefully to the edge of the room and found the comfy chair. 'If you can find somewhere to sit, please help yourselves. The bed is fair game, and there's an upright chair by the desk but it's not terribly comfortable.'

She settled into the armchair while Lady Hardcastle and I sat together on the edge of her bed.

'Before we begin, dear, there's a piece of quite distressing information we've been withholding,' said Lady Hardcastle. 'It was at JB's request, but that doesn't excuse us, I don't think. It's that—'

'Edgar didn't die of natural causes,' interrupted Clarice. 'I know. JB told me this morning. I'm not surprised, to be honest. Actually, I'm surprised it didn't happen sooner. He had a way of making people want to kill him.'

'Ah, well, that makes things simpler, then. So, it seems reasonable to us that both Edgar and Robert Sidwell-Plant were killed by the same person. The problem is that everyone except Patience has an alibi for one or both of the murders. At least that's what we believe. But our beliefs are based only on what everyone has told us about where they were and who they saw, so we were wondering if you had any of your unique observations to add.'

Clarice thought for a moment. 'Like what?'

'Sounds or smells, perhaps. You upbraided JB when he mentioned his belief that your other senses were enhanced, but you went on to say you pay more attention to them, so what have you noticed over the past few days that the rest of us would have missed?'

'I see. So, what do you know so far?'

We ran once more through the list of runners and riders and their movements as we understood them, from the evening when the jewellery went missing to the afternoon of Sidwell-Plant's murder.

Clarice sat in silence again while she thought all that through.

'I'm sure more things will come to me later,' she said after a few moments, 'but a couple leap immediately to mind. Do you remember when Lily Thacker arrived from the mainland on Vickerman's boat? She'd been out in the fresh air for some time but her clothes didn't smell as though she had.'

'What did they smell of?' I asked.

'Fish stew.'

'Vickerman's is a fishing boat,' said Lady Hardcastle. 'Perhaps she'd brushed against something on the trip over.'

'Perhaps,' said Clarice, 'but she didn't smell of the outdoors. I thought it odd, but it seemed rude to point out that she smelled of fish so I kept my counsel. The only other thing I can quickly think of is that I distinctly heard the slight squeak of soft-soled shoes passing by my door yesterday afternoon, shortly before my clock struck four.'

'Interesting,' said Lady Hardcastle. 'Could you tell which way they were heading?'

'Towards the Bridgewaters' room. A pair of men's shoes went in the same direction a short while later. Then the soft shoes hurried back the way they'd come a few minutes after that.'

'But not the other man's shoes?'

'No.'

'This could be very important,' I said. 'Who wears soft-soled shoes?'

'That's just it,' said Clarice. 'No one. The ladies all have small heels, the men all have normal men's heels, and when he goes out, Wilson wears hobnailed boots.'

'So if we can find some soft shoes,' I said, 'we might find our killer.'

We stayed a while to chat with Clarice and eventually left her chuckling over one of Lady Hardcastle's filthier jokes.

I looked up and down the corridor. 'What now?'

'Now I think we ought to do something we should have done much sooner: we need to walk through the scenes of the crimes. Let's see if we can put ourselves into the mind of the thief-cum-killer. It might jog something.'

And so we did.

We started by walking between the Bridgewaters' original room and the Sidwell-Plants' as though we were stealing jewellery. It was easy to move between them without being seen, as long as no one else was in their room, and we knew that everyone else was downstairs in the library or visiting the cloakroom off the hall.

'How do we get back to the gathering?' I asked. 'If we walk downstairs we might be spotted. Anyone looking out through the library door would see us, and we'd bump into any number of people on their way to and from the WC. No one said, "Oh, and I saw So-and-so coming downstairs before the recital."'

'Perhaps we could hide out somewhere here?'

'No, we'd not want to be seen near the scene of the crime.'

'Upstairs in one of the empty rooms, then? That might give us the idea for where to stash the body when we kill Everett.'

'That seems like the best option. Shall we take a look?'

We went upstairs to the second floor.

The last time we'd visited, JB had just led us straight to the box room without giving us a chance to look round, so now we took our time and explored the second floor properly. It was quite a bit more spacious than I'd imagined and, as well as additional guest rooms, another two of which were being used for storage, there was a large, modern bathroom.

There were no rooms on the north side of the floor – the side that would be looking back to the Devonshire shore if it had windows – and the wall was adorned with luxurious linenfold panelling reflecting the Tudor origins of the building.

'This is rather swish,' said Lady Hardcastle as she ran her hands over the wood. 'I wonder if it's original.'

'You never know with JB,' I said. 'He'll have paid a fortune for it, either way. It's sort of a shame he didn't put some windows in, though. We're above the dining room and drawing room so the view of the coast should be good from here.'

She nodded. 'True, but this is beautiful. The shame is that more people don't get to see it.' She nodded towards a door at the end of the corridor. 'Where does that go, I wonder? Another room?'

'I can think of a way to find out.'

We tried the door but found it locked.

'Blast,' she said. 'Lockpicks?'

Lady Hardcastle had given me a pretty brooch for my birthday several years before which concealed small picklocks. This meant I was usually never without this essential tool, but the sartorial requirements of a country house weekend had left me temporarily ill-equipped.

'Not with me, sorry. With all these stupid changes of outfit I've left the brooch on one of my other dresses.'

'Not to worry – we can come back later. But I think it's safe to say that the thief could have come up here after pinching the trinkets and then slipped back down to join us in the drawing room for Everett and Clarice's performance.'

'Agreed. They could have stashed the swag up here, but there are so many hiding places I doubt we'd ever find it.'

'They might have retrieved it, anyway,' she said. 'Let's move on to the murders for now, though. Everett's body ended up on this floor so let's work backwards.' She led the way back to the box room where the body had been found. 'He hauls Everett up the stairs and along the corridor to here.'

'How does he know this would be a good hiding place? You wouldn't heave an eleven-stone body up a flight of stairs on the off chance you might find somewhere to stash it,' I said.

'Good point. An earlier scouting trip?'

'Seems reasonable. Either that or he was also the jewel thief and knew all about what was up here from his previous exploits.'

We made our way down the stairs.

I looked across from the foot of the stairs to the side door of the long gallery. 'It's easy enough to get the body out of there and up the stairs without being noticed as long as no one comes out of their room. It's a gamble, but you'd only be in view for a few moments before you rounded the curve of the stairs.'

We went into the long gallery and over to the spot on the rug where we'd seen the bloodstain.

Lady Hardcastle checked her watch. 'It happened about this time of day so it would have been a little gloomy in here, just as it is now, but it's still perfectly possible to see what's going on. It wasn't an ambush – the killer would have been in plain sight.'

'True, but everyone here knows everyone else and thought they were all friends. Everett wouldn't have been on his guard that day any more than Sidwell-Plant was yesterday. You wouldn't expect to have to fear a fellow guest.'

'You're right, of course. Even if someone were larking about with the narwhal tusk, one wouldn't have anticipated that their next move would be to ram it into one's chest.'

'So, what do we think? The killer was in here and Everett came in to see what was going on? A quick chat, a bit of larking about with the tusk and then . . . wallop?'

'I'm not sure it matters. If it were the other way round with the killer coming in and finding Everett examining the exhibits, it could still result in murder.'

'It wasn't like Thursday evening, though, when everyone was safely on the ground floor and sneaking up here might be easy.' I pointed out the end door of the gallery to the corridor beyond. 'With people in and out of their bedrooms taking naps and whatnot, getting in here and hanging about would have been quite a risk.'

'And why would the killer hang about here in particular? How did he know his victim would come to this place at that time?'

'He wouldn't unless they'd arranged it.'

'Arranged it. Yes.' She led the way out of the end door and along the passageway to the Bridgewaters' old room. 'And what about Sidwell-Plant? What was he doing in here?'

'Another arrangement?' I said.

'It's the only thing that makes sense. But how? It can't have been a verbal invitation – one's immediate response would be, "Why can't we just talk here, old chap? Why do we need a secret assignation?" So there must have been notes. It would be most helpful if we could find them.'

'Would you keep a note from a friend asking you to meet in the long gallery, or would you throw it away?'

'I wouldn't much care what I did with it, to be honest. I'd not save it for my diary, but I'd not be desperate to get rid of it, either. The putative notes could be in the bin or they could be in their rooms somewhere.'

'Or on their bodies,' I said. 'Patience would have spoken up by now if there was a note from the killer among Sidwell-Plant's effects.'

Lady Hardcastle grinned and gripped my arm. 'You little marvel. To the outside storeroom, tiny servant, with all possible dispatch.'

◆ ◆ ◆

We weathered Peggy's concerns about our going out without coats and reassured her we'd only be a few minutes. She didn't seem entirely convinced but we didn't hang about for long enough for her to argue.

Once inside the storeroom we flicked on the electric light and went straight to the tarpaulin-covered bodies. It was remarkably cold in the room and the chill had slowed putrefaction so that examining them wasn't quite as unpleasant as it might have been in summer.

'We should have searched their pockets before, you know,' I said as I crouched to rifle through them.

'There are a lot of things we should have done, dear. I for one have been so focused on trying to talk to potential killers and witnesses that I completely forgot that the victims themselves might be able to tell us something.'

There was a folded piece of paper in the right hip pocket of Sidwell-Plant's jacket, and I pulled it out and handed it to Lady Hardcastle as I continued my search. The other pockets held only the usual odds and ends a gentleman might carry with him.

I moved on to Everett.

Once again his pockets were full of the nonsense a gentleman apparently needs to have about him all day, and it wasn't until I reached the inside pocket on the left-hand side that I found another folded piece of paper, which I also passed to Lady Hardcastle.

I found nothing else of note and stood. With a frown, she handed both notes back to me.

The first was written in block capitals in blue ink.

> MEET ME IN THE LONG GALLERY AT 3 O'CLOCK – THERE IS SOMETHING WE MUST DISCUSS. GB

The second was in the same hand and the same ink on a sheet of the same Guardians Rock notepaper.

> MY ROOM. 4PM. WE NEED TO TALK. GB

I read both again. 'That's rather damning.'

Lady Hardcastle didn't seem quite as excited as I might have expected. 'Yes. It is, rather. But . . .'

'But what?'

'Well, don't you think it's rather *too* damning? Imagine yourself in the role of murderer. You have written a note arranging a meeting with your intended victim and, to your great relief, they turn up and allow you to kill them without too much fuss. Everything up to this point has been planned with at least moderate care, but at the last you entirely forget to check their pockets for the incriminating note. Twice. Overlooking it the first time might be understandable in the heat of the moment. But surely when you went over the events in your mind you'd be cursing yourself for a fool for forgetting something so fundamental, and you'd take care to search your second victim.'

'When you put it like that,' I said, 'it seems a good deal more contrived. So someone is trying to fit Bridgewater?'

'I'm not able to say for sure, but I'm not going to rule it out for now. I think we need to get back to my room so I can ponder. Also, I'm bloody freezing, but don't tell Peggy.'

# Chapter Fifteen

We passed through the kitchen once more and asked for a pot of coffee.

'To warm you up, I'll be bound,' said Peggy with a sage nod. 'I said you'd get cold out there. It's perishing.'

'You were right, Peggy dear,' said Lady Hardcastle. 'We should have listened to you.'

This seemed to please her and we left her smiling smugly as we went back upstairs to Lady Hardcastle's room.

She put the incriminating notes on the desk and looked out of the window at what the poets might have called the gathering gloom. It was still over an hour until sunset, but the clouds were thick and we were glad of the electric lamps.

'Where are your thoughts taking you now?' I asked as I settled in the armchair.

'Hither, thither and, to a certain extent, yon. I remain unconvinced that the thefts and murders were conducted in the cleverest way. There's superficial evidence of careful planning, but so much was left to chance – there were so many possibilities of being seen going to and from the scenes of the crimes. I'm sure that in a place like this you and I could come up with half a dozen better ways of going about things.'

'We've more experience of skulduggery,' I said.

'Even so, there's incongruity here that I can't reconcile. And these notes.' She indicated the papers on the desk. 'They're so clumsy, whichever way one looks at it. Either Bridgewater is a forgetful nincompoop who neglected to clean up after himself, or it's the most ham-fisted way possible of implicating him.'

'Ham-fisted to us, perhaps – we've seen quite a few murders in our time – but to someone who's only read about murder in the newspapers and detective stories it would seem jolly clever.'

'Hmmm,' she said. 'Yes.'

This last was spoken in the familiar distracted tone that told me I wasn't going to get much more out of her for a few minutes, while the cogs whirred and her mighty brain worked through the problem. If she'd been at home with our crime board she'd have been scrawling notes and drawing lines to connect people and events, but as it was she just stared out of the window.

Crawford arrived with our coffee and I poured her a cup without her apparently noticing either of us.

I took the pen and pad that had been placed on the desk for guests' use and doodled. I drew a cat wearing a cowboy hat and a tin star, with a speech bubble that said, *I'm the sheriff round these parts, son. I ain't got no patience for your flim-flam.*

I was part way through a passable rendition of an octopus having an earnest conversation with a set of bagpipes when Lady Hardcastle returned to reality.

'I say, thank you for the coffee. When did this get here?'

'About ten minutes ago,' I said. 'Did you really not notice?'

'No, dear, sorry. On the plus side, though, I think I have an idea.'

'Which you're not going to share.'

She laughed. 'Of course not. Don't be silly. Go and fetch your lockpicks – I want to see what's behind that door upstairs.'

◆ ◆ ◆

It was the work of mere moments to pick the lock on the door at the end of the panelled corridor, and we opened it to find not a room, as I had been expecting, but a flight of circular stone steps leading upwards.

'A spiral staircase,' I said. 'Exactly what a good fort needs.'

'If one were being pedantic, they're helical steps rather than spiral, but who are we to go against hundreds of years of geometric misnomerism?'

'Who indeed? I suppose you're going to tell me now that the clockwise spiral isn't to make them easier for right-handed swordsmen to defend.'

'I did read something about that recently, too, but I'm not convinced, no. Surely it's difficult for anyone to wield a sword on a helical staircase, no matter which hand they hold it in. And, honestly, what's the point? If attackers are already inside one's castle and fighting their way upstairs, the battle is lost. Better to have a decent escape route than a fancy staircase. It's much more likely that they were built this way because they take up less space and the direction of turn is just an aesthetic choice.'

'You make a good point. It seemed like such a clever idea, though.'

'Sorry. Would you go first, though, dear? If there's another locked door at the top we don't want to fall to our deaths in a clumsy attempt to swap places.'

I led the way. There were no lights on the stairs, and no windows, so the only illumination came from the open door at the bottom. After a couple of turns, this had faded to nothing and I found myself walking like a music hall ghost, with my arms out in front of me to feel my way.

Eventually I reached a small landing and groped my way forwards to find, as predicted, another locked door. I soon had it open and we stepped out on to a large square platform at the very top of Guardians Rock Fort.

'I say, this is a marvellous spot,' said Lady Hardcastle. 'In decent visibility one could see for miles from here. This must have been the lookout.'

I pointed to the embrasures in the waist-high parapet that bounded the platform. 'You could put smallish guns up here to take pot shots, too.' We walked over to the wall on the 'inside' of the fort and looked down. 'See? The main gun platform's down there, but there's no point in wasting this fantastic vantage point.'

Turning back, we took in the flagpole mounted in a small stone plinth at the centre of the platform and got a better look at the neat structure that housed the doorway through which we had passed a few moments before. Behind it was a newly built section made of almost-but-not-quite the same stone.

'What do we think that is?' I asked.

'It's a stone hut.'

'I don't know what I'd do without you. Why do you think it's there?'

She winked at me. '"I can think of a way to find out," as a wise woman once said.'

There was a door on one of the long sides of the little building, which succumbed in seconds to my trusty picks. On a hunch, I felt around on the inside of the door frame for a light switch and soon the small room was illuminated.

A tall iron frame in the centre held a large electric motor and gearbox connected to a sizeable pulley wheel holding a steel cable, one end of which disappeared down the centre of a square shaft with the other going down one side.

'The dumb waiter mechanism?' I suggested.

'That would be my guess,' she said, looking down through the hole beneath the machinery. 'It's a good deal more substantial than I would have expected for something intended just to haul a few dinner plates up from the kitchen. It seems to have a counterweight. Not the level of sophistication one might think necessary for so simple a purpose.'

'The transporty bit – you know, the box thing – is quite a size, though. Perhaps they use it for moving supplies between floors. Even furniture, at a pinch.'

'JB does like his gadgets and modern inventions, doesn't he. But look at the way this lift shaft is built. The runners come all the way up, so the car needn't stop at the dining room on the first floor – you could bring it up here if you needed to.'

'Or you could stop at, say, the second floor,' I said.

'But where would it open out . . . ? Oh, that panelling.'

'That's what I was thinking. Shall we take a look?'

Back down in the wood-lined passageway, we carefully examined the panels, looking for any kind of gap that could indicate where an opening might be, but everything had been made to the highest standards of workmanship and the fit was perfect. Even around the area where we assumed the lift shaft would be, we could find nothing.

'You have a musical ear,' I said after a few minutes of fruitless searching. 'Close your eyes and listen for a change in tone as I tap on the wood. I'll try to knock in the same place in each panel – surely there'll be a difference. Even if they're all mounted on battens and set away from the stone, there must be a difference in the sound when there's no wall behind.'

She nodded and closed her eyes as instructed.

I tapped.

And tapped.

And tapped again.

'There,' she said. 'That one's subtly different.'

She opened her eyes and together we re-examined the panel. Still nothing.

Almost in desperation, I pressed the centre of one of the elegantly carved linen folds in the middle of the panel. It gave slightly and there was a soft click as though of latches being released. I pressed harder and two of the panels slid back towards the wall.

I looked at Lady Hardcastle and shrugged.

'Sliding door?' she suggested.

I placed my hand on the panel and tried to push it to the right and, sure enough, it slid noiselessly aside on greased runners to reveal a large, framed opening in the wall about four feet square. Through this opening we could see what I presumed to be the elusive lift shaft. As I moved my head, light glinted on a heavy steel cable within, confirming my guess.

There was a small metal box mounted on the wooden frame of the opening with a pair of vertically mounted buttons labelled 'Up' and 'Down'. There were tiny light bulbs beside the buttons and the one labelled 'Down' was illuminated.

I looked at Lady Hardcastle.

She looked back and, with a grin, pressed the button marked 'Up'.

The cable vibrated and there was the faintest sound of greased wheels on the steel tracks, but the motor in the building above us was all but inaudible.

A few moments later, the lift car arrived and the 'Down' light was extinguished – apparently it indicated where the car was in relation to the stop. Clever.

Lady Hardcastle released the button and it halted, almost precisely lined up with the opening with its base level with the floor.

She grinned in satisfaction at her achievement. 'I could have been a lift attendant, you know.'

I nodded. 'It's good to have a trade to fall back on.'

I'd never had a good view of the dumb waiter when it was in use in the dining room, and it was much larger than I'd imagined. The opening in the dining room wall was big enough to allow a couple of trays and a pile of plates to be placed inside the car, but now I was able to see that the car itself was much, much larger. On a floor like this one where the opening was big enough, you could easily fit a decent-sized chair in the car.

Or a person.

'In you go, poppet,' said Lady Hardcastle.

'Poppet?'

'I thought it would make my request sound a little more . . . you know . . . reasonable. A friendly invitation to fun and larks between pals.'

'Why don't you get in, *poppet*?'

'Because I am frail and old—'

'You're forty-five.'

'I am. But you know, less than a hundred years ago half the population was dead by the age of *thirty*-five. By their standards I'm positively ancient. But I was going to go on to say that, compared with you, I'm also an absolute giant—'

'You're a danger to shipping. If poor Captain Scott had made it back from the Antarctic, his next voyage would have been to try to explore the other side of you.'

'You're making my point for me, dear. Just get in the lift and see where it goes.'

'It goes downstairs to the dining room and the kitchen.'

'Yes, of course. But where else does it go?'

'How should I know? Where else is there?'

'And that, my dearest Flossie, is why I want you to get in and find out. I have an idea, and this little elevator might well be the key to understanding what's going on.'

With a tut, I crouched down and shuffled into the sturdy wooden box of the dumb waiter. The floor was reassuringly solid and stable, and in the dim light coming in through the large opening I could see that the walls and ceiling were also suitably rugged. There was no wall at the back and I could see the stone of the lift shaft.

I knelt on the floor of the car and looked around. 'There are buttons in here. In a box on the wall like the ones out there.'

'Are they labelled?'

'"Up" and "Down", just like on the outside.'

'I'd suggest "Down", then. We know what's above us.'

I pressed and held the 'Down' button and the dumb waiter started to move.

The movement of the lift was smooth and comfortable. It didn't judder. It didn't wobble against its tracks. It just glid, glode or glided almost noiselessly downwards.

It wasn't long before an opening appeared in the shaft. From the size of the aperture I guessed that this would be the dining room, and I delayed my release of the button until my head was level with the doorway so that I could see what I was dealing with.

I sat silently.

The doors, not designed to be concealed like the ones above, were not as closely fitted and I was able to tell that the lights in the room were not switched on. It wasn't dark out there, but the only light came from the slowly descending dusk outside the windows.

I pushed the door on my left and it swung easily open, revealing that I was, as I had suspected, in the dining room. I pulled the door closed and pressed the 'Down' button once more.

I was facing the side where the doors would appear, keeping a lookout for the telltale signs that I'd arrived at the kitchen. I knew Peggy would be hard at work there and didn't want to have to explain why I was mucking about with the dumb waiter, but I still wanted to be sure of where I was and what I could see.

There was a weird breeze behind me as I descended but I didn't have time to turn and investigate before the opening appeared in front of me and I knew I was at the kitchen level.

Light shone through the cracks in the lift doors and the sounds of culinary bustle came from the room beyond. This was most definitely the kitchen.

So I was right. The dumb waiter served the kitchen and the dining room with an opening on the second floor, presumably for moving guests' baggage and other large items to the upper level.

But Herself 'had an idea', so I owed it to her to carry on exploring. There was no evidence that this was the lowest extent of the lift shaft so I pressed 'Down' again and descended.

It wasn't long before the lift stopped moving with a soft bump, as though it had hit a set of gentle springs. I was disappointed to find that there was no opening in front of me, but a cold draught behind me made me shuffle round to take a look.

There was an opening, this time uncovered. I struggled out and found myself in what felt like a large wooden box. Or a cupboard – that was much more likely. I pushed open the door and found myself in a darkened room.

If I had been better prepared for my jaunt, I might have had a box of matches and a candle, or even a flashlight, but as it was I was as blind as Clarice.

I had an idea where I might be, but it seemed that to do the job properly, I ought to get out and confirm it.

I needed to explore, but I couldn't see a thing, so I decided to follow the line of cupboards. Most rooms are rectangular, so I reasoned that if I followed the walls all the way round I'd eventually find the door and, I hoped, a light switch.

I'd gone no more than a few feet when I hit wooden shelving. This went some way towards confirming my guess as to where I might be, but scuppered my wall-following plan. I turned and followed the shelves to their end and then had to take a step of faith into the open space beyond.

I edged forwards across the stone-flagged floor, arms outstretched, hoping to find the far wall with its door and light switch. How did Clarice do this? Years of practice, obviously, but what did she actually do? She was at pains to point out that her other senses weren't enhanced and that she didn't have magical powers, she just paid more attention to the senses she had.

I had the same senses she had, so what were they telling me?

I stopped moving and concentrated.

What could I hear?

Nothing.

No, wait, I could hear the sound of wind whistling faintly underneath a door.

I clicked my tongue. The reverberations of the sound told me the room was quite large and had hard walls and floor. That much I already knew, but I felt a bounce of confidence as my ears seemed to confirm it.

What could I smell?

The freshly cut wood of the shelves. Coffee. Vegetables. I must be in the storeroom, just as I suspected.

And then another smell hit me. The unmistakable smell of death. I was definitely in the storeroom with the tarpaulin-covered bodies of Everett and Sidwell-Plant.

And if that was the case, then I knew that as long as I kept going slowly forwards, I'd soon reach the outer wall and from there I'd easily be able to find the door.

I moved on. After less than a minute of careful shuffling I could feel the draught from the door on my face and hands and moments later I had the lights on.

Finally, there before me was the familiar storeroom, with its shelves of supplies – including the supposedly smuggled cognac – and the two bodies.

At the back of the room I could see the cupboard door I'd opened to get out of the dumb waiter and, to my chagrin, the light switch right beside it. All that stumbling about could have been avoided if only I'd fumbled around for a bit. Heigh-ho.

It was time to take my new knowledge back to the waiting Lady Hardcastle.

I took one more quick look round, but there was nothing fresh to be seen so I went back to the dumb waiter. I switched off the light and stepped into the cupboard, closing the door behind me. I crawled into the lift and held the 'Up' button. I began to ascend.

I passed the kitchen and then, on a whim, turned to the back of the car to try to find the source of the draught I'd felt on the way down. Between the kitchen and the dining room, there was another opening in the lift shaft, on the same side as the entrance to the storeroom. I stopped the lift, lining it up as carefully as I could with the opening, and pushed at the wooden panel. As before, it was a door and it opened into another large space.

This time I took the trouble to hunt for a light switch. It wasn't hard to find and I was soon looking into a small, low-ceilinged room. There was a mattress in one corner with what looked like some women's clothing untidily stuffed into a soldier's kit bag. The rest of the room was reasonably tidy, but some discarded greaseproof paper and an empty beer bottle indicated that someone had stayed here long enough to eat and sleep.

I went in to have a good look round.

I rummaged through the bag and confirmed that it held a woman's outdoor outfit, complete with coat and boots, as well as two pairs of plimsolls – one small enough for me, and one suitable for someone a good bit taller. There was a velvet pouch at the bottom and I drew it out and looked inside.

Well, that answered one question, at least.

Finally, screwed up behind the bag was a man's bloodstained shirt and a rag – exactly as we'd expected we'd find somewhere after we'd examined Everett's body.

After my sensory successes in the storeroom, I sniffed the air, but the delicious aromas of Peggy's cooking masked anything else I might have been able to detect.

With a nod of satisfaction at a job well done, I switched off the light, clambered back into the dumb waiter, closed the door behind me and went up to tell Lady Hardcastle what I'd found.

# Chapter Sixteen

By the time we were changed for dinner, Lady Hardcastle, of course, had figured everything out. Despite my irritation, she, of course, was still refusing to explain it to me.

'Do you know,' she said as I pinned up her hair, 'I can't fathom out why JB is insisting on having this farewell dinner. Two of his guests are dead. Everyone must know by now that both of them were murdered. Everyone knows that one of the others is the murderer—'

'Except the murderer himself,' I said. 'He – or she – knows he's the murderer.'

'Well, quite, and—'

'And who *is* that?'

'Who is what?'

'Who's the murderer?'

'I should have thought it was obvious.'

'Oh, yes, of course. I've known since this afternoon, obviously. But I just wanted you to say it.'

'And I shall. But what I was going to say right now is that no one wants to be here any more. I should have thought we'd be better off with another carpet picnic while we all packed and got ready to scoot off as soon as Vickerman arrives with the boat tomorrow morning.'

'I'll be honest: everything you lot do has always been a mystery to me. Your intimate soirées and your country weekends, your shooting and fishing, your bridge nights and elegant lunches with friends. It's a million miles from how most people live their lives.'

'And you'd think that with all this money and power we'd have freedom to go with it, but we impose ever more vacuous rules on ourselves, tying ourselves up with absurd social rituals.'

'Like getting dressed for dinner instead of telling your best friend the solution to the murder mystery,' I said.

'Exactly like that. It's ridiculous.'

I tutted, shook my head, and tried to think of anything else that might properly express my exasperation, but I knew deep down that I'd just be playing into her hands if I made too much more of a fuss. *Just give her her moment*, I thought.

Down in the library, JB poured us each a gin and tonic with his customary bonhomie, as though there were nothing untoward going on at all.

Patience arrived, dressed in her most extravagantly elegant evening gown yet, and adorned with a perfectly chosen set of matching sapphire jewellery – earrings, necklace, brooch and bracelet.

She asked for: 'Something wild and decadent, JB darling.'

'Coming right up. And here's Gran and Dot. What can I get you folks?'

'What's everyone else drinking?' asked Bridgewater.

'Emily and Florence are having gin and tonic. Patience has asked for something wild but I've not quite decided yet what that might be. I'm thinking maybe I'll get Peggy to send me up an egg and some cocoa powder so I can make her a chocolate cocktail.'

'Oh, I say, that does sound properly decadent,' said Patience. 'What's the booze?'

'Yellow chartreuse.'

'I can hardly wait.'

'Bit too rich for my blood,' said Bridgewater. 'How about a scotch and soda? But don't stint on the scotch.'

'Sure thing. Dotty?'

'I'll have one of those chocolate thingies, if I may – that sounds heavenly.'

The bell was rung; Crawford arrived and was sent away with an order for eggs and cocoa. To my enduring befuddlement, a party atmosphere began to emerge.

Clarice, who by now had learned her way around the fort and was travelling unaccompanied, came in next and ordered an absinthe.

Last to arrive were Wilson and Lily, looking suspiciously flushed and giggly, who both asked for champagne.

So jolly was the mood that I began to wonder if I was the one who was out of step. Despite my years of exposure to the lives of the upper classes, it seemed that I hadn't been exaggerating when I spoke to Lady Hardcastle earlier – I really didn't understand them at all.

By that point in our lives, theft and murder were all in a day's work for me, but I liked to imagine I took things a little more seriously. Obviously I made jokes, but that didn't mean I took matters lightly. Maybe they really didn't care. The world was a better place without Edgar Everett in it, after all. And Patience's life would be improved by the absence of her husband and the addition of the wealth she'd inherit as his widow. The Bridgewaters' futures would be secured without the threat of exposure from Sidwell-Plant, too. As for Lily and Wilson . . . well, they didn't really know any of these people, so what did they care?

Maybe I should just join them and get roaring drunk.

Two – in a couple of cases, three – drinks later, we moved upstairs to the dining room and readied ourselves for the sumptuous feast whose preparation had filled the fort with delicious aromas all afternoon.

JB had been saving some of the finest wines from his cellar for the final night, and we were encouraged to eat, drink and be merry.

'Do you know,' said a decidedly tipsy Patience, 'in spite of everything, I've had rather a jolly time this weekend. Thank you, JB. I mean, obviously it would have involved a little less paperwork if Robert had simply divorced me, but at least I'm free of him now. Please don't any of you feel you have to attend the old buzzard's funeral, but you shall all dance at my wedding. If darling Dr Lamkin will have me. But why wouldn't he? I'm an absolute catch.' She snorted.

Clarice was similarly squiffy. 'I've had a marvellous time, too, darling. And I'm free of my own monster. I just wish I could have seen the look on his nasty face when the narwhal tusk ran him through. I shan't be dancing at your wedding, Patience dear, but I'll happily play for you. A jaunty jig, perhaps.'

'Oh, darling, yes. And my offer still stands: you must come and live at the house with me. We'll have such larks.'

'You know,' said Bridgewater, 'that reminds me of a story. There were these two women—'

A chorus of groans and a well-aimed bread roll from Patience stopped him in his tracks.

'Yes, well, I'm glad everyone is . . . happy,' said Dotty, 'but I still haven't got my blasted ruby necklace back.'

'Oh, bugger the necklace,' said Patience. 'And bugger the brooch. They're just pointless trinkets.'

'Expensive trinkets, Patience darling. We're not all rich widows, you know.' Dotty glanced at Bridgewater. 'Although if he tells just one more of his blasted stories, I might be a widow sooner than he thinks.'

I looked to the end of the table and was slightly relieved to see that Lily and Wilson were as bewildered by all this as I was. More than bewildered, I thought – they were actually uncomfortable.

'What about our sleuthy friends?' asked Patience. 'Have you had a good time?'

I looked at Lady Hardcastle and shrugged. I had no idea how to respond.

'Do you know,' she said, 'I have rather enjoyed myself. I do like a puzzle.'

'Ah, yes, the puzzle. It's a shame you didn't manage to solve it before the police get here tomorrow. It would have been rather satisfying to know which of my friends I should thank for my good fortune. My money would be on Gran.'

'Now, look here,' said Bridgewater, 'I can't pretend my life isn't easier with Robert gone, but . . . the man was my friend once. I couldn't kill him. I thought it was you and Clarice working together.'

Clarice let out a joyous bark of a laugh. 'If only. You've no idea how often I fantasized about doing him in. But it wasn't me. I thought it was JB.'

'Not me,' said JB. 'I didn't kill anyone.'

'No,' said Lady Hardcastle. 'No, you didn't. Of course not. Why would you steal your guests' jewellery and bump two of them off? Self-evidently it was our two young friends at the end of the table. Lily stole the jewels and Wilson got rid of the two thorns in everyone's sides. It's all rather simple really.'

◆ ◆ ◆

'You must be joking,' said Wilson. 'Me? I wasn't anywhere near the fort when they were murdered. I was out walking. You all saw me go out. You all saw me come back. You all know I couldn't have done it.'

'And I wasn't even here when the jewellery went missing,' said Lily.

'All of that appeared for a long time to be entirely true,' said Lady Hardcastle, 'and I confess we were utterly flummoxed. Flummoxed, that is, until this afternoon, when Miss Armstrong and I began to explore some of the nooks and crannies of the fort – the places usually skipped by the official tour.' She reached into the elegant evening bag she'd been carrying and placed two items on the table in front of her. 'Dotty, I believe this is your ruby necklace. And Patience, your diamond brooch.' She passed them across to their owners.

'So how do we know you didn't steal them?' asked Lily. 'You took them and you're worried you're going to get caught, so you're giving them back.'

'Actually, that *is* a satisfying explanation – but, unlike you, we have decent alibis for the thefts and the murders.'

'So do we,' said Wilson. 'Neither of us was anywhere near the place.'

'It certainly appeared that way, but whereas we were seen by more than one person at the time of the various crimes, you're relying on the fact that you were seen leaving before they were committed and returning afterwards. No one saw either of you while the black deeds were being done.'

'Because we weren't there,' insisted Wilson again.

'And that's what was so clever, what so very nearly fooled us. But you *were* there, and we have a witness to prove it. Or, at least, to prove you weren't where you claimed to be.'

'We have witnesses to say we were exactly where we said we were. Peggy saw me leave before Everett was murdered. Patience and Dotty walked with me. Then you saw me come back – you were with Dotty and Clarice in the kitchen. Peggy saw Lily and me go out before Sidwell-Plant was killed and come back afterwards. We weren't anywhere near the fort.'

'And you all saw me arrive the day after the jewels went missing,' said Lily. 'You met me when I arrived on the island on Friday.'

'All true,' agreed Lady Hardcastle. 'But that's only half the story. Only a fraction of the story, actually. If you'll all indulge me a little, I need to go back to some conversations we had. I should have been more suspicious from the start, but why would I doubt friends of JB? When we first met you, Lily, you were introduced as a photographer hired to record the transformation of Guardians Rock from a Tudor fort to a weekend retreat. You and I talked about our mutual love of photography a little later and you described your equipment. You said you have a Graflex Speed Graphic with an f/2.9 lens, yes?'

Lily looked doubtful for the first time. 'Yes?'

'I've had my eye on the Graflex for a little while and it doesn't have a lens anywhere near that fast. I let it pass, but later events made me wonder if you might not be all you seem, especially when I realized I'd not once seen you with a camera in your hands. You, too, Mr Wilson, may not be all you seem. It might be that you have an interest in antiquities, but you claim not to have been to the fort before and to know nothing about it.'

'It's true,' said Wilson. 'First time I've been here.'

'I can't prove it's not,' said Lady Hardcastle, 'but when we were talking about the electricity generator, you seemed to know an awful lot about the construction of its shed.'

'JB told me. You know what he's like.'

'I do. And he might have. But these little discrepancies from both of you began to ring alarm bells when combined with something Miss Armstrong discovered this afternoon. Florence?'

'Oh. Yes,' I said. 'The dumb waiter. You've all been as impressed as I am by the dumb waiter. A wonderful invention. Very popular in America, I believe. You've seen it here in the dining room as Crawford lifts out crockery and dishes of delicious food, but you probably haven't noticed that the car itself – the box that goes up and down from the kitchen to here – is a good deal larger than it appears. In here it looks about the size of the kitchen cupboard in a small flat. But the box is actually huge and there's an opening on the floor above us that's big enough for a person to get inside. So I did. And it turns out the lift goes from the wood-panelled corridor on the second floor all the way down to the outside storeroom. Which you'd expect, really, wouldn't you? It's handy to have a way of getting supplies up from the store as well as getting food up to the dining room. And being able to lift other heavy or bulky items up to the second floor must be a real boon. So that all made perfect sense. What I wasn't expecting, though, was the secret mezzanine room between the kitchen and the dining room.'

Now Lily looked positively anxious.

'It was there that I found a set of outdoor clothes in Lily's size, along with a pair of plimsolls that I believe would also fit her, a pair of the same soft shoes that would fit Mr Wilson, and the jewels that Lady Hardcastle has just returned to their owners. I also found a blood-stained shirt in Mr Wilson's size – the one the killer was wearing when he moved Everett's body from the long gallery to the storeroom on the second floor.'

'That doesn't prove anything,' said Lily.

'Or disprove either of our stories,' said Wilson.

'Your stories, yes,' said Lady Hardcastle. 'Let's get back to the stories, shall we? I have alternatives for all three. We'll start with Lily arriving on Friday. Now that we know one can get from the outside storeroom to the mezzanine room without going into the fort, it seemed possible to me that Lily could have arrived secretly on Thursday with the supplies and hidden herself away before any of the rest of us got here. We don't know anything about Vickerman the Fisherman, but I doubt he'd be above taking a few bob to make an additional human delivery along with the food and wine. She made herself comfortable – Florence found a mattress and the remains of a packed lunch – and waited until the evening. Once dinner was done – she'd have known dinner was over by the sounds coming from the kitchen below her hiding place, and because the dumb waiter had finally stopped going up and down – she took that same dumb waiter up to the second floor and let herself out into the corridor there. We were all down on the ground floor in the library so she would have had the run of the place. Even if she didn't know for certain that Dotty and Patience would have valuable pieces with them, it was a fair bet that some of us would have. So she took a couple of the priciest items and scurried back to her hidey-hole.'

'All nonsense,' said Lily. 'I arrived on Friday. You saw me.'

'We did. Clarice, what did you tell me about Lily's arrival?'

'I said her clothes smelled of fish stew,' said Clarice.

'Which you didn't mention out of politeness – she had, apparently, just arrived on Vickerman's fishing boat after all, so perhaps it was that. But what did we eat on Thursday evening?'

'Bouillabaisse,' said Patience. 'It was delicious.'

'Indeed. Clarice, was the smell bouillabaisse or just fish?'

'Definitely the stew. There was garlic, fennel, onions—'

'Thank you, dear,' said Lady Hardcastle. 'Now, the mezzanine room isn't quite above the kitchen, but it does seem to trap the smells, doesn't it, Florence.'

'Definitely,' I said. 'I couldn't smell anything in there this afternoon apart from tonight's dinner.'

'So what simpler explanation could there be for the smell of bouillabaisse on Lily's clothes than that she and her clothes had spent the night in the room above the kitchen?'

All eyes were on Lily now.

'So let's move on to Wilson's stories,' said Lady Hardcastle. 'Clarice, do you have a cold?'

'No?'

'But I distinctly remember you sniffing when Wilson came back in from his walk on Friday afternoon. I thought you might have a sniffle.'

Realization began to dawn on Clarice. 'Ah, no. I was puzzled by something, that's all, so I tried to get a better whiff.'

'Puzzled by what?'

'You remember I said that people smell different when they've been outside in the cold? You can sense the coldness and smell an outdoor freshness on their clothes. It doesn't last long, but the longer they've been out, the stronger the effect. Wilson didn't smell of the outdoors when he came back from his walk, he smelled faintly of cooking. Actually, he and Lily didn't smell of the outdoors when they came into the library after their long walk on Sunday, either. Barely any fresh air smell at all. On Sunday it could have been that too much time had passed and the scent of outdoors had gone, mind you.'

'Thank you,' said Lady Hardcastle. 'So here's my alternative for both those stories. We were all going about our business, moving between rooms, chatting in little groups, when Wilson announced that he was going for a walk. We heard him go and get his coat and boots, then we heard him talking to Peggy in the kitchen. Peggy remembers seeing him leave through the kitchen door. Patience and Dotty joined him briefly and saw him set off, but then doubled back because it was too cold for them. The official version is that he then went for a long walk and sat in the grotto with his thoughts, then returned to the kitchen, where he was seen by me, Florence, Dotty, Clarice and Peggy before going back to his room to change. But I don't think that's what happened at all. I think he waited until Patience and Dotty were safely inside, then went into the storeroom, where he summoned the dumb waiter and rode it up to the mezzanine room. He took off his coat and changed his boots for plimsolls, then he waited. Just before three, he took the lift up to the second floor and slipped quietly down the stairs to the long gallery to wait for Everett.'

'No, wait a moment,' said Bridgewater. 'How did he know Everett would be there?'

'Oh, you'll like this part,' said Lady Hardcastle. 'Everett had a note in his pocket telling him to meet the sender in the long gallery at three. It was signed "GB".'

'Well, I'll be—'

'Quite. But we'll get to the notes in a moment – there was another on Sidwell-Plant's body, you see, and I want to cover them both together. When Everett arrived in the long gallery, he might have been a little surprised to see Wilson, but perhaps he thought Wilson had been summoned there, too. Whatever he thought, he wouldn't have been expecting Wilson to run him through with the narwhal tusk. With the dreadful deed done, Wilson carried Everett's body upstairs and hid both it and the murder weapon in one of the box rooms on the second floor. Then he returned to the mezzanine room to wait until enough time had passed to put him completely in the clear. He dressed once more for outdoors and then reversed his journey down in the dumb waiter, out through the storeroom and back into the kitchen, to be seen by a great many more witnesses than he could possibly have hoped for.'

'Bilge,' said Wilson.

'We'll see,' said Lady Hardcastle. 'On Sunday, Wilson and Lily performed the same going-out-for-a-walk act, having played the part of couple-reluctantly-forced-together-by-an-impish-host so well. We all heard them go out, and then all saw them come back. It didn't matter that they didn't have so many witnesses that time, because we all just expected that what had happened on Friday had happened again: Wilson had gone for a long walk – this time with Lily – and had come back some time later. But, as before, they didn't do anything of the sort. This time they both went up to the mezzanine room, where Lily waited while Wilson went up to the second floor and then walked in his soft-soled shoes—'

'I heard him pass my door,' said Clarice.

'You did. He went first to the long gallery to take one of JB's knives. Then walked past your door to the Bridgewaters' room, where he waited for Sidwell-Plant, who had been summoned to a meeting by another note signed "GB".'

'Of all the damn nerve,' said Bridgewater.

'Wilson stabbed Sidwell-Plant, but this time he left the body where it fell – all the better to implicate Bridgewater, one presumes – then retraced his route back to Lily in the mezzanine room. They bided their time in their hiding place, then came back through the kitchen like young lovers returning from a first walk. I've not said so already, but another of my presumptions is that Lily and Wilson were lovers long before this weekend. But that's by the by. So, anyway, they pulled their little dumb-waiter trick and, hey presto, they had alibis for all the crimes and now the finger of blame points squarely at GB, who summoned both victims – for want of a less melodramatic way of putting it – to their appointments with death.'

No one said anything for a few moments.

'That's all well and good,' said Patience eventually, 'but why on earth would they do such a thing?'

'This is what troubled Florence and me for quite some time. Between you, you all had decent motives for at least one of the crimes, but Wilson and Lily were just bystanders. Patience, you were incensed by Everett's bullying, Clarice was the victim of that maltreatment – you might both have wanted Everett dead. Patience, you wanted to be free of your loveless marriage, so you could easily have wanted Sidwell-Plant dead. Bridgewater, you knew Sidwell-Plant was going to blow the gaff on your embezzlement from JB's many accounts—'

'Now look here,' blustered Bridgewater.

'—and so silencing him would save your job and your wealth. The same thing gave you a motive, Dotty, and both of you would benefit from the insurance pay-out from the stolen jewels. But Wilson and Lily? It wasn't until I remembered all those things about them not being who they seemed that I began to wonder, but I still couldn't put it all together.'

There was a familiar snickety-click from the end of the table, and I turned to see JB holding an intricately engraved, pearl-handled Colt Peacemaker revolver.

He was pointing it towards Wilson and Lily.

'I knew you two would figure it out for us,' he said. 'Thank you, Emily and Florence. Now, what say you varmints – I've always wanted to call someone a varmint, must-a read one too many penny dreadfuls over the years . . . What say you two varmints put your hands on the table where we can see them, while Robert and Granville fetch some rope so we can tie you up till the police get here.'

'Just a moment,' said Lady Hardcastle. 'I haven't quite finished.'

'Sure you have,' said JB. 'You've explained it all just right. These two stole the jewellery and murdered Everett and Sidwell-Plant. It all makes perfect sense.'

'Well, you see, dear, it does and it doesn't. All weekend it's been obvious that this is a bit of a mismatched group. You have your old friends – your business pals and your musicians. But then you also invited these two frauds' – she pointed at Wilson and Lily – 'and us.' She indicated herself and me. 'You had an explanation for Wilson – he was looking for a piece for your collection. Lily was here to take photographs – although, as I say, I never once saw her with a camera in her hands. But what about us? Why were Florence and I invited this weekend? We've known you for a while, it's true, and you definitely wanted to show off your new place to get thoughts on its potential as a hotel, but why this weekend in particular? Why bring us with this group and not with people we already knew from the rest of your wide circle of friends? And then it dawned on me: we have a reputation for solving murders. We've been involved in many cases over the past few years so we have more experience than most. You knew of our relationship with the Bristol police and our friendship with the police surgeon there. We were invited because we knew enough about murder to be able to estimate the time of death. Wilson's alibi only works because we know when both men were killed. It's only because we were able to say that Everett died at three on Friday and Sidwell-Plant at four on Sunday that Wilson was in the clear. We were encouraged to investigate further, but I suspect he imagined his plan so well thought out that we'd never crack it – the important thing was our confirmation of the time of death. Without our testimony, the blame couldn't be laid at Bridgewater's door, could it, JB?'

'Well, I must say, I deeply regret underestimating you, my dear,' said JB. 'I thought I had it all figured out.'

'Wait,' said Bridgewater. 'You mean JB is behind all this?'

'I rather fear so,' said Lady Hardcastle. 'I said that Sidwell-Plant knew about your embezzlement, but he knew a great deal more about JB's accounts than he ever let on. JB, I believe, is very close to bankruptcy. It's supposition at this point, but when you add the fact that the Crawfords haven't been paid for a few months – we overheard them when we went out for our walk yesterday – to what everyone's been saying about how keen JB is that this hotel plan should be a success, it's not a massive leap to suppose that he has very little free cash and that everything is tied up in this venture. I can't prove it—'

'Oh, I can,' said Patience. 'There's a copy of the accounts in our safe at home.'

'Make sure the police get them, dear. Do you remember what he said in the long gallery on that first day when we were talking about how tidy everything was? He said, "I can't stand mess and disorder. I have to straighten everything up, 'sort it all out' as you fellas say." He needed to sort everything out. He knew Everett was a bullying monster – you all did. He needed sorting out. He knew Bridgewater was embezzling and he knew Sidwell-Plant was about to turn him in. And he couldn't have that – he couldn't have a scandal ruining the neatness of his business affairs. So he hired Wilson and his girlfriend—'

'Wife,' said Lily.

'I do beg your pardon, dear. He hired Mr and Mrs Wilson – presumably not their real names – to come and clean up for him. He knew well that payments from his accounts could be scrutinized and traced, so he offered payment in the form of jewellery which could be stolen from his solicitor and accountant. He loves Clarice like a daughter and couldn't bear to see her so mistreated, so Everett had to go. Sidwell-Plant was going to cause a scandal, so he had to go, too. But Bridgewater had to face punishment for the embezzlement somehow, so why not implicate him in the murder of his friends and let him hang? Even if Wilson was as ignorant of the fort as he claims, JB could have told them about the dumb waiter and the mezzanine room and explained how they could be used to commit the crimes. I wonder if the Wilsons were supposed to slip away before the police got here. They had decent alibis – backed up by Florence and me – and the local police would surely swallow the ham-fisted evidence of the notes found on the bodies. But the storm put paid to that and here we all are.'

'That's all very well,' said Patience, 'but how would that help the business? Surely theft and murder would be just as big a scandal as accounting fraud.'

'Just as big, but a great deal more glamorous,' said Lady Hardcastle. 'We've learned over recent years that the public absolutely loves a murder. The minor scandal of a boring old fraud would turn his target market against him, but stolen jewels and a couple of murders? People would flock to Guardians Rock to see where it had all happened.'

'Well,' said JB, 'it looks like I really did underestimate you.' He turned the gun towards me and Lady Hardcastle.

I tried really hard not to sigh. Villains expect terror and obedience when they begin waving weapons about, so weary insouciance tends to irritate them and I try to keep it in check if I can. But. I mean. Really.

I looked around at my fellow diners. Obviously Lily and Wilson were quite pleased with themselves. With their employer now back in charge after a brief attempt at disruption by Lady Hardcastle, they might get away with it after all.

The Bridgewaters were staring nervously at their plates. Clarice had her head cocked, listening for any sounds that might tell her what was going on.

Patience, who had been picking up another bread roll when the revolver appeared, was looking at me. She flicked her eyes towards JB. I hoped with all my heart that she wasn't planning something foolhardy.

Lady Hardcastle made no attempt not to sigh. 'Honestly, JB, how does this help? The game is over, the jig is up. Do you plan to shoot us all?'

'I haven't decided yet,' said JB, 'but I'm pretty certain I won't have to. I'm going to have to take out you two smart alecs, of course. But Patience will keep her mouth shut if she wants to keep hold of her money. Clarice will come around to the idea that I arranged things out of a fatherly love for her, so she'll keep quiet, too. Dotty . . . well, no one will believe Dotty Dorothy, the village simpleton. I reckon I can turn things around.' He waved the gun. 'You know, this beautiful revolver was made for me at the instruction of Samuel Colt himself. He gave it to my father as a christening gift for his firstborn son, and when I came of age, my father gave it to me—'

'I know one isn't supposed to interrupt the villain of the play when he's making his climactic speech, JB dear,' said Lady Hardcastle, 'but that's a Colt Single Action Army revolver, first made in 1873. From the look of it, that one is a much later model – I'd say 1890s at the earliest. You were born, if memory serves, in 1851, and Mr Colt died, I believe, in '62, so no part of your story can possibly be true.'

'And yet it's the story I tell. And if I tell the story, then the people I control will believe the story and defend the story. The truth is whatever I decide it will be. The investigation will be perfunctory and our story will be swallowed whole by the police, the press and the country at large. Like you say: people will lap it up. We'll be booked solid for years to come.'

'I foresee a slight problem with your plan,' said Bridgewater. 'You see, you're not the only one here who's armed.' He produced a nickel-plated pistol from beneath the table. 'I have this spiffing little Colt 1911. Put your peashooter down and we'll have no more talk of massacres.'

JB levelled his own gun at Dotty. 'I have a better idea. Why don't you put *your* peashooter down and we'll have no more talk of me spraying your beloved wife's brains all over my newly decorated dining room. Assuming the bullet can find any brains in there, of course.'

'I say,' said Dotty, 'there's no call for that.'

JB laughed. It was a proper, eyes-closed, head-thrown-back guffaw, and it afforded Patience the perfect opportunity to fling her bread roll at his face.

It did him no harm, of course, but it distracted him sufficiently that I was able to pick up the table knife from beside my plate and throw it into his chest.

That really got his attention, and he turned the gun back to me. 'You little bi—'

A Colt pistol makes a terrifyingly loud noise in a small room, but it was oddly reassuring – if I'd heard the sound and was able to be mentally complaining about it, I wasn't dead.

Nor was JB, but he wasn't at all well. With a knife in his chest and a bullet wound in his shoulder, he looked as though he might soon go into shock. He dropped his gun on the table and Lady Hardcastle quickly scooped it up before standing and rushing to JB's end of the table. She laid him down and began to administer first aid.

'Can I have napkins, please,' she said. 'The bullet went straight through but it's made a bit of a mess – I need to stop the bleeding.' She looked at the knife. 'That didn't go in very deep, dear.'

'I just wanted to startle him,' I said. 'I didn't throw it hard enough to kill him.'

She pulled the knife out, and JB seemed not to notice.

'Is it safe to do that?' said Patience. 'I thought you weren't supposed to pull knives out.'

'It's fine,' said Lady Hardcastle. 'It barely pierced the skin. My Flossie knows what she's doing.' She applied pressure to JB's shoulder and the bleeding seemed to be slowing. 'While I'm doing this, can somebody stop those two, please?'

Amid all this confusion, Wilson and Lily were attempting to make a break for the dining room door, but Clarice had the situation in hand. With the timing of a virtuoso musician, she swept her cane behind her chair and tripped Wilson as he tried to run past her. Lily fell over him and the fight went out of them both once they saw Bridgewater's pistol pointing at them.

'Dotty, my angel,' he said, 'there are shackles and chains in JB's collection in the long gallery. I fancy I saw some darbies in there, too. Would you be an absolute poppet and fetch them for me. Let's secure these scoundrels before they get up to any more mischief.'

Dotty stood and placed her napkin neatly on the table. 'Of course, darling. I'll be back in a jiffy.'

# Chapter Seventeen

Lady Hardcastle managed to stabilize JB and, with a first-aid kit supplied by Crawford, properly dressed his wounds. We carried him to his bed, and Lady Hardcastle, Dotty and Patience took turns in sitting with him to make sure he stayed fit enough to stand trial.

Meanwhile, we locked Wilson and Lily in their rooms – still bound in the shackles Dotty had found, of course – and Bridgewater and I stood watch in the corridor in two-hour shifts just in case.

Having been given the details of the events she'd not been able to see in the dining room – though she had surmised most of it for herself – Clarice had retired to her room and was the only one of us to get a full night's sleep.

Apart from the Crawfords, of course, who carried on as though nothing out of the ordinary had happened.

Breakfast was served as usual at eight o'clock. After a brief conference, it was agreed that we could leave the Wilsons unattended – if they were shackled and locked in rooms in a Tudor fort, they weren't going to go anywhere – and that Patience would keep an eye on JB while the other two ate with the rest of us.

And so Bridgewater, Dotty, Clarice, Lady Hardcastle and I met in the dining room and helped ourselves to the usual delicious selection of food.

'There's something that's been bothering me, Gran darling,' said Clarice as she tucked in to the sausage and egg sandwich I'd made for her.

'Just the one thing?' said Bridgewater. 'You're doing far better than I, old girl. I don't think I've ever been so befuddled.'

'Well, quite. I always felt it was your natural state. But in your perpetual befuddlement, you still managed to bring a gun to dinner. What on earth made you think of that?'

Bridgewater laughed. 'Nothing more than self-preservation. Everett was dead, my friend was dead, and the culprit was still among us. Who knew which of us might be next. I didn't want Dotty or me to be run through with any more of JB's vicious knick-knacks so I pinched one of his guns and some ammunition and slipped it in my pocket. At least it would give us a fighting chance.'

'It certainly did,' said Lady Hardcastle. 'Well done, you.'

'And well done, you,' said Dotty. 'You worked out what was going on and saved the day.'

'I almost got us all killed in the process, though, let's not forget. I really should have considered the possibility that JB would try to do us all in. One gets so used to having the rozzers about at moments like that that one forgets killers are apt to try to kill again when they're cornered.'

'I just wish I'd seen it,' said Clarice. 'But then I wish I could see anything at all. Good to know my friends are looking out for me.'

'Always, old thing,' said Bridgewater, and patted her on the arm.

'What happens now?' asked Dotty.

'I spoke to Crawford and he said Vickerman is due at ten. I thought one of us could go straight back to the mainland with him to fetch the police, and then they could take it from there.

We should be away and on our way back to our homes by late afternoon, all being well.'

'What will happen to the Crawfords?' asked Clarice.

'I was about to say that I have power of attorney over JB's affairs and that I'd take care of them,' said Bridgewater, 'but I'm about to be arrested, too, I don't doubt. Still, they're paid through one of JB's many trusts so they'll still be employed. I suppose it's up to them what they do.'

'They'll probably want to stay on for as long as they can,' I said. 'I think they've got a lucrative smuggling business going on here.'

'Then *they* should be arrested, too,' said Dotty, indignantly.

'We've no proof,' I said. 'It's mere conjecture on my part.'

'Is there proof of *your* impropriety, Granville?' said Lady Hardcastle.

'If one knows where to look,' he said, wearily. 'I covered my tracks well, but a skilled accountant – someone like RVSP, for instance – would be able to find it.'

'But without such expert testimony, it would just be your word against JB's?'

'For the time being, yes.'

'It's entirely a matter for you, dear, but in your shoes I should be inclined to ponder the moral position as well as the strictly legal. Is it always wrong to steal from a criminal? Is there a sense in which he might – morally, at least – now owe you a significant sum in reparation for planning to see you hang for crimes he had commissioned others to commit? I'm no lawyer, and no moral philosopher, but it's food for thought . . .'

'I certainly won't say anything,' said Clarice.

We finished breakfast and agreed that it would be best if Patience, Lady Hardcastle and I went down to the dock to meet Vickerman and his boat. Dotty and Bridgewater would keep an eye on the prisoners, and Clarice could make more jokes about not being able to keep an eye on anything. It seemed like a sensible division of labour.

I was sent to the cliff at the entrance to the tiny harbour from where I was to try to attract Vickerman's attention and warn him of the sunken obstruction a few yards from the jetty. We had taken a good look and decided there was plenty of room for him to dock, but it was plain that if he just came barrelling in as though everything were normal, we'd have two sunken boats in the bay and still no way of getting home.

I saw the little fishing boat from some way out but withheld my waving until Vickerman was within hailing distance. As he drew nearer I could see that he was not alone and that one of the two men accompanying him appeared to be dressed in a policeman's uniform.

*That's handy*, I thought.

When I judged the boat close enough that Vickerman might hear me, I managed to attract his attention and he acknowledged my shouted warning by slowing down and turning carefully as he rounded the cliffs to enter the bay.

As he slowly eased into place, I scurried down to join Lady Hardcastle and Patience on the quayside.

We helped secure the boat's lines before Vickerman and his two guests hopped ashore.

'JB not about?' asked Vickerman as he checked our rope work.

'He's in the fort,' said Lady Hardcastle.

He indicated the uniformed policeman and his plain-clothes companion. 'I see. Only I got these two fellas with me and they wants a word about two of his weekend guests.'

The man in the suit and raincoat raised his hat to Lady Hardcastle. 'Inspector Ellis, madam. And this is Sergeant Satterly. Are you Mrs McIntyre?'

'I'm Lady Hardcastle and these are Mrs Sidwell-Plant and Miss Armstrong. We're guests of Mr McIntyre.'

'Ah, so you're Lady Hardcastle, are you? I was hoping I might bump into you. I've been liaising on a case with one of my fellow officers in Bristol, an Inspector Sunderland. I believe you two are acquainted.'

'I should like to think we were good friends, yes.'

'Excellent. He said you would be a useful ally and that I would be well advised to trust your judgement.'

Lady Hardcastle smiled. 'Well, that was very kind of him, I must say. But why were you talking to him and why did my name come up?'

'Both your names, actually. He also said Miss Armstrong would be handy in a scrap, but I confess I didn't quite know what to make of that. Nevertheless, I've been talking to forces in Manchester, London, Leeds and Bristol about a couple of villains we've been tracking after a job they did up Exeter. Con merchants and thieves they are, and they're wanted on suspicion of at least one murder. Guy and Susan Walker.'

'I think we have them with us,' said Lady Hardcastle, 'though we know them as George Wilson and Lily Thacker.'

The inspector consulted his notebook. 'Yes, that's them. They used those aliases in Leeds. They're up at the fort, you say?'

'They are.'

'I see. Well, they're dangerous individuals, so I think you'd better wait down here while Sergeant Satterly and I go up and speak to them. Where will we find them?'

'They're shackled, and locked in their rooms. I don't think they'll be any trouble.'

He looked puzzled.

'It's a long story, Inspector. We'll walk up with you and explain on the way.' She turned back to Vickerman. 'And you need to have a word with Peggy and Crawford, dear. I think they've got something for you.'

We walked up to the fort together and, between the three of us, told Inspector Ellis the story of the weekend.

◆ ◆ ◆

We came in through the main door and Vickerman went across the hall to the servants' quarters.

The inspector nodded towards him as he went. 'Anything we should know about there?'

'No,' said Lady Hardcastle. 'Just a private matter among friends.'

'He's a sly one, that Tommy Vickerman, mind,' said the sergeant. 'I've lost count of how many times we've had him in our cells over one thing or another.'

'It's all fine, honestly. Now the . . . what did you say their real names were? The Welshes?'

'The Walkers, m'lady,' said the inspector.

'Ah yes, do forgive me. The Walkers are up here on the first floor. Mr Bridgewater has been keeping an eye on them. Everything all right, Mr B?'

'Quiet as church mice, Lady H,' said Bridgewater with a cheery wink. 'They both took some breakfast about half an hour ago and gave me a mouthful of abuse for my troubles, but they've been good as gold since then.'

Bridgewater unlocked Wilson's door and let the inspector and the sergeant in while we all waited outside.

'How's the patient?' asked Lady Hardcastle.

'Dot says he's in a considerable amount of pain, but I can't say I'm at all unhappy about that,' said Bridgewater. 'Serves the blighter right, I say.'

'Well, quite. I'm sure they'll let him have some morphine when he gets to the hospital at Plymouth.'

'Will they? That's a shame. Ah, well. Can't be helped, eh?'

A short while later, the two policemen emerged and asked to be let into Lily's room.

We made small talk while we waited, and at length the two men reappeared.

'They're not admitting to anything, as is their right, I suppose, but they've both been formally arrested and we'll be taking them into custody as soon as we've spoken to Mr McIntyre. Where's he?'

I stayed with Bridgewater while Lady Hardcastle showed the policemen the way to JB's room and we discussed the possibility of actually making it home before Wednesday. At the rate things were going, I wasn't hopeful but, despite everything, Bridgewater was a cheerful optimist and was absolutely convinced he'd be back in his own bed before the clock struck midnight.

Lady Hardcastle returned with Inspector Ellis and Dotty.

'I can see we're going to have the usual trouble with those three,' said the inspector. 'They're all blaming each other, but that's what crooks tend to do in my experience. We'll have the truth out of them, though, don't you worry.' He drew his watch from his waistcoat pocket and consulted it. 'I put in a request to the Coastguard at Plymouth before we set off this morning, asking them to send a boat and some men over to Guardians Rock. They had some business to attend to first, but the commander assured me he would have someone with us by midday. So I propose we all have a nice cup of tea while the sergeant and I take your statements, then we'll take care of the suspects and the . . . er . . . the bodies – begging your pardon, ladies – and Vickerman can take you back to the mainland. If all goes well you should be in time to catch the afternoon train to Plymouth.'

◆ ◆ ◆

By half past twelve, a charming coastguard lieutenant and his men had secured the prisoners aboard his launch, along with the bodies of Everett and Sidwell-Plant.

Lady Hardcastle and Bridgewater had a long chat with the Crawfords, who were, as predicted, rather keen to stay on at the fort even in the absence of their employer. Vickerman assured them that he knew a man who could salvage and repair JB's diesel yacht, and Bridgewater offered them the job of caretakers until . . . Actually, he put no time limit on it. JB might wriggle free of the accusations but it was unlikely he'd return to the fort. Then again, he might swing for his part in the murders, in which case his trusts would be wound up and the monies and properties disbursed according to the terms of his will. Whatever happened, Bridgewater controlled the purse strings and was perfectly happy to let them stay and take care of the place.

'It'd make a lovely hotel,' said Peggy once he'd explained everything.

Bridgewater laughed. 'Do you know, I rather think it would. Let's let the legal matters play out and then I shall put it to the board.'

'Thank you, sir. I've always fancied runnin' a nice little hotel somewhere.'

'It's a splendid idea, Mrs C, and you and Mr C would make the perfect managers. Leave it with me.'

With Crawford's help, Vickerman managed to get everyone's luggage aboard his little fishing boat and the six of us crammed ourselves in among the nets, lobster pots and four cases of cognac as Crawford untied the lines and waved us off.

'Do you have any suggestions for how we might get to the railway station?' asked Lady Hardcastle as the little boat swished through the choppy water.

'Don't you worry about that, m'lady,' said Vickerman. 'Old Jethro'll come and pick you up. Him and Jemima was the ones what brought you from the station t'other day. His cart's big enough for all of you if you don't mind squashin' together.'

'I'm sure we won't mind, but will Jethro?'

Vickerman flicked a glance towards the cognac and winked. 'Any friend of Jago Crawford is a friend of ours, m'lady. We'll see you right.'

Clarice was sitting with her back to the gunwale, a happy grin on her face and her violin case clasped tightly to her chest.

I sat beside her. 'What will you do now?'

'In the long term? I don't know. I shall carry on performing, I imagine. The world is full of accompanists and I can't imagine not playing. I say, I don't suppose your pal would like a job?'

'Oh, you can do much better than her – she'd drive you mad in no time.'

'And you couldn't live without her, could you? I hear it in your voices.'

'You might be right.'

She chuckled. 'And in the short term, I'm taking Patience up on her offer of a room at her London place.'

Patience had heard us. 'We'll have the jolliest time. Two single ladies razzling about the town.'

'We know a few rather degenerate nightclubs if you want a properly debauched evening or two,' said Lady Hardcastle. 'Oh, and we can introduce you to some ragtime musicians if you ever fancy a change of pace from the classical repertoire.'

'I might take you up on that,' said Clarice. 'I enjoyed playing with you.'

The Bridgewaters kept to themselves on the crossing, but by the time we were all disembarked and waiting outside Vickerman's cottage for Jethro's cart, they seemed to have settled things between them and their customary bonhomie returned.

Bridgewater looked at his watch. 'By the time we get to Plymouth I think we'll all be too late for trains to London and Bristol. What say I try to sweet-talk the stationmaster into letting me use his telephone so I can try to get us some rooms in the city? We can have supper together and then go our separate ways in the morning.'

Everyone agreed.

'Marvellous. So, there were six travellers on the road to . . .'

After a surprisingly convivial supper in Plymouth, we all retired to the neighbouring rooms Bridgewater had managed to book for us in a rather nice hotel.

The following morning, the whole group had made our way to the railway station together to catch our trains and only then realized that we'd all be on the same one – the train for London Paddington would be stopping at Bristol Temple Meads, where Lady Hardcastle and I would leave them so we could catch the local line to Chipping Bevington.

We couldn't find a compartment with enough seats for all six of us, but by happy chance the steward was our old friend Pearson, who was happy to see us and was kind enough to arrange a large table for us in the restaurant car so that at least we could have lunch together.

We sat down to eat shortly after stopping at Exeter St Davids, and I soon saw a familiar figure hovering around near the restaurant door.

I beckoned Pearson over. 'Do you see that gentleman at the end of the carriage?'

'I do, miss. Isn't he the one who shared your table last week?'

'He is. We have room for one more if he wants to dine with us. My companions won't mind.'

I honestly had no idea whether my companions would mind, nor did I much care – a chap has to eat.

Pearson made his way adroitly along the moving carriage and spoke to the man. I saw the smile of recognition and the tentative wave as Pearson explained my proposal, then the two men came back to the table.

'I hope you don't mind,' I said to the group, 'but this is our old friend Mr Dymond and I've invited him to eat with us.'

'Not at all, dear boy,' said Bridgewater jovially. 'The more the merrier, what?'

'It's more a case of whether you'll mind dining with *us*,' said Clarice. 'We're an appalling bunch.'

'Quite dreadful,' said Patience. 'Sit yourself down. Mr Dymond, is it?'

'It is,' said Dymond. 'Like the jewel but with a Y.'

'Splendid, splendid,' said Bridgewater. 'I suppose it falls to me to make the introductions. I'm Bridgewater, and this is my lovely wife. Then there's Lady Hardcastle and Miss Armstrong, but I gather you already know them. Then we have Mrs Sidwell-Plant, and Mrs Everett.'

Dymond looked open-mouthed at Clarice. 'Mrs Clarice Everett? The violinist?'

'The very same,' said Clarice.

'What an honour. I'm a great admirer of your work. One of my most treasured memories is of a recital you performed at the Royal Albert Hall last year. You were spellbinding.'

'You're very kind to say so. Thank you.'

'How was your weekend, Mr Dymond?' asked Lady Hardcastle.

'Very enjoyable, thank you. My friend was greatly impressed by my *Titanic* Bear and the two American examples he recently acquired were simply marvellous. As promised, he let me have one, so I'm taking him back with *Titanic*.'

'Oh my goodness,' said Patience, 'do you have a *Titanic* Bear? I adore Steiff bears. I have three, but not the *Titanic*. Clarice, darling, you'd love them.'

'I'm sure they look charming,' said Clarice.

'Oh, you goose. I meant you'd love the feel of them – they *feel* wonderful. The fur is so soft and comforting.'

Dymond beamed. 'It's rare to meet a fellow arctophile. I usually brace myself for mockery and incomprehension.'

'Not at all,' said Patience. 'I adore toy bears.'

'Or teddy bears, as the Americans call them,' said Dymond. 'Speaking of which, how did your weekend with your American host go? I got the impression from Lady Hardcastle and Miss Armstrong that it had the potential to be quite an exciting weekend.'

There was the briefest of silences around the table before everyone began laughing.

As the laughter subsided, Bridgewater held up his hand for calm. 'You'll have to forgive us, dear boy. No mockery intended. But it has been quite the weekend. It all began on Thursday afternoon, d'you see . . .'

◆ ◆ ◆

We had telephoned the house from Plymouth station to let Edna the housekeeper know we would be returning later, and although she and Miss Jones, the cook, had gone home for the day, they had left food for us and made sure there was fresh milk and bread in the larder.

By the time the cabman had finished hauling our luggage into the hall, I had the kettle on and Lady Hardcastle was in the sitting room going through the post.

I brought the tea tray through. 'Any invitations to country house weekends in there?'

'Not yet, dear, no.'

'If you come across any, do turn them down, won't you.'

She laughed. 'Absolutely. But you're safe for now. So far I have a bill from the vintner, a bill from our dressmaker, and a letter from my brother.'

'How is he? Oh, and how is Lavinia?'

'He seems well, though he makes uncomplimentary comparisons between her and assorted large animals – notably the hippo. But the doctor says she's in fine form, as is the baby, and that all is exactly as it should be for a woman who's seven months along.'

'Another niece or nephew for you to corrupt by the middle of April, then.'

'I do hope so. It's a pity he or she won't be with us when we go up for your birthday treat.'

'It just gives us an excuse for another trip to London later in the spring.'

'I suppose so.' She put down her letters. 'I don't know about you, but I could do with being in the company of people who aren't trying to defraud each other, steal from each other, murder each other, fit each other up for those murders, or generally pretend to be that which they are not. Shall we go to the pub?'

'Will we find anyone like that there?'

'Perhaps not, but they'll be our friends and we'll forgive them their foibles.'

And so we put our hats and coats back on and set off down the chilly lane to the village green and the Dog and Duck.

Loud, smoky and a little bit dishevelled. And the pub wasn't in great shape, either.

My friend Daisy was behind the bar, wiping glasses with a suspect tea towel.

'Evenin', ladies, what can I get you?'

'I'll have a brandy, I think,' said Lady Hardcastle.

I nodded. 'Me too, please.'

Daisy began fussing with the glasses. 'It's lovely to see you both. We was expectin' to see you yesterday, though, to tell the truth. How was your swanky weekend away?'

'Absolutely marvellous, Daisy dear,' said Lady Hardcastle. 'Though I confess I should prefer to go to Devonshire in the summertime if we visit again. It was more than a little nippy.'

'I can imagine. We 'ad a bit of a storm here Saturday – took some roof tiles off our ma's next-door neighbour's house.'

'Was anyone hurt?'

'Nooo – they's all right. Bedroom got a bit damp but it weren't nothin' a bucket couldn't take care of. Sam Hardiman come round and fixed it yesterday mornin'.'

'No other damage?'

'None as I know of. Few branches blown down, that sort of thing. But I wants to know about this fort you went to. What was it like? What did you get up to?'

'Oh, you know,' I said. 'The usual.'

# Author's Notes

The island and fortress are fictitious but are inspired by Lindisfarne Castle on Holy Island in Northumberland. That castle was built in 1549, partly using stone from the dissolved Lindisfarne Priory, as a strategic defence against the Scots. It served many purposes in the intervening centuries until it was bought by Edward Hudson, owner of *Country Life* magazine, in 1901.

He commissioned his friend, the architect Sir Edwin 'Ned' Lutyens, to convert the castle into a weekend retreat. Gertrude 'Bumps' Jekyll designed the gardens. Among the regular visitors once the conversion was complete were the writer Giles Lytton Strachey – who seemed to spend most of his time complaining about how hard it was to get there – and a noted cellist of the day, Madame Suggia.

Despite the claims of many an Internet expert, blind people have been photographed wearing dark glasses since at least the 1870s. The use of a cane for feeling the way was commonplace, but they were not painted white until the 1920s – apparently a gentleman named James Biggs from Bristol came up with the idea of painting his cane white in 1921.

I share JB McIntyre's enthusiasm for technology. The 'fella from Fort Wayne, Indiana' who invented the refrigeration machine was Frederick William Wolf Jr. Refrigeration machines had been around for a while, but he is usually credited with inventing the first domestic machine, the Domelre, in 1913. I've taken a liberty and had JB aware of it before it went into production in 1914. But he knows people who know people – he'd have his finger on the pulse.

The 'fella in San Francisco' was Lee de Forest, who invented the triode vacuum tube (known as a 'valve' in the UK), which was essential to the development of the electronic amplifier.

I first heard the story about the ice salesman during a lecture in an American History module I took as part of my degree course. The lecturer was a big fan of Henry David Thoreau and recounted a story about ice harvesting on Walden Pond. From there he went on to talk about Frederic Tudor's ice-selling empire and told the salesman story pretty much as JB tells it. The problem is that I've never been able to find another reference to that specific story. Yes, Tudor made his fortune by experimenting with new methods of harvesting, storing and transporting ice. He sold ice across the USA and beyond, and he's widely credited with popularizing chilled drinks. But the story of the salesmen in bars – even though I've heard other people tell it – remains unconfirmed. JB wouldn't be above a good yarn, though, even if he couldn't verify it.

You probably already know this, but Louis XIII is cognac maker Rémy Martin's special 100-year-old blend. Or, at least, it is now. Since 1874, the cellar master at Rémy Martin has overseen the blending of the finest eaux-de-vie and ageing the results in special barrels for no less than 100 years. The company makes much of the romance of a cellar master putting their knowledge, experience and expertise into something for future generations that they themselves will never taste. In Lady Hardcastle's time, Louis XIII – in its distinctive crystal decanter – was 'merely' Rémy Martin's highest-quality cognac, but it was still pricey. Probably not as pricey as she estimates, but worth a good few bob nonetheless.

According to both the *Oxford English Dictionary* and *Green's Dictionary of Slang*, the word 'boiler' to mean 'old or unattractive woman' appears to be first recorded in 1962. I'm usually fastidious about these things, but it was an altogether too perfectly Flo-ish thing to say for me to forgo it just because she was fifty years early.

Bristol City finished sixteenth (out of twenty) in the Second Division of the English Football League in the 1912/13 season. They rose to eighth the following year. Meanwhile, the Philadelphia Phillies were fifth in the National League in 1912 (out of eight teams) and were runners-up in 1913. JB's hopes weren't quite so misplaced after all, although neither was his pessimism. They led the league for the first part of the 1913 season but then had a disastrous run of losses, leaving them in second place behind the New York Giants.

In England, although sausage meat is sold for various culinary purposes, when we talk about sausages, we always mean what Americans refer to as 'link sausages'. The Scots have Lorne sausage (usually called 'square sausage') but in England a sausage sandwich (or a 'sausage butty' in many regions) is always made from actual sausages and not 'sausage patties'. I once caused consternation in an American hotel by asking for a sausage sandwich. I was told they were very sorry but they didn't have any sausage. I pointed to the tray of link sausages. 'But they'll fall out as you eat it,' said the server. 'That,' I said, 'is at least half the fun.'

Dymond uses the word 'arctophile'. The word appears to have been coined in the 1970s to describe teddy bear collectors but, as with 'boiler', I thought it was too good not to use.

# Acknowledgements

Some while ago, my friend Léonie Watson, who is blind, asked if I'd ever considered including a blind character in a Lady Hardcastle story. I said I hadn't but would certainly give it a go if she would agree to be my consultant. She agreed. All authenticity in the depiction of Clarice Everett's blindness is thanks to Léonie's advice. All inaccuracies are thanks to my own stupidity.

As always, my heartfelt thanks go to my editor, Victoria Pepe, for her expert guidance and unstinting support, and to Laura Gerrard, who always wants the murder to happen sooner. They worked long and hard on this one and their help is massively appreciated.

Special thanks, also, to my daughter, Alice, who suggested the idea for the central mechanism of the mystery.

Paul Dymond appears in the story, having made an extremely generous bid for a named character in the Children In Read auction in aid of the BBC Children in Need appeal in 2024.

# Another series by T E Kinsey

# The Dizzy Heights Mysteries

Read on for an extract from *The Deadly Mystery of the Missing Diamonds . . .*

France,

July 16, 1917

Dearest Flo,

I don't know when, or even if, you're going to get this – the mail has been taking an age to get across the Channel lately. I'll go ahead and write it anyway, and hope for the best.

Thank you for your last. I loved the story about Gertie Farley-Stroud and her new dog. Won't it get confusing if they call the dog Gertie, too? Maybe she shouldn't have let her granddaughter name it. Anyway, I'd love to see them again when I next get some leave – both the lady and the dog. She's my third favourite Englishwoman. (And look at that – I've been so long among you all that I've forgotten how to spell. There's no 'u' in favorite. I'm going native.)

I know I complain, but life behind the front lines isn't so bad, really. Obviously I can't say much about what we see, but among the, let's say, 'unpleasantness' (I wonder if that's mild enough for the censor – you'll have to let me know) there are always moments of joy and hope, no matter how small or fleeting. The boys can be so funny and charming, even in their darkest moments. I wonder if that's an English thing. You seem to cope with adversity with defiant resignation. Except that you're not English, are you? But you're only half Welsh, surely? (I await your scathing response to that one.)

My fellow nurses are all absolute darlings. Well, most of them. I can't name names in a letter that might be intercepted by the Bosch (they might attempt to undermine our morale by exploiting our dissatisfaction, or some such bunkum) but if she uses my hairbrush without asking one more time, she'll learn not to mess with this 'Yank'. I know where we keep the senna, and no one wants to spend any extra time in these latrines, let me tell you.

Have you heard from Ivor? (I still can't bring myself to call him Skins – it really doesn't suit him.) Or even Barty? It's so frustrating. I only joined the Fannies to get closer to him – to keep him safe, maybe? I don't know how I thought that would work, but it made sense when I left Maryland. I knew I could do nothing at all from three thousand miles away so I simply had to get closer. I just can't seem to actually get to him, though. I put in a request to be moved nearer to him every time I find out where his regiment is, but by the time I get there they've moved on, or he's performing in a concert party in Paris, or . . . You get the picture. I don't think the Powers That Be in the First Aid Nursing Yeomanry are going to indulge me many more times.

I was wondering if he might have written to you or Emily, thinking the letter would be more likely to reach you than me. He's an idiot, but he's my idiot and it's frustrating to know I'm never more than a hundred miles from him and I still can't see him.

But I'm getting maudlin now, and I have to stop that. No one wants a sad-eyed nurse at their bedside and I have to be on duty in a moment.

So how about something a little lighter? There was an incident nearby that made me think of you and it was sufficiently exciting that it was reported in the local newspaper (clipping enclosed). There was an old-fashioned hold-up on the road to Calais. I wanted to imagine men with bandanas over their faces, armed with Colt six-shooters, riding palominos and holding up the stagecoach, but the newspaper tells a more mundane story (the French press can be very stodgy and strait-laced sometimes). If my French is as good as I think it is, it was a man in an old coat with a muffler over his face. But he did have a six-shooter, even if it was a French army pistol, and he held up a small van on its way to the port.

But that's not the interesting part. Well, it's quite interesting, but it's not what made me think of you and Emily. The newspaper reported the theft of 'some cash' and 'the driver's lunch', but there's a rumour going around the aid station that the courier was carrying diamonds. Can you imagine it? An actual diamond thief. Right here in France, just like one of your cases back home. I thought of you two roaring into town in your beautiful motor car and solving it all, like one of your mysteries. Wouldn't that be fun?

But the clock has beaten me. There's a messenger waiting in the office to take the mail and I have to go and change some dressings.

Give my love to Emily. I promise to visit on my next leave.

Your friend

Ellie

# Chapter One

***May 1925***

Singer Mickey Kent announced the Charleston, and the gentlemen of the Aristippus Club and their lady guests whooped their approval. As the band struck up the familiar tune, a startlingly beautiful young thing, her face aglow and her headdress askew, loudly proclaimed the dance to be 'the capybara's spats', earning her a cheer of her own.

Skins Maloney looked out from behind his drum set at the wildly flailing dancers and smiled. He caught the eye of his old friend Barty Dunn and nodded towards a particularly uncoordinated gentleman dancing near the front of the low stage. He was half a beat behind the band, and his swivelling feet seemed in constant danger of tripping him up, but such was the look of unselfconscious pleasure on his doughy face that it was impossible to do anything but share his glee.

Dunn grinned round the neck of his double bass and inclined his head towards another candidate. This one had no chin, and a neck so thin that his shirt collar appeared to be floating freely in mid-air, but he, too, was lost in the joy of the dance. His delight was equally infectious.

His dance partner was less impressed. Twice now she had been jabbed in the ribs by an errant elbow, and she was trying to put some empty air between them to save herself from further injury.

It had been, as always, quite a night. The Dizzy Heights had been the club's resident band for some months, and it was the club, not the band, who thought themselves the lucky ones. Aspiring bands fought eagerly for even the sniff of a chance of a 'residency', no matter where, but the Dizzy Heights had long since passed 'aspiring' and were well on the way to 'highly respected'. Their reputation among jazz aficionados in London was such that clubs were chasing them rather than the other way round.

They had regular spots at a couple of the more fashionable jazz clubs on weeknights and kept Saturdays open for 'special' bookings (of which there was never a shortage). But Friday nights were spent at the Aristippus Club, a gentleman's club in Mayfair that was experimenting with providing regular entertainment for its younger members. The older members had a more traditional view of what a gentlemen's club should be and still tutted impatiently if anyone so much as breathed too loudly in the reading room, but there was a new generation coming through and they wanted some fun. A delegation had approached the band and a deal had been struck, not least because Skins was so amused by the club's nickname: 'Tipsy Harry's'.

It was always a lively crowd, who made up for in enthusiasm what they lacked in dancing talent and musical knowledge, and the band always had a splendid time. This evening's crowd – many of whom were there to celebrate the birthday of one of the members – had been among the most enthusiastic they had played for, and this, the third Charleston of the night, was the raucous climax to an already-exuberant affair.

There were cheers and applause as the band brought the song to a close.

'Thank you, ladies and gentlemen,' said Mickey through his tin speaking trumpet. 'You've been a wonderful audience and we've been the Dizzy Heights. Enjoy the rest of your evening. Goodnight.'

More cheers and applause followed, mingled with a few shouts of 'Shame!' and 'Just one more song!'

'Black Bottom!' called the capybara's-spats woman.

'I told you to be careful where you sat,' was the inevitable reply from her friend.

Laughter. More cheering. The band left the stage and retired to the back room that had been reserved for them. Bottles of beer and a heaped plate of sandwiches awaited.

'This is better than working for a living – eh, lads?' said Skins as he put his drumsticks in his old army pack and helped himself to a cheese sandwich.

Dunn was looking for a bottle opener. 'How would you know?' he said. 'You've never done a day's work in your life.'

'Well, no,' conceded Skins. 'But I've got a cracking good imagination. And my old man worked on the railways. I saw what proper work did to a bloke. And all I'm saying is I'd rather play a couple of hours for a bunch of "bright young things" than break my back laying track like my dad.'

Eustace Taylor, the band's trumpet player, had come into the room behind him.

'Well, you'd do better to put a bit of effort into it, if you don't want to find out first-hand what it's like laying track,' he said. 'Your timing was out in the middle eight of "Fascinating Rhythm". And do try to keep that blasted cymbal under control during my solo in "Dippermouth Blues", there's a good chap.'

Skins rolled his eyes and shook his head, but said, 'Right you are, Eustace. Always happy to receive your notes.'

Eustace frowned. 'Yes, well,' he said. 'Just you be careful.'

Skins had been playing ragtime since before the war and had been one of the first to bring proper American jazz to the London clubs as soon as he'd been demobbed. Eustace, meanwhile, had spent the years before his call-up playing second trumpet in the Dorsetshire Philharmonic. But his claim to a formal musical education (he was always suspiciously vague about where and with whom he had studied) gave him an all-too-apparent feeling of superiority over the lesser mortals in the band, despite having come to jazz comparatively late in life.

'How is it that you've never decked him?' asked Dunn once Eustace had retired to a corner of the room to annotate his trumpet score.

'Well, he's about six inches taller than me, for a start,' said Skins. 'I'm not sure I could reach. But you reckon I'm a good drummer, right?'

'Best in London.'

'That's what it says on the posters,' said Skins. 'But I'm all right. And the audiences? What do you think they reckon?'

'I don't think most of them would know a decent drummer from a coalman, but they don't complain.'

'Right,' said Skins. 'So, if you think I'm all right, and I think I'm all right, and the buck-and-wing and Charleston brigade think I'm all right, what do I care what the second trumpet in the Seaside Philharmonia thinks? Let him have his moment.'

'You're a better man than I am,' said Dunn.

'Never been in question, old son, never been in question. Hello, ladies.'

The band's saxophonists, Blanche Adams and Isabella 'Puddle' Puddephatt, always stuck together.

'How the devil are you, Skins?' said Blanche. 'Nice work in "Fascinating Rhythm" tonight. Well done. Loved that syncopation in the middle eight. Gave it a lovely feel.'

'Why thank you, ma'am,' said Skins, doffing an imaginary hat. 'What about you, Puddle? Did my humble efforts please you?'

'Everything about you pleases me, sweetie, you know that,' said Puddle. 'Is there any gin?'

'Just beer,' said Skins. 'But there's plenty of it.'

'That'll have to do,' she said. 'Pour me one, would you?'

Skins opened another bottle of beer and poured two glasses. He handed them to the woodwind section.

'This happens week after week,' said Blanche, pointing at the bottle. 'It's a bit much asking a girl to swill beer when there's gallons of champagne out in the other room. You got us this gig, Skins dear – do something about it, would you?'

'I sorted out the regular booking,' said Skins. 'But I didn't get involved in the catering.'

'Well, then, who did?'

'Elk, I think,' said Dunn. 'He served with the club's wine steward at Ypres. Or something. I forget the details.'

'We need a manager to sort these things out. Someone who can get us something other than beer to drink, at least. We can't leave it to the banjo player.'

Elk turned round. 'Did someone mention the banjo player?' he said.

'They did, mate,' said Skins. 'Blanche thinks you did a rubbish job sorting out the catering.'

Blanche scowled. 'I said nothing of the sort. I merely suggested that it shouldn't be up to the banjo player to have to arrange everything like this. We need a manager.'

'You'd get no complaints from me,' said Elk. 'It was a nightmare. You have no idea how much trouble I had to go to just to get them to put beer back here. They thought champagne would do. I mean, I ask you.'

Blanche shook her head.

'Not a bad night, though,' continued Elk, obliviously. 'Cool new bit in "Fascinating Rhythm", Skins. Nice one.'

Skins raised his glass. 'And that, my old mate,' he said to Dunn, 'is why I've never taken the trouble to lamp our trumpeter.'

The Dizzy Heights had been formed in 1923 by Ivor 'Skins' Maloney and Bartholomew 'Barty' Dunn. The two men had made a name for themselves in the years before the war, performing the new ragtime music that had made its way over from America in the 1900s. They had played in several bands of varying degrees of competence and popularity before striking out on their own as musical mercenaries, billing themselves as 'The Greatest Rhythm Section in London'.

Skins had been a lively boy, always quick with a joke and quicker to dodge out of the way of the cuff round the ear that inevitably followed his cheeky remarks. His grandmother had delighted in telling him, 'You should be on the stage, little Ivy.'

Indulgently, he had always said, 'You reckon, Nan?'

And she would say, 'Yes, son. Sweepin' it.' She would cackle wheezily at her own comic brilliance, and little Ivor would smile kindly and scamper off to find fresh mischief.

But he'd loved the music hall, and he actually did want to be on the stage. He was so often seen hanging around the stage door that the stagehands came to know him, and occasionally enlisted his help fetching and carrying for them. As a reward, they would let him in from time to time, to watch a show from the wings. He learned the comic routines and knew all the songs, and dreamed that one day, just as his nan had said, he really would be on the stage where he belonged.

In 1900, at the age of ten, his first proper job in the theatre – also exactly in accordance with his nan's predictions – involved sweeping the stage.

He was cleaning up one morning while the band were running through some new numbers. The percussionist, hemmed in by a big bass drum, a snare drum, a pair of cymbals, and assorted whatnots and thingummies that Ivor was unable to identify, missed his cue and completely fluffed the snare drum flourish that was supposed to end the song. The band fell silent apart from a few impatient tuts from the piano player, so that the only sound in the theatre was little Ivor's boyish laugh.

This induced the rest of the band, who weren't known for their serious outlook on life, to laugh, too. They liked Ivor the Errand Boy and were inclined to indulge him. Even the percussionist's frustrated embarrassment at his own mistake evaporated once he realized who had been mocking him.

'You reckon you can do any better, you little chimp?' he said. 'Get down here and try it. Go on. Shilling says you can't.'

Never one to pass up the possibility of extra cash, Ivor clambered into the orchestra pit and wormed his way into the percussionist's corner. He watched carefully as the tall drummer demonstrated the figure but then stood unmoving as the man handed him the sticks.

'Go on then, little man. Show us what you've got.'

'I can't,' said Ivor with uncharacteristic meekness.

'You seemed a good deal more cocky up there on the stage,' said the drummer. 'Not so easy now you're down here, is it?'

He reached out for the sticks but Ivor held on to them.

'No, I mean I can't reach the drum,' he said. 'You must be about nine bleedin' foot tall. How am I supposed to reach the drum from down here where the normal people live?'

The band laughed again, and a few moments later they had found an old beer crate for the boy to stand on. He held out the sticks.

'Like this?' he said.

The drummer adjusted his grip slightly and Ivor smiled. That felt right.

He tentatively tapped the snare drum. It was loud. Much louder than he had expected. He tapped it again. He had the feel of it now.

'Want me to show you again?' said the drummer.

'No, I've got it.'

He tried the figure slowly. The sticks bounced off the taut drum skin faster than he could control them, and the little flourish ended in a chaotic, rattling jumble.

To Ivor's surprise – and immense relief – no one laughed.

'Give it another go,' said the drummer.

Ivor tried another four times, each time getting a little better but each time ending in a clattering mess.

He took a deep breath. Steadied himself. And had one last try.

He rattled through the little drum figure at full pace and finally got it dead on. The band applauded.

'You want to watch out, mate,' said one of them. 'The sweeper-upper's after your job.'

From then on, Ivor spent all his spare time in the orchestra pit, watching, learning, and asking endless questions. The percussionist gave him an old pair of sticks to practise with, and he drove his family mad, tapping out rhythms on any available surface. But it paid off. Later that year when the percussionist was ill, Ivor stood in. His proficiency earned him the nickname 'Skins'. The name also suited his skinny – though he preferred 'wiry' – frame, but people seldom commented on that, nor his short stature. What struck almost everyone who saw him was the smile. Few had ever said he was handsome, but the warm, cheeky smile, so freely offered to almost everyone he met, guaranteed that a fair proportion of them would later declare him 'oddly attractive' or 'weirdly good-looking'. His personal favourite had been a girl from Tottenham who had said, 'I don't know what it is . . . there's something about you . . . is it your hair?' He was very proud of his hair. By the time he was eighteen, he had left the theatre and was working as the drummer in a ragtime band with his old mate Barty.

Barty Dunn had known Ivor since they had played together on the streets of Hornsey, where they grew up. Unlike his diminutive pal, no one was ever in any doubt as to why they found Dunn attractive – he was most definitely the good-looking one of the pair. Tall, athletic, and with the darkest blue eyes anyone had ever seen (or so he had been told, many, many times), he was everyone's idea of handsome. He was generally genial and charming, but was given to bouts of melancholy brooding which, to Skins's perpetual bafflement, seemed to make him even more attractive. While Skins was bouncing around, larking and joking, trying to charm the girls, Dunn just had to, as Skins put it, 'stand there looking sullen' and the girls would 'throw themselves at him'.

Although Dunn's family had been no better off than their neighbours, they had aspirations for their children (more often characterized as 'ideas above their station') and the young Dunns were all encouraged to learn musical instruments. Barty was given piano and violin lessons and worked hard at both, but the first time he saw a double bass he knew that was the instrument for him.

His parents couldn't properly afford the battered second-hand violin they'd bought him from the pawn shop, and they certainly couldn't stretch to something as exotic – and inconveniently huge – as a double bass, so he admired the instrument from afar. But he put a few pennies away each week from his job at the Barratt's sweet factory in Wood Green, and by the time Skins was ready to join a ragtime band, Barty had his own double bass and nothing could stop him following his old pal on the path to fame and fortune.

Black American soldiers had introduced the boys to the new 'jazz' music while they were serving in France, and as soon as they were demobbed, they had set about assembling a group of like-minded musicians to take London by storm.

It had taken them four years and many changes of personnel to get what they were after, but eventually they had the band they wanted. Gigs were hard to come by at first – clubs were still a little suspicious of the new music – but slowly the doors started to open to them as the 'bright young things' demanded the music they were listening to on their gramophones. The Dizzy Heights had arrived.

◆ ◆ ◆

When the party had finally wound down and the last of the guests had tottered tipsily on to the streets, the band retrieved their instruments and cleared the makeshift stage. Eustace Taylor packed up his trumpet, Benny Charles his trombone. Blanche and Puddle had a saxophone and a clarinet each. Elk Elkington put away his banjo and Mickey Kent tied a length of string to his speaking trumpet and slung it over his shoulder.

It was getting on towards dawn and the buses and trams were already running, taking the early starters to work, but they served just as well to take the late finishers in the band home. All except Skins and Dunn.

Skins and his drum set had been turned away from more buses and trams than he could count ('You can't bring all that tat on here, mate – what do you think this is, a bleedin' totter's cart?'), and the one time he'd tried to get it down the escalator at a tube station had ended in disaster. Dunn and his double bass had fewer problems by comparison, but it was still like travelling with a drunk friend, and he, too, had been turned away from many a bus with a weary 'Only room for one more, mate, sorry.'

They had the use of a storeroom at Tipsy Harry's if they wanted it, but it wasn't always convenient and they often needed somewhere else to store their bulky instruments. Fortunately, Barty Dunn 'knew a bloke' who ran a shop on New Row, near Covent Garden. In return for free admission to any club the boys happened to be playing, and the occasional complimentary drink, he let them store their instruments in the shop's stockroom. The only problem that remained was how to get them there.

To this end, they had invested in a large handcart which would carry Skins's drums and Dunn's double bass and still leave room for any extras – their best suits if they'd been playing somewhere posh, or a crate of beer left over from the show, perhaps. Most often the space was occupied by Dunn's romantic conquest of the evening, who would giggle her way round town before he whisked her back to his digs in Wood Green.

Tonight, though, Dunn had left the party with only Skins, his bass, and a few bottles of champagne liberated from the party on his way out.

'Unusual for you to be birdless after a gig,' said Skins as they wound through the deserted West End streets, pushing their clattering cart. 'Although it's been happening a lot lately, hasn't it?'

'A worrying trend, mate,' said Dunn. 'That one with the massive feather on her headband kept giving me the glad eye, but by the time we came off she was canoodling in the corner with some chinless twit with a monocle. A bleedin' monocle.'

'Losing your touch, then?'

'Do you know, I think I might be. It's been weeks since I've had so much as a chaste peck on the cheek. What if I'm getting too old?'

'You've only just turned thirty.'

‘Five years ago,’ said Dunn. ‘I’m ancient now. No one wants to go to bed with an ancient bass player.’

‘Look on the bright side, though. There were times not so long ago when we didn’t think we’d live to see thirty. But we got through it. And you’ll get through this little drought. And you’re a jazz musician. We’re cool. The kids love a musician.’

They had arrived at the shop by now. Skins let them in and Dunn helped him lug his drums and traps case through to the back. With the gear safely stowed, they locked up and leaned the cart against the wall. They said their goodbyes on St Martin’s Lane and Dunn strolled off towards the bus stop, whistling a tune they’d been trying to learn after hearing it on a gramophone record brought over by some visiting American musicians. Skins carried on up past Seven Dials and on towards Bloomsbury.

By the time Dunn got to Finsbury Park, the sun was up and people were already making their way to work. He couldn’t face the two-and-a-half-mile walk home, so he opted to wait for a tram to take him to Wood Green.

Barty Dunn made his way round the corner from the tram stop at Wood Green, to the little terraced house on Coburg Road where he rented a room from Mrs Phyllis Cordell. She had lost her husband and both her sons in the Great War, and had welcomed Dunn into her home. She was grateful for the much-needed rent, and for the company of the rakish musician who added a bit of glamour to the otherwise perfectly ordinary, working-class street. Although, by Dunn’s reckoning, she was not much more than ten years his senior, Mrs Cordell doted on him like an indulgent mother, chuckling over his tales from the clubs and clucking over his hangovers and minor ailments.

She didn't mind the strange hours he kept, nor did she bat an eyelid at the seemingly endless succession of pretty young ladies who emerged from his room just after lunch several times a week. She made them a cup of tea and offered them a sandwich, chattering away as though she was delighted to have them in her home. Which she was. But she didn't expect to see them again. She knew it would be a different face that came blushing into her parlour next time.

This was the sole source of friction between tenant and landlady.

'I don't mind who you spend the night with,' she had said one afternoon as she handed him yet another cup of tea. 'And I don't mind what you get up to when you do. Lord knows I'd enjoy a bit of that meself if I ever got the chance. Not that I ever will. Woman of my age.' She laughed at the very idea of such a thing. 'But I don't want to see you ending up lonely. You need to find a nice young woman. A war widow, maybe. Settle down. Make a life for yourself. A family. You need a family around you. Everybody needs that.'

'But what would you do then, Mrs C?' he'd asked with a smile. 'I can't leave you on your own.'

'I'll have Gallipoli,' she said, and patted the gormless mongrel's friendly head.

She had adopted the dopey dog a few years earlier and had named him after the disastrous campaign that had taken both her boys from her. The neighbours had tutted.

'You don't want to be calling him that,' one had said. 'It'll be like dwelling on it. You should put it all behind you. No good'll come from reminding yourself of it every time you call the dog in.'

But she had insisted that it would be a comfort. The name of her new canine companion would take the sting out of it.

'It might have took my boys,' she had said, 'but now I can hear the name and think of this little fella instead. I can remember my boys as the two handsome lads who went off to war, and Gallipoli as the silly little mutt who keeps me company now they've gone.'

It didn't make sense to anyone but her and Dunn.

He let himself into the darkened house with his latchkey. Mrs C always left him a glass of milk and a tongue sandwich on a shelf in the larder – 'just in case you're hungry when you get in' – and he sat at the kitchen table and ate it while he waited for tiredness to tell him to take himself off to bed.

Gallipoli had heard him come in and stirred himself from his basket by the stove to see if there might be any food on offer. Dunn peeled a slice of tongue from the generously filled sandwich and shared it with the dog, who ate it greedily. He lolled sleepily against Dunn's leg for a few moments more, but when it became evident that there was to be no more to eat, he padded back to his basket and settled down again.

'Room in there for an old soldier?' said Dunn, but the dog was already asleep. 'Better get myself upstairs, then. See you tomorrow, old mate.'

After a quick visit to the toilet in the tiny backyard, Dunn trod lightly up the stairs and into his room. Mrs Cordell had taken the wartime blackout restrictions more seriously than most and had run up thick, heavy curtains to try to stop light from spilling out on to the street.

'What you doing that for?' her neighbour had asked. 'We've got the streetlights half covered up.'

'And when the zeppelins come,' said Mrs C, 'they'll see your house, not mine. You can come and sleep in my parlour when they bomb you out.'

'What are they going to bomb us for, all the way out here?'

'The sweet factory. Good for morale – sweets. They want to break us, them Germans.'

'Liquorice Allsorts,' laughed her neighbour. 'Vital war supplies.'

Mrs Cordell had blacked out her windows nevertheless, and her neighbours had nervously followed suit. Now, nearly seven years after the end of the war, the blackout curtains served to supply semi-nocturnal Barty Dunn with the darkness he needed to sleep his way through the morning.

He threw his clothes over the back of the chair and all but fell into his bed. Sleep came almost immediately.

◆ ◆ ◆

It only took Skins about twenty minutes to walk home from the shop. He and his wife, Ellie, lived in a Georgian town house on a leafy street not far from the British Museum. The house was part of a row of similarly impressive dwellings, each fronted with white-painted stone at the ground floor, with dun-coloured bricks on the three upper floors. A gate in the black-painted railings opened to give access to the 'area' below street level – the servants' and tradesmen's entrance to the house – while the front door was reached by climbing a flight of six stone steps. The tall windows on the first floor gave on to narrow balconies which none of the street's residents ever used. It was rather more house than anyone expected a jazz drummer to live in, and they were right to think so – it was Ellie who had bought it for them using money from her inheritance.

Under the terms of her father's will, the entire – quite substantial – family fortune should have become hers when she married. When the trustees in America had learned that her husband-to-be was a musician, however, they had invoked 'the gold-digger clause'. It had been inserted by her father's lawyers to protect her from such undesirable ne'er-do-wells and had frozen the bulk of the money until the tenth anniversary of their marriage.

Under pressure from her Aunt Adelia, they had grudgingly released enough to enable her to buy a property in London suitable for a member of the Wilson family of Annapolis. There was an annual allowance, too, sufficient to keep her comfortable. But the trustees handled the household bills and servants' wages themselves and were unwilling to allow her control of the full amount until they knew that this Maloney fella meant business.

Skins let himself in. It was half past four in the morning so there was no one about. Even the housemaid – who, it seemed to Skins, was always working – was still fast asleep. He knew he should be, too, and that if he got his head down as quickly as possible, he'd be able to spend some time with Ellie and the children before he had to go out to work again.

Like Dunn, though, he found himself too wide awake to go straight up and instead went to the kitchen to make himself a cup of cocoa. He took it through to the drawing room, where he planned to sit in his favourite armchair and read yesterday's paper.

When he arrived he found Ellie lightly snoring in her own favourite chair, her dark hair strewn across the winged back and the paper resting on her delicate nose. He gently touched her arm and she stirred.

'Hello, love,' he said. 'What are you doing down here?'

She folded the paper and sat up. 'Catherine had a nightmare so I went to try to comfort her. By the time she was settled I was so wide awake I thought I might as well come down here and wait for you.'

'Poor kid. Is she all right?'

'She's fine. But how are you? You must be done in.'

'I'm fine, too. And all the better for seeing you. I wish I'd known you were down here, though – I'd have made you some cocoa.'

She smiled. 'I was hoping to be able to welcome you home, but I nodded off. Sorry.'

'Don't be daft,' he said as he sat down. 'Anything good in the paper?'

'Not a thing.'

'There never is,' he said. 'I don't know why we bother with it. We hardly get time to read it, and when we do, we just complain it wasn't worth reading.'

'We need to keep up with current affairs,' she said.

'And why's that?'

'I come from a very political family. We like to keep our fingers on the pulse.'

'Which is why you used to be a nurse, obviously. It all makes sense now.'

'The metaphorical pulse, goofus.'

They had met in Weston-super-Mare in 1910 when Ellie was touring Europe with her aunt. That trip got 'a little out of hand' and the two women were spirited home by the American embassy after a series of unpleasant incidents at their hotel. But the encounter at the Arundel Hotel where Skins and Dunn had been playing with Robinson's Ragtime Roisterers had changed their lives forever.

Skins had managed to hand her his calling card before she was whisked away, and the two youngsters struck up a transatlantic correspondence that carried on uninterrupted until the war. Their letters became more sporadic as the mail ships began to face attacks in 1915. The last letter Ellie received from him told her that Skins and Dunn had volunteered together for the Middlesex Regiment and were certain to be in France by the end of the year. Ellie had no intention of leaving it at that. She had a plan, and it only took three years of working her way round the local aid stations in France to get it to work perfectly.

Skins had thought himself lucky to get all the way to the summer of 1918 with only minor scratches and a bruised ankle to show for it. Then, one bright, sunny day in August 1918, a stray shell landed directly in front of his company's trench. Skins was leaning against the wall telling a joke about a talking dog when the shell exploded. The sturdy construction of the trench had protected him and all his friends from the blast, but the signpost on the trench's lip, pointing westwards and indicating that Tipperary was 'a long, long way', did not fare so well. It was knocked over by the force of the explosion and landed on Skins's unprotected head, knocking him unconscious.

The official record showed simply that he had been wounded in combat, but the unofficial record kept by one of the junior officers said that he had been 'rendered unconscious by a sign of dubious comic value while telling a joke of equally dubious comic value and being, in direct contravention of Standing Orders, sans tin hat'.

He regained consciousness quickly, but the sign had opened a gash in his head that required stitches. He was taken to the local aid station where he was seen by an excitingly familiar American nurse. She stitched his head wound and demanded that he spend at least two hours of his next leave taking her to dinner.

They married as soon as he was demobbed in 1919.

And now, to the intense irritation of her extended family, she was a musician's wife and living in London. Her uncles and cousins were completely unable to understand why she didn't want to marry a member of the Maryland senate and settle down where she belonged. Only her Aunt Adelia supported her decision to lead an independent, modern life.

'You probably ought to get back up to bed,' said Skins. 'I'll not be long.'

'I probably should,' she said. 'I've got things to do tomorrow.'

'Today.'

'Today, then, pedant. Can I have a sip of your cocoa?'

'Always.'

Ellie stood and took the cup from him, kissing the top of his head as she did so. She took an enormous gulp of the hot chocolate and set off upstairs.

Skins looked at the tiny dribble of cocoa she'd left him and settled down to read. In spite of his fervent belief that he wasn't anywhere near tired enough to go to bed, it wasn't long before he found his eyes swimming out of focus. It was time for bed after all.

# About the Author

*(c) 2024 T E Kinsey*

T E Kinsey grew up in London and read history at Bristol University. *Murder on the Rocks* is the thirteenth story in the Lady Hardcastle Mystery series, and he is also the author of the Dizzy Heights Mystery series. His website is at tekinsey.uk and you can follow him on:
Facebook: www.facebook.com/tekinsey
Bluesky: bsky.app/profile/tekinsey.uk
Instagram: www.instagram.com/tekinseymysteries
Threads: www.threads.net/@tekinseymysteries

# Follow the Author on Amazon

If you enjoyed this book, follow T E Kinsey on Amazon to be notified when the author releases a new book!

To do this, please follow these instructions:

## Desktop:

1) Search for the author's name on Amazon or in the Amazon App.
2) Click on the author's name to arrive on their Amazon page.
3) Click the 'Follow' button.

## Mobile and Tablet:

1) Search for the author's name on Amazon or in the Amazon App.
2) Click on one of the author's books.
3) Click on the author's name to arrive on their Amazon page.
4) Click the 'Follow' button.

## Kindle eReader and Kindle App:

If you enjoyed this book on a Kindle eReader or in the Kindle App, you will find the author 'Follow' button after the last page.